Girls with Guns

Girls with Guns

by

Michelle Grubb

Carsen Taite

Ali Vali

2016

GIRLS WITH GUNS

ISBN 13: 978-1-62639-585-5

This Trade Paperback Original Is Published By
Bold Strokes Books, Inc.
P.O. Box 249
Valley Falls, NY 12185

First Edition: April 2016

Credits
Editor: Shelley Thrasher
Production Design: Stacia Seaman
Cover Design by Sheri (graphicartist2020@hotmail.com)

Acknowledgments

We would like to thank our friends, family, hardworking beta readers, and steadfast spouses for their support. Thanks also to everyone at Bold Strokes Books for all the behind-the-scenes work, and a special shout out to our intrepid editor, Shelley Thrasher. To all our loyal readers who love suspenseful stories featuring powerful women—this collection is for you.

Girls with Guns

Bow and Arrow

Carsen Taite

Chapter One

I didn't mean to give Cash the biggest half of the burger, but even at my hungriest I wasn't about to yank a piece of meat away from an eager dog. "Fine," I told him, "but I've got dibs on the big half next time."

Cash wolfed down his portion of the Whataburger with cheese before thanking me with a deep bark in his throaty Husky voice. As polite as he was, it was hard to begrudge him the extra bites. His other mother wasn't about to feed him anything that wasn't labeled organic—no wheat, no corn, no fun—so eating with me while I was on the job was his only chance at a decent meal.

I just hoped we wouldn't be sitting here much longer. Less than an hour into this stakeout, and I was already twitching in my seat. A couple of months of living with Jess and I'd gotten soft. Now I was paying the price for blowing off work and reveling in the pleasure of home-cooked meals and a soft bed with clean sheets and a woman who I actually didn't mind waking up with. My regular employer, bail bondsman Hardin Jones, had called last week to say if I wasn't back at it ASAP, he was going to find a new bounty hunter to trust with his business. So instead of sitting in the comfort of Jess's house, I was looking at a long Sunday afternoon spent waiting for a glimpse of the first guy on Hardin's list.

Joe Cantoni was the nephew of Salvatore Cantoni and a big-time hood, but he'd been lucky enough to get caught doing only small-time stuff until just before Christmas, when he was swept up in a big counterfeit-purse sting. On a scale of serious to not much, purses would hardly seem to rate, but the haul was worth about a hundred grand, which made it a first-degree felony. The DA's office was salivating at the prospect of taking down one of the Cantoni family's top lieutenants, who they were certain had committed a ton of not-so-white-collar offenses. If they got a guilty on the purse deal, they could introduce all Joe's other transgressions during sentencing and wouldn't have to prove it all beyond a reasonable doubt. Tricky and kind of not fair, but I had a hard time sympathizing with the guy who was in charge of taking out anyone who crossed the family. What goes around, comes around and all that.

I'd been scouting Joe out for a couple of days and finally found his hidey-hole here at a simple-looking bungalow in East Dallas. I knew the place. It belonged to a friend of mine, Morris Hubbard aka Bingo, who was finally back in business after being caught in the middle of a power grab between a couple of rival families last year. Bingo ran one of the oldest private gambling rings in Dallas, and I'd sorely missed him while he was out of commission since I used to spend several days a week cashing in paydays for chips to play on his tables. I'd made it over here only twice since he'd reopened, but I wasn't quite ready to admit why I'd shirked one of my favorite habits now that it was readily available again.

Like magic, my phone rang, and the name on the screen was a flashing reminder of everything I'd given up and gained at the same time. "Hey, Jess."

"Hey, Luca. You working?"

I spent a second reading the tone. She wasn't checking up on me, just curious. "Yep. You?"

"Called it for the night. I was thinking about Thai. You interested?"

It was food, so the answer should've been a given, but the lilt in her voice told me the food was only a prelude. I glanced at the orange-and-white striped bag from Whataburger, then at Bingo's place. Cash watched me carefully before he put a paw on my thigh and whined something that sounded like "go home." I'm strong but not strong-willed, and the combination of the promise in Jess's voice and the fact I didn't want to be working anyway spurred me to say I was on my way. But before I could speak the words, the front door of Bingo's place opened and Joe Cantoni's petite frame stepped onto the porch.

"Babe, I'm very interested. Give me an hour and I'll be there." Before she could respond with more bewitching subtext, I clicked off the line and motioned for Cash to stay put. He whined as I opened the door, and I caved like always. "Okay, but stay close and wait for my signal."

I slipped out, circled my Bronco, and waited. Joe's car was three down and across the street. If I moved quickly I could intercept him before he even stepped into the road, and since I was almost a foot taller, he wouldn't have a chance. Sometimes I tried to sweet-talk jumpers into coming with me with stories about how I could help them out with the court, make sure everything was cleared up once they explained why they'd missed their appearances. It was always a lie, which didn't bother me in the least, but Joe Cantoni wasn't the type of guy who'd fall for my bullshit. This takedown would have to be all muscle.

I hunkered down and listened to the slap of his fancy loafers on the hard pavement. When the shadow of his little shoes came into view, I lunged forward and grabbed both his arms, yanking them up and across his back.

"What the hell?"

His voice was loud and full of surprise, and I decided to let the surprise work for me. After I made sure I had a good grip on his hands, I pulled my gun and rested the barrel behind his ear. Then I leaned in close and whispered, "Stay quiet or you're a dead man."

All bluff. If I was going to kill someone, and I'd thought about it plenty, it wasn't going to be a nothing like Cantoni. He was a piece of shit, but he'd never shit on me personally. He wasn't worth a single bullet from my prized Colt 45.

"You're the one who's dead," he said. "Do you know who I am?" Cantoni's voice rose with each syllable.

"I absolutely know who you are. Do you happen to know how high a bond your uncle posted to get you out of jail?"

He squinted and stared. While he tried to figure out if I worked for Salvatore or someone else, I glanced over at Cash, who shook his head and yawned. I could feel his pain. Now that we'd nabbed our guy, all I wanted to do was get Cantoni downtown and booked in time to make it home for dinner with Jess. I tried to tell myself it was because I like the food from the Thai place, but a nagging inner voice insisted on other reasons for my sudden preference for a sit-down meal at home versus a high-profile nab worth a bunch of cash.

Hell, I'd gone domestic.

With the realization, my stubborn streak reared its head. Maybe I would make it home for dinner, maybe I wouldn't, but right now I was focused only on this guy and the money I'd get for bringing him in. Maybe after I got my cash, I'd head back here and play a few games at Bingo's tables. I didn't answer to anyone and I could do whatever I wanted, but I needed to get Cantoni in my car before some of his pals came along. I motioned for my assistant. "Cash, do your thing."

Cash advanced on Cantoni until he was just out of kicking distance, then bared his teeth and growled. Completely out of his nature, but very convincing to strangers—we'd spent a lot of time and hot dogs perfecting this trick. While Cash kept an eye on Joe, I cuffed him and shoved him into the front passenger seat of my Bronco. Cash leapt into the back and put his growling mug between us while Joe inched his way over to the window.

"Where're you taking me?"

"Lew Sterrett," I said, referring to the Dallas County jail. No sense letting him wonder anymore. "Don't worry. Maybe when you explain to the judge you had to skip court to play poker, he'll let you out on bond again."

The look of confusion disappeared from his face and he shot me a knowing smile. "You're Luca Bennett. I heard of you. You're the gal that works for Hardin."

My turn for the knowing smile. "Freelance. Hardin calls me when he needs help. You know, someone he can rely on."

He shrugged as if to say potato, potato. He shot a cautious glance at Cash. "That some kind of Eskimo dog?"

I shook my head. "Husky. They're known for their ability to catch fugitives."

"How much you getting for hauling me in?"

I adjusted the mirror and drove to the end of the street, hoping he'd get the hint I wasn't interested in making small talk all the way to the jail.

"Seriously, Bennett, whatever he's paying you, I can double it."

There was a time the offer would've tempted me. I was a little tempted now. I might be living in domestic bliss, but I still kept my payouts in a coffee can. Still, I wasn't about to jeopardize my relationship with Hardin for a few extra bucks, no matter how many poker games I could buy into with the cash. He'd given me work when no one else would.

"I don't need your money," I lied.

Cantoni slumped back in his seat, but his eyes were still bright. I figured he was churning through ideas about what I might need that could convince me to cut him loose. He shouldn't have bothered. I had work. I had a good woman who loved me, a nice place to live, a car that started most of the time, and a loyal dog. Wasn't a damn thing he had that I wanted. Or so I thought.

"You found me pretty easy. Was that an accident or was it because you're good at what you do?"

"What do you think?"

"I think you're okay, but it was more me being stupid about wanting a game of cards than you being some Nancy Drew girl."

I didn't bother pointing out that Nancy Drew girl was redundant and that she and I were pretty much nothing alike. I drove a Bronco; she drove a convertible sportster. Her father was a well-known lawyer; my father was a retired drunk. She dated a quarterback while I did the quarterback's sister. The list was endless. The only similarity was that she always solved her case, and, at least in this instance, so had I. I pointed this out to him.

"True, but there's one case you didn't solve. Whatever happened to Teresa Perez?"

Teresa Perez. Another girl I didn't have much in common with. I was a cop for six months; she'd been married to the job. She was bitter and cynical; I was only cynical. I caught criminals; she was one. Last time I saw Detective Teresa Perez, she'd helped a handful of Mexican Mafia madmen, who she'd been supplying with drugs, take down her fellow officer, Jessica Chance, and then me. The fact she'd escaped before the good cops showed up was a huge sore spot. Perez had been in the wind for several months now, and a day didn't pass without me thinking about revenge. Cantoni's comment had me more than curious. "You know something?"

He lifted his cuffed hands and scratched his chin. Pure affectation. "Maybe."

I'd put the word out on the street that I was looking for Perez, and nothing would make me happier than to be the one to haul her in. His maybe was the first real lead I had. The question now was whether Cantoni was fucking with me. "Spill."

"What's in it for me?"

I steered the Bronco to the curb with one hand and eased back the flap of my jacket with the other, enough so he could see my gun. "I haven't decided yet. Just depends on what you have to say."

"I know you're looking. You're not the only one, though. Those guys she left behind? They don't mess around when it comes to dealing with loose ends. Word is that Jose Calderon has a bounty on her."

I perked up. Jose Calderon was the Mexican Mafia captain who'd lured Perez to the dark side and then been double-crossed by her. If Calderon was looking for Perez, it was only a matter of time before she turned up. Probably dead. I needed to find her first if I wanted any kind of justice. "Too bad you don't have the kind of reach Calderon does."

"Aw, come on. I got connections. You cut me loose, I'll get the lowdown and fill you in. Swear."

I took the car out of park and started to pull back onto the road. He'd gotten my hopes up, but I was over it. Time to turn in the fugitive and collect my winnings. I'd barely driven two feet when he shouted.

"Wait!"

I slammed on the brakes and shot him the evil eye. "Don't yell when I'm driving, asshole."

"Look," he said, "I'll tell you what I know only if you let me go. I promise it's good."

I stayed in the road this time, foot on the brake. "I'm supposed to believe anything you say? A minute ago you had to go looking for information, but now you're saying you had it all along? Give me a break."

"It's complicated. A bunch of people are on the hunt for Perez, not just the Mexicans."

"Let me guess. You were hanging on to what you know, waiting for the highest bidder?"

He ducked my glance. I knew I was right, and the rush of anticipation pushed me to take a leap. "Start talking. Tell me everything."

❖

A couple of hours later, Cash and I strolled through the door of Jess's house. Our house. Whatever. Two months in and I couldn't quite get used to the whole concept of two people living together. My parents had tried it for years, but it had never gone smoothly. Jess and I had shared living quarters since just before Christmas, and it couldn't have gone more smoothly. Made me nervous, like any minute it would all come crashing down around us. Maybe tonight I was trying to help it along.

"Luca?"

Her voice was velvet, warm, and not at all what I expected since I was way late. What would she think when I fessed up that I'd spent the evening with a fugitive and hadn't earned a dime since I'd turned him loose in return for what might turn out to be a shady promise? "Be right there."

I sent Cash ahead of me into the kitchen to test the atmosphere. Once I heard her cooing gently in his ear, I strode in.

"You catch your guy?"

She smiled as she asked the question, and deep in my heart I knew she didn't mean anything by it, but the words left a slight sting. She'd spent her day as a homicide detective for Dallas PD. She'd worked hard and earned her keep. I only worked when I had to, and now I'd given up my paycheck on my first day back. I hadn't earned any money, but if what Cantoni had to say turned out to be true, I had something more valuable. The question was whether I would share what I knew.

Jess had suffered even more than I had at the hands of Teresa Perez. She'd been taken hostage by thugs with a hard-on for vulnerable cops, and despite her law-and-order tendencies, Jess had sworn she'd tear Perez's face off if she ever showed it again. She'd meant every word. As much as I'd love to see that action, I took a breath and measured my response. "Not tonight."

She pulled me close and nuzzled her head against my neck. The scent of green-tea something or other swirled around my head, and my hunger shifted from Thai food to something else. Something that wouldn't keep. In a brilliant display of mind reading, she asked, "Hungry?"

"Always."

The bedroom was close and we were there in an instant, kissing, stripping, ready for a fast fuck. Funny, since now that we lived together we could totally take our time. While I yanked at her shirt, she jammed her hand into my jeans. I bucked against her and dove my face into her breasts, loving how quickly they hardened with arousal. For years we'd done this dance and it worked every time. Every single time. Fast or slow, hard or soft. No one got me like she did, and in the blink of that realization, I almost told her what I'd found out tonight, but the roar of my own orgasm drowned out my thoughts, and I surrendered to the haze of complete and total pleasure.

"You still hungry?"

I rolled onto my side and pulled her close. We were almost snuggling, but I'd never call it that. I let a slow grin show and said, "I could go again, but I probably need to eat first."

She punched my arm lightly. "I'll go get the food. I waited for you."

I pulled her back. "Wait." I hesitated.

"What?"

I wanted to tell her about Perez and wasn't quite sure what was holding me back. Cantoni had given me the name of a guy who knew another guy who he said could get me a lead on where Perez was hiding out. Instead of taking Cantoni to jail, I made him take me to guy number one to prove his story. To Joe's credit, the guy sported the Mexican Mafia gang sign. If anyone would know where she was, her former law-breaking pals were the most likely suspects, so I took him at his word when he assured me I would get a call from his pals about Perez.

I looked at Jess, who was still waiting for me to answer. We'd have a better chance of nabbing Perez together, but Jess had a job that required her to bring suspects back alive. If she found Perez, she'd be in a hard spot, and I didn't want to be the one that put her there. "Nothing." I looked away to keep her from reading the opposite in my eyes.

She reached out and stroked my face. Sweet and gentle. "You don't have to feel bad about tonight. You'll get back in the swing of things."

"I thought I was pretty amazing."

"I wasn't talking about the sex, doofus."

I laughed. "I know. Don't worry. I've got a full day planned tomorrow. I'll bag a bad guy. I swear."

"I'm sure you will, but it won't be tomorrow."

"You have other plans for me?"

"No, but the Crowley courthouse does. Did you already forget about your jury summons?"

My stomach sank as I recalled the official envelope that had arrived in the mail a few weeks ago. I'd closely examined it at the time, certain I'd meet one of the exceptions listed on the flip side of the formal notice, but not one applied. So instead, I turned to my favorite defense mechanism and forgot all about it. Leave it to my cop girlfriend to put it on the calendar. "Why don't you call one of the many judges you know and get me out of it?"

She shook her head. "Save the favors for the next time you get arrested. Don't worry. You'll be there a couple of hours at most. No way you'll get picked."

I mustered a dose of righteous indignation. "What's that supposed to mean? I'm perfectly capable of sitting in judgment on my peers."

"I have no doubt, but you're a bounty hunter and you live with a cop. Both sides will probably strike you."

She was right. Seemed like a total waste of time to get up early and trudge through the crowd at the courthouse for nothing, but maybe it would mean I'd be off the hook work-wise for a while. I glanced at the clock. It was late. I should eat and get some sleep, but as I turned back around and saw the curve of Jess's breast barely covered by the sheet, thoughts of food and rest fell away. My dreaded morning obligation would be here soon, but I was going to enjoy every minute of this evening.

Chapter Two

When I finally made it to the central jury room the next morning, I was in a long line of other folks who hadn't found a way out of civic service. From the middle-aged guy in his fancy suit, whose eyes were glued to his phone screen, to the twenty-something in skinny jeans and too-high heels, swaying in time to whatever tune was flowing through her headphones, it looked like all of us would rather be anywhere but here. The best thing I could do for now was stay below the radar. If I was one of the unlucky few who got called up to a courtroom, I'd start speaking out about how I couldn't possibly be fair and impartial. When I reached the double doors, I handed my slip to the bailiff but kept my eyes trained on my boots.

"Luca Bennett, what the hell are you doing here?"

The words were followed by a big belly laugh, and I looked up into the eyes of Curtis Landridge. He'd been a Dallas cop who'd worked with Jess when she was on patrol. "I could ask you the same thing. When did you start working for the sheriff's office?"

"Just last week. I left DPD after I hurt my back, so I got this new gig herding jurors. It's boring as hell, but it'll let me get in my last couple of years so I can take full retirement."

I nodded, even though the idea of getting paid for not working was a completely foreign concept. "Don't suppose you want to cut me loose?"

"No can do. If you made it this far, you have to go all the way. Hey, are you still friends with Jessica Chance?"

Memories of Jess's naked body flashed in my brain, and I hoped the heat I felt wasn't showing on my face. "Yep."

"Tell her I said hey. She's a helluva cop."

I heard someone clearing his throat behind us, and then a clipped male voice said, "Do you think you could postpone your personal conversation to another time? Some of us have places to be." When I looked down the line, I saw business guy looking all indignant and full of himself. When I turned back to Curtis, he had a big grin on his face.

"Better hope you don't get stuck on a jury with that one," he said.

"I don't plan on getting stuck on any jury."

He handed me the summons and patted me on the shoulder. "Good luck."

I walked through the doors into the large room lined with rows of chairs, the kind that were hooked together to make sure people didn't get all willy-nilly about the seating arrangements. I settled into a seat toward the back of the room and pulled out my phone. So far, no word from Cantoni's pal, but it was probably a little early in the day for criminals to get moving. I turned off the ringer, shoved the phone in my pocket, and distracted myself by looking around the room.

Several televisions were positioned around the room featuring a local newscaster giving a spiel about the wonders of jury duty and what we were in for over the course of the next hour or so. The broadcast was on a loop, and by the third time it played, I wanted to hurl my boot into the screen closest to me. I started looking around the room to see if there was anywhere I could sit that would shield me from the drone of the television. Before I could assess my options, a woman plopped down in the seat next to me and started talking.

"I'm not late, am I? They haven't called any names yet? Halfway here I hit the worst traffic on I-30. Of course when we finally started moving, there was absolutely no sign of an accident, so I don't have a clue why we were stopped. You're sure they haven't called any names yet, right? My name's Cris, by the way."

I looked down at the hand she held out while my brain caught up to her rushed tumble of conversation. The very last thing I wanted to do, besides being here in the first place, was engage in small talk with anyone else in this room, but her hand hung in the air, and despite popular opinion, I'm not a jerk. I reached out and shook it, surprised by the firm grip. "Luca. And, no, you haven't missed anything unless you enjoy watching endless loops of useless information."

She followed my glance to the nearest television monitor, and I'm certain I saw her mouthing the words along with the narrator. A few seconds later, she looked back my way and the slow creep of a blush reddened her cheeks. "Thank goodness," she said. "They always turn the introduction off before they call the names."

As much as I didn't want to make new friends, curiosity got the best of me. "So, you've done this before."

"Absolutely. This is my third time."

I cast about for the appropriate condolence, but her exuberant expression told me she didn't need my sympathy. She actually enjoyed jury duty. Wow. Now that I'd found out this much, I had to know more. "Guess this must be more interesting than your day job."

I didn't have a day job, and I imagined them to be endless, boring stretches of time spent trapped in a cubicle, talking on the phone, and possibly typing. So many people had them, though, they must have some appeal to the general public. Judging by her neat but casual attire, I pegged this woman for a secretary of some sort who likely viewed jury duty as a perfect escape from a demanding and possibly lecherous boss. "What do you do?"

"I'm head of accounts for Advanced Teleconnect," she said, naming one of the top telecomm companies not just in Dallas, but in the world.

I was impressed but still leery. Someone with that kind of clout should've been able to make a phone call or, better yet, have her secretary make a phone call, to get her out of this cattle call. If she was stuck here, that didn't bode well for my chances of ducking out without a fight. Determined to ignore this whole scene in hopes it would go away, I crossed my arms and let my head fall onto my chest in my best I'm-sleeping-now-and-we-don't-have-to-talk-anymore pose. The escape lasted all of five minutes.

"Is this your first time?" she asked.

First time sleeping in public? First time at the courthouse without being in trouble? The possibilities were endless. I was done engaging, but she clearly wasn't getting it, so I grunted an affirmative.

"I can tell. You didn't dress in layers." She tugged at her jacket and patted the messenger bag at her side. "And you didn't bring snacks."

My ears perked at the word "snacks," but I shook my head. "I don't plan on being here long. I'm not exactly jury material."

She started to reply, but at that moment a tall, thin man in a black robe stepped up to the podium at the front of the room and tapped on the microphone. Cris sat ramrod straight in her chair and grinned like a kid at a carnival. I resumed my casual pose, hoping to fly under the radar. Ten names in, my hopes were dashed at the sound of the judge's gravelly voice over the loudspeaker. Cris punched me in the arm in what was supposed to be a congratulatory move, and I slowly made my way to the door, headed for the 283rd District Court on the sixth floor. As I passed the bailiff, I heard the impatient businessman from earlier asking him directions to the same court I was headed to, and I sped up before I got roped in to showing him around. I wasn't here to be a tour guide, and if all went well at the next stop, I wouldn't be here much longer at all. I had leads to chase, and kicking around upstairs while I waited for some prosecutor or defense attorney to realize I'd shacked up with a cop was a complete waste of time.

I took the escalator to the third floor, as high as it would go, and then broke off to the stairwell. The elevators in the building were notorious for not working, which meant the ones that did work were crowded with a bizarre mix of wide-eyed innocents, creepy-looking defendants, armed cops, and impatient attorneys packed into too little space. Three flights of stairs later, I regretted how many times I'd missed my morning run over the past couple of months. I'd had to give it up for a few weeks, post gunshot to the abdomen, but then I'd just gotten lazy. Happy and lazy, which is the worst kind since it's really hard to be motivated to do something when someone is whispering sweet nothings in your ear.

When I finally huffed my way to the double doors of the courtroom, I grabbed a seat on a bench in the hall and settled in for the next round of waiting. A few minutes later, the businessman I'd seen downstairs strode up to the doors and pushed his way through. I mentally counted the seconds, betting he'd be back in less than ten. Only took five before the courtroom bailiff ushered him back out into the hallway.

"Wait here until your name is called," he said.

"But you don't understand. My name was already called. That's why I'm here. I'd like to go ahead and talk to the judge and explain why I need to go. It'll save everyone time."

"Nice of you to want to save time, but that's not how it works. Have a seat and wait for your name to be called."

I didn't bother hiding a smile as I watched Busy McBusiness frown at the bailiff's back and then look at the remaining benches with a look of disdain. Ultimately he chose to remain standing, punching the buttons on his phone in a fit of self-importance. Fine by me. I wasn't in the mood for sharing the space I'd managed to stake out.

"Luca!"

Disconcerted at the sound of my name, I looked up and sighed when I saw Cris standing nearby. She pointed at the space beside me. "Is anyone sitting there?" I shook my head, suppressed a sigh, and scooted over.

"Hard to believe we got assigned to the same court. What are the chances?"

The chances were crazy, actually, but maybe I was having all this bad luck now, and when we got into the courtroom, the defense attorney or prosecutor would recognize me and cut me loose before I had to endure a couple of hours of inane questioning. I could hear it now. *Can you be fair?* I couldn't be fair about anything if I was locked in a room all day, subjected to set meal times all for a few measly bucks.

"I wonder what kind of case this will be," Cris said. "Last time it was trespassing."

"It'll be more serious than that," I told her. "They only handle felonies on this floor."

"How do you know?"

The bailiff saved me from answering as he rolled out a large plastic trash can full of clipboards. As he called out directions for completing the questionnaires, I took a minute to look around at my fellow inmates. A pretty diverse mix of folks, and all of them, with the exception of Cris, looked as bummed as I was to be here.

I used the clipboard as a shield for the next thirty minutes, providing honest but inflammatory answers to the questions. I paused for a few seconds over the section that asked about whether I was related to anyone in law enforcement. Related. Funny word. I'd known Jess since we were young recruits, days into our stint at the police academy. For years she'd been my go-to source for pretty much anything from information about a bail jumper to sex at a moment's notice. She knew me better than anyone else, and now we lived under the same roof. Did all that and the fact I'd finally said those three little words that used to make my stomach churn make us related?

Damn it. I was overthinking this. My pen cut through the paper as

I carved Jess's name in all caps. If nothing else, listing her should give the defense attorney a reason to try to strike me from the panel.

A few minutes later, the bailiff gathered up our clipboards, and a while after that he ushered us into the courtroom and assigned us seats. I wound up two spots down from Cris on the third row, a position that caused me to sigh with relief. Felony cases called for twelve jurors, and plenty of folks were ahead of me. To my extreme satisfaction, McBusiness was front and center.

After close to an hour of sitting on the hard benches in the courtroom listening to Judge Bowser drone on about how jury service worked, we broke for lunch. I checked my phone first thing and found three texts. I took the stairs two at a time while I read each message:

Hardin: You got Cantoni yet?

I ignored that one and glanced at the next message.

Jess: Lunch?

I started to type *hell yes*, but before I could thumb the words, my eyes strayed to the last text. It had come in three minutes ago. I didn't recognize the number.

Got the info. Call now.

Guess I wasn't going to be eating anytime soon. I looked up from my phone to see everyone crowding the elevators, and I sidestepped a woman pushing a stroller to head for the stairs. Once I hit fresh air, I called the number and waited impatiently through the rings. I'd about given up when a gruff male voice answered.

"Yeah?"

"It's Bennett. Whatcha got?"

He growled an address and said, "Come to the back. Be there in fifteen."

The line went dead before I could respond. Great. Looked like this was turning into a scavenger hunt. Luckily, the meet wasn't far from the courthouse. I jogged across the street to my Bronco, silently bemoaning the fact I'd have to pay to park again when I got back. As I slid behind the wheel, I felt the burn of someone watching me and slowly turned my head to the left. Cris, the eager juror, waved from a car two spots away. It was a little disconcerting to see her out here since I thought she'd planned ahead so she'd never have to leave the courthouse, but I wrote off my paranoia to the adventure I was headed toward. I gave her a quick wave and pulled out of the lot.

I recognized the building as soon as I pulled up at the address. A well-worn sign that read Antiques hung by the door. If there were antiques inside when this place opened, they were ancient now. I pulled around back and cruised the parking lot, without a clue as to what I was supposed to be looking for. A few minutes passed and I silently cursed both Joey Cantoni and my failure to take the sandwich Jess had offered when I left the house this morning.

I'd just about decided to head to the nearest burger joint when I saw a rail-thin, gray-haired woman walking toward the Bronco. She stared straight at me, so I put the car in park and rolled down the window, bracing for her to tell me to get lost. When she reached the window, she asked, "You Bennett?"

Taken off guard, I just nodded. She handed me a bulky brown envelope, and when I took it from her I noticed her hand was wrapped in a piece of cloth. I started to ask her what was in the envelope, but she spoke first. "Take it and leave. Don't come back."

This wasn't the deal. I'd already peeled through two layers of leads, and I'd expected to get some actual intel at this point. I said as much, but she shook her head.

"Take it or leave it, but this is all you get. Now go."

I didn't have any other options at this point so, vowing to find Joey Cantoni and turn him in for the bounty Hardin would pay, I drove away with the envelope on the seat beside me and pulled into the nearest fast-food joint. I shouted my order to the hard-of-hearing drive-through operator while I tore into the envelope and poured the contents into my lap. In between moving a few feet forward in line every few minutes, I sifted through the contents, not at all sure what to make of it. Most of it seemed like junk. Matchbooks, coasters, random Google maps highlighted to show various locations around what looked to be primarily seedy parts of town. And there, at the bottom of the pile, was the jackpot: a full-color, sharp-as-shit headshot of Teresa Perez, complete with the same smug smile I'd loathed since the first time I laid eyes on her. The print in the corner of the photo read yesterday's date, and I knew I had what I was looking for. Proof of life.

A loud honk shook me out of my gloating, and I drove up to collect my double burger and fries. I barely had time now to make it back to the courthouse, so I wolfed the food on the way while I plotted how to get out of jury duty. I didn't have time to pass judgment—I had a real crime to solve.

Chapter Three

As we filed back into the courtroom, Cris walked next to me. "Now for the fun part," she said. Her tone told me she wasn't kidding. Too bad people couldn't volunteer for this gig. Would make a helluva lot more sense to have people judging a case if they were actually interested in the process. I only cared about the before and after part of justice. I pointed to my seat and edged away to keep her from engaging further.

After the judge explained that the defendant was charged with murder, he turned the questioning over to the lawyers. The prosecutor was first up at bat—a leggy, dark-haired girl whose suit skirt was just a shade on the short side. She stood and introduced herself as Rebecca Reeve and spent the first few minutes of her allotted time droning on about how grateful everyone was that we'd shown up to perform this civil service.

I acted bored, which wasn't hard, while she progressed from grateful to feisty as she singled out a few folks on the panel who'd written rebellious things on their questionnaire. One woman had a relative who'd been arrested before, and there was a guy who'd served on a jury who'd found someone not guilty, and another who didn't believe in the death penalty.

I knew her game. She planned to either strike these folks from the panel or challenge them for cause, so she used them to get out some key points she wanted to make at trial, like how the burden of proof works or how important it is to listen to the evidence and watch for inconsistencies.

My questionnaire probably had her confused. I'd listed my

occupation as fugitive-recovery agent. A savvy prosecutor would know that meant bounty hunter, and the job would probably make her imagine a rebellious type she didn't want on a jury. But mix that in with Jess's name, and she'd be at an impasse. To figure out which side of the crime spectrum I fell on, she'd have to ask me some questions, which could mean opening up a can of worms. I braced for a question, but none came.

On the other hand, the defense attorney wasn't scared of anything. Bea Watson's suit skirt hit just at the knees, and she paced the room with a confidence that signaled she'd done this dozens of times before. I watched while she tackled the panelists, one after the other, on various issues with provocative questions designed to eliminate everyone she spoke to. Fine by me. When she finally got to me, I was ready to go.

"Ms. Bennett?"

I raised my hand despite the unfamiliar "Ms." She smiled in my direction, like a cat at a mouse. "What's a fugitive-recovery agent?"

I could tell by the tone of her voice she already knew the answer, but she wanted me to say *bounty hunter* for the benefit of the rest of the potential jurors. I figured she wanted to focus on what I did for a living to ask me a bunch of questions that would serve as a kind of allegory for the rest of the group. I played along, thinking this was the perfect way to turn myself into a lightning rod.

"I track down fugitives," I said in my best cop voice. "Criminal offenders who've violated the conditions of their bond."

To her credit, her expression didn't change. She asked a couple of questions about how the job worked, who hired me to do this kind of work, etc., and then, in a casual tone, she asked, "Are some of those offenders ever armed and dangerous?"

"Yes."

"Even when they aren't armed, would you say some of them are dangerous?"

I paused for a second. I'd been with her up to this point, but we were entering murky waters now. She better not be about to ask me specific questions about my cases, or I'd have to take the fifth. I kept my answer short and simple. "Yes."

"So dangerous that you'd use whatever means necessary to defend yourself or someone you cared about, if it came to that?"

I shifted in my seat at the loaded question. What in the hell was she getting at? I dodged. "'Whatever means necessary' is pretty broad, don't you think?"

"I guess it is," she conceded. She looked over her shoulder at the judge, and I noticed the prosecutor looked ready to pounce. "But I guess we'll have to leave more detail until we get into the facts of this specific case." She flipped through her notes and I relaxed, thinking she was moving on. I was wrong. "What's the nature of your relationship with Dallas Police Detective Jessica Chance?"

Well, this wasn't cool. Whatever it was, it wasn't any of her business. "We live together."

"You used to be a police officer, didn't you?"

"Yes."

"And you worked with Detective Chance?"

"Well, she wasn't a detective then."

"You're close."

"Is that a question?"

"Let me put it this way. Don't you think the fact that you haul in alleged criminals for a living and you have a relationship with a Dallas police officer would influence how you evaluate the evidence in this case?"

That and a million other things. The right answer was no, but truth was I'd probably be influenced by everything about my own life experience, so I could honestly give the answer that was most likely to get them to toss me out for cause. "Yes."

"Thank you for your candor, Ms. Bennett." She turned away and addressed the judge, "Your Honor, I'm—" But before she could finish, a now-familiar voice piped up.

"Your Honor, shouldn't the question have been would your relationship with a Dallas police officer cause you to be more likely to assign credibility to the prosecution's witnesses to the detriment of the defense?" As all eyes in the courtroom turned toward her, Cris ducked her head and her voice trailed off. "Or something like that."

I shook my head as everyone turned back to me. What the hell? I was certain Watson had been about to vigorously argue that I should be stricken for cause, but now this busybody was about to rehabilitate me as a potential juror. The judge cleared his throat and leaned forward. "Ms. Bennett, how about you answer that question. Would you be more likely to side with the prosecution because of the things Ms. Watson has pointed out?"

Damn. I should say yes. Lots of people would. Smart people. People who had other things to do with their time than sit in a room and listen to boring lawyers talk about boring things. But every rebellious bone in my body screamed no way would I be more likely to side with law-and-order folks in any situation, despite the fact that I went to bed with a cop every night of the week. I mentally counted the number of people seated in front of me and decided I could be honest and safe at the same time. "No, Judge. I can put all that aside and listen to the evidence."

He nodded and then told the panel that anyone who had any private information they didn't want to share in front of the rest of the group could stay behind while the rest of us kicked it in the hallway again. As I burst through the double doors, I felt a tug on my arm and looked over to see Cris standing beside me. I let loose. "What was that about?"

She looked genuinely surprised. "I didn't want you to lose out on being picked. She didn't ask the question right."

Lose out, my ass. I shrugged her off and looked for a quiet corner where I could spend more time with the contents of the envelope full of Teresa Perez. Afternoons at the courthouse were reserved for those of us not smart enough to get out of jury duty, which meant the crowds that had been present this morning had thinned out. I walked far enough away from my group, but stayed close enough to be able to hear when the bailiff called us back inside.

I reached inside the envelope and pulled out my first clue. The coaster read *Shorty's Rack*. To someone who didn't hang out in the seedier parts of town, the name could mean anything: rib joint, strip club, but I knew Shorty's was a pool hall on the south side. It was a popular place for former or fleeing felons to pick up necessities like a fake ID, drugs, or a hooker, and I'd managed to haul in a few jumpers just by hanging out in the parking lot and waiting. But what did Shorty's have to do with Perez?

Clue number two was a matchbook from another dive, but this one was in Oak Cliff, a well-known watering hole for Dallas's underbelly. I reached into the envelope and grabbed a handful of the random scraps of paper and found more of the same. Places, lots of places, but nothing that specifically pointed to Perez other than the headshot that taunted me with its implicit reminder she was still on the lam.

The bailiff appeared in the hall and yelled that the judge was ready. I crammed the contents back in the envelope and filed back into the room with the others. I figured the formalities would take about fifteen more minutes, and then I'd be on my way.

"Ladies and gentlemen," Judge Bowser said, "I'd like to thank you for your time. We need only twelve of you for service today. The rest of you can take your pay slips to the clerk's office. If I read your name, please make your way to the jury box and wait to be sworn in."

I tapped my fingers on the bench, half out of my seat, ready for this prison sentence to end. McBusiness was the first juror in the box, and I had to fight the impulse to laugh out loud at his obvious discomfort. The next half dozen were complete nondescripts. I didn't recall seeing them here at all, and they certainly hadn't spoken up during voir dire. No matter, we were almost done at this point. The judge called a couple more names, and then he said, "Cris Perez-Soria."

I watched the couldn't-be-happier-to-be-here chick not even try to hide a smile as she practically skipped toward the jury box, but my brain whirred in response to the judge reading her last name. Perez? I'm not big on superstition, but that seemed like a pretty odd coincidence, and I shot a look at my envelope. I didn't need to pull out the photo to see the image of Teresa Perez that was burned into my brain. I supposed there were some physical similarities, but surely juror number eleven wasn't any relation to Teresa Perez. Or was she?

A light punch on the arm interrupted my thoughts, and I looked at the old lady seated to my right. "Isn't your name Bennett?" she asked.

"Yes," I whispered, not wanting to interrupt the proceedings and risk holding up our release.

"Then you better get moving so the rest of us can get out of here."

Her words didn't compute at first, but as I looked around, I noticed everyone's attention was trained on me and the bailiff was waving in my direction and pointing to the jury box. I looked from him to the judge to the motley crew already in the box, and agony ate my insides. No fucking way.

A few minutes later, I held my hand in the air with everyone else and took an oath in response to the blah, blah, blah the judge recited while my mind spun with all the things I should be doing instead. I pretended to pay attention while both sides delivered their opening statements, but I only caught phrases like “we will prove,” “the evidence will show,” “murder,” “reasonable doubt,” “eyewitness.” Silently, I willed them to speed it up. I had my own crime to solve.

Chapter Four

"You're later than I expected," Jess called out from the kitchen as I walked through the door. "You get your guy?"

Her question took me by surprise since the only "guy" on my mind wasn't a guy at all. I'd left the courthouse and run by one of the bars highlighted on a map in the stack of supposed clues I'd picked up from Cantoni's contact. The place didn't open until nine, which didn't compute in my world, since drunks will drink any time of day.

I stalled, instead stopping to pet Cash, who jumped up and placed both his front paws on my chest and licked my face like he hadn't seen me in weeks. I got it. We hadn't been apart for more than a few hours since he'd adopted me. "I'm sorry, buddy. I promise I would be with you if I could. I'll be gone tomorrow too, and probably the next day. You can blame your other mother for not being able to get me out of jury duty."

"Oh, sure, blame the cop. Everyone does."

Jess was standing right behind me now, a fake scowl on her face. "Did they not finish picking today?"

"Oh, they finished all right."

Her scowl morphed into amazement. "No way."

"Yes, ma'am. Meet Juror Number Twelve. No one seemed to care that I live with a cop, that I catch criminals for a living, or that I hated being there more than I hate fries without ketchup. I guess the choices in front of me were so bad, I seemed like a good prospect in comparison. Hard to believe, huh?"

"Impossible. Which court were you in? Did you get into any evidence today?"

"Judge Bowser. Opening statements only. Evidence starts tomorrow, bright and early."

"Come eat and tell me all about it. I made spaghetti. Don't get too excited—the sauce is from a jar."

I didn't know there was any other kind. Besides, I was starving and would've eaten five-day-old Thai food at this point. But before we adjourned to our gourmet out-of-a jar dinner, I had to clear something up. "Thanks for making dinner, but you know I can't talk about the case, right?"

She laughed and tugged me toward the kitchen. "Right."

I dug in. "I mean it."

"You crack me up when you try to be all law-and-order. Come on. Dish." She kept walking.

"Jess…"

She stopped and turned to face me. "Wait a minute. You're serious, aren't you?"

"Well…" I wavered for a second. For the first time since I'd moved in, I had the upper hand. Don't get me wrong. Life with Jess had been a breeze so far, but I'd spent the first few weeks of it recovering from a gunshot wound and the time since trying to get into the groove of working like a normal person, something I'd never tried before. The upshot of it all meant Jess was basically supporting me and I had no power. If hanging on to little bits of information about the case and my clandestine search for Teresa Perez were what I needed to give me a boost, I planned to grip tight, even though I knew I was being petty. "Of course I'm serious. Besides, you're a detective. If you want to know something about the case, you can detect it for yourself."

"Okay." She pivoted and strode off to the kitchen without another word. I stood in the living room and stared at Cash, who cocked his head as if to say he didn't have a clue what to make of her reaction either. I signaled for him to follow, and we took off toward the smell of an amazing dinner to which I was no longer sure I was invited.

Jess was feeding pasta into boiling water, and in a sea change from moments ago, she didn't even look up when I walked in. If I didn't know her better, I would've thought she was pouting, but Jess didn't play games. If she was pissed, she said so. Still, a childhood spent with a drunk dad and petulant mother doesn't come without some baggage, and right now I carried the guilt of having maybe possibly hurt her feelings. I slid my hands around her waist and kissed the back of her neck, making sure to find the magic spot. "Hey, babe, dinner smells wonderful. You want me to open some beers?"

She turned in my arms, her eyes black with desire. She pulled me tight against her and gave a little grind against my thigh as she leaned in close, her breath hot against my skin. The heat trailed up my neck and threatened to explode just as she whispered in my ear, her words killing the mood. "The prosecutor is new. Well, new to state court. She used to work at the U.S. Attorney's office. The charge is murder. I know every last detail about the evidence, and the whole thing's pretty open-and-shut, if you ask me. You want me to tell you what I know about your top-secret case?"

I play-shoved her away and Cash nipped at my ankle. She pointed at him. "See, even your dog is on my side. The only thing I don't know about your super-secret case is how the hell you got picked for the jury. Did you tell them we live together?"

Her eyes reflected the slightest hint of insecurity, like she wasn't quite sure if I'd been willing to admit our relationship to a bunch of what to me were virtual strangers. I pulled her back against me. "Of course I did. I gotta figure either they didn't care or there were too many crazies seated in front of me they had to strike first."

"You probably just confused the hell out of them."

"I guess." I pulled a couple of plates out of the cabinet—my small contribution to homemaking. "Say, when you said it was open-and-shut, how does that translate in terms of days? Two, three?"

"Oh, so now you want intel from me?"

"Come on. I'm trying to plan my life here."

She drained the pasta and it slid neatly into a big red bowl. "Well, Judge Bowser runs a brisk court—long days and short breaks, but even so, you're looking at a couple of days at least for the state's evidence. If you find the guy guilty, you'll probably be there all week."

I groaned.

"Sorry, pal. But hey, no matter how late he makes you stay Wednesday, keep the evening open. I have plans. Special plans."

She delivered the words "special plans" with the same sexy smile she'd used to try to seduce me for information. I was super tempted to give her anything she wanted. But my libido would have to wait. "I may have to work every night this week." I pointed at the pasta. "I'm going to have to go out after dinner tonight."

"Really?"

Her disappointment almost made me take it back. Almost. If I was going to run down these leads on Perez, I had to strike now. I'd never expected her to stick around. A smart villain would have left the scene of her last crime and not looked back. Perez was smart, but she was also greedy. If she'd stayed in the area, it meant there was some lucrative reason for her to be here, and I was going to find out what it was. Of course I didn't plan to tell Jess any of that. "Gotta earn my keep."

"Uh-huh."

"Jurors only make a few bucks a day. Did you know that? I mean, what's the point of paying us at all?"

She sighed and passed me a hunk of garlic bread. "Sure, Luca. Eat your dinner. You're going to need it if you're going to work at night and get up early to be a good citizen."

I did my best to ignore the edge in her tone and ate the spaghetti. Three bowls of it. It tasted amazing, but then it sat like a rock in my belly while I tried to process the change in mood between us. Jess was pissed. Mildly pissed, but still pissed. It was pretty out of character for me to obsess about work, so I got it, but telling her what I was up to wasn't likely to change her mood, so I didn't bother. She'd come around when I found Perez, and if all went well, that would be tonight.

❖

I spotted the SUV three streets away from the house. The driver was careful to stay just far enough back, but I've tailed enough cars to be able to spot when I've got a shadow of my own. Besides, I'd kind of expected I might be followed. Whoever had provided me with the envelope full of Perez likely had a vested interest in finding her. Mexican Mafia, the feds? I didn't have a clue, but I was happy to do their dirty work if it meant I got to see the look on her face when she got caught.

When I turned into the drive for Shorty's, the SUV shot past on the main road. I waited in the parking lot, thinking they might double back and I could confront my silent partners, but after fifteen minutes of lonely, I gave up.

For a Monday night, the place had a decent crowd. I spent about an hour at the tables, with nothing to show for it but a lighter wallet. I'd never been much of a pool player, but I was trying to blend in. I'd gotten nowhere with my subtle questions, so I retired the cue stick and took a seat at the bar.

The bartender was a big, burly chick who went by Fred. Her real name was Freda and she'd owned this place for over twenty years. I don't remember exactly how old I was when my dad first brought me here and set me up with a cherry Coke while he lost grocery money playing eight ball. In a best-selling novel or TV movie, the whole situation would have been sentimental. Freda would've been like a second mother, sneaking me food and listening to my stories while my sad dad tried to strike it rich to give us a better life. In reality, Fred bullied my dad to pay for my one Coke—no free refills—and my only meal on those nights was the single cherry at the bottom of my glass. Dad eventually gave up pool as a source of income and took up poker at Bingo's place. I'd been back here over the years, looking for deadbeats, but I doubted Fred had a clue that I was the same scraggly kid who'd hung out at her bar.

"Whatcha want?"

Fred's eyes bored holes into me, and I knew her question was more about telling me I couldn't just sit here without ordering something rather than trying to find out how she could assist me. "Beer. Draft."

She jerked her chin and tapped a perfect pour. "Three bucks."

I slide a five across the bar with Perez's picture on top. No sense being cagey. She slid the bill out from underneath the photo and started to walk off. "Hang on," I said. "Aren't you even going to look?"

"Don't need to. You drink that and head on out of here."

She acted all nonchalant, but her eyes shifted to and away from the photo twice before she ordered me to leave.

"You've seen her, haven't you?"

"What makes you think I'd tell you if I had?"

"You let her hang around here, you're in for trouble. Real trouble." I leaned in close. "Of course, maybe that's what you're looking for. Maybe you and she are, you know." I twisted fingers together in a mock display of simpatico. I was reaching here, but sometimes you have to get a rise out of someone to get the truth.

"You don't know what the fuck you're talking about."

I knew exactly what I was talking about, but before I got to make my point, I heard a click behind me, real close to my ear. It wasn't a gun. Worse, it was a knife. I could see the glint of steel out of the corner of my eye. Damn, I hate knife wounds, especially when you see them coming. Slow-moving, personal, and painstaking. I'd already taken a bullet because of Perez, and getting stabbed wasn't part of my plans. I slowly held a hand in the air. "Maybe I don't know what I'm talking about. Maybe you could fill me in."

Fred shot a look at Knife Wielder, and the blade clicked shut. I turned my head just enough to see Fred's protector and tried not to laugh at the short, scrawny dude. Knife or not, I could take him, but instead I sat quietly and waited for Fred to talk. She didn't have a lot to say.

"Bitch moved on."

"Any idea where?"

"Nah."

"When did you last see her?"

"Dunno."

I motioned at the other losers in the bar. "She hang with any of these folks?"

"I wasn't her babysitter."

Yet you were glad when she left. Fred knew more, but I wasn't going to get it straight from her. It was late and I had to be up early. Time to move along and approach this from another angle. I emptied my glass, climbed off the bar stool, and made my way to the door.

Chapter Five

Mornings always sucked, but the early alarm, the rushed coffee, and the sad-faced dog totally ruined this one. To top it off, Jess had left before I woke up, so I had no way of knowing if the edge from last night had worn down.

Things didn't get any better when I got to the courthouse and made a bad choice about which door to use. Usually, the line to the underground entrance was smooth and fast since not many folks other than cops and lawyers knew about it, but today the metal detector was broken and we were all being searched like turban-wearing guys with one-way tickets at the airport.

When I finally shoved through the doors next to Judge Bowser's courtroom, the bailiff was standing in the door to the jury room, tapping his foot.

"You're late."

And you're king of the obvious, I thought but didn't say. This was the guy in charge of attending to our every want and need over the next hopefully not-too-many days, and I didn't want to piss him off. "Sorry. Metal detector's down. Private guards aren't so good with the personal searches."

"Damn right, they're not." He delivered the words with a grunt. It was a point of contention with court security that the county had hired a private-security firm as the first line of defense. He offered a grudging smile. "Go on in. Judge is about to take the bench."

I filed into the jury room and assessed the defendant's peers. There was one other white guy besides McBusiness, three white chicks, including me, two black women, one black man, one Asian, three Hispanics—one male, two female, including Cris Perez-Soria. All in all, a pretty diverse cast of characters. I studied Cris the longest, certain something was off about a person who actually looked forward to the mind-numbing task we were about to start and wondering if she was any relation to my nemesis.

Everyone had formed little cliques already, and they were huddled in groups around the jury room. Glad I'd missed the friend-picking portion of the morning, I walked over to the coffeemaker and poured a cup while I scoured the counter for sugar. I was dumping the sweet stuff in my cup when I heard McBusiness say, "Ask her. She lives with a cop."

I resisted the urge to turn around, instead stirring my coffee and reading the tedious information about jury duty some helpful courtroom personnel had posted on the bulletin board. My resistance worked. I heard Cris chime in. "They'll keep us back here while they hear pretrial motions and deal with any issues they don't want us to know about because they might prejudice us about the case."

The fatter of the two white women piped up. "I'm not prejudiced."

"Not prejudice like that," Cris said. "Prejudice like if we heard what they're saying, it might color how we look at things."

"Well, whatever happened to the whole truth, nothing but the truth, so help you God?" This from McBusiness. Since when did you take an interest in what's going on around you, I wanted to say, but instead I shook my head and held my tongue. I'd need every ounce of patience I had to make it through the next few days with these yahoos. Thankfully, the door opened and the bailiff walked in before we could get any deeper into a discussion on the finer points of the law.

"Judge's ready. Follow me."

I stuck to the middle of the pack, surprised to find Cris at my side. I'd expected her to make a beeline for the courtroom the minute this thing got started, but here she was, sticking to me like a burr. I studied her as best I could while we filed through the hall by the judge's chambers into the courtroom. I didn't see any obvious resemblance to Teresa Perez, but still. I know it's a common name, but it seemed weird I'd get a lead on Perez and then be stuck in the same room with a woman with her last name for the next however long. I might be crazy, but I might also be looking her up when I had a free moment.

Which wasn't now. The judge reminded us about the oath we'd taken the day before and the rules about not talking about the case and not reading or watching any news stories about it. If anything about this case had made headlines, then the next few days might not be so boring after all.

The first witness on the stand was a cop. No surprise there. I'd been a cop long enough to see how things worked, but not long enough to ever have to testify in a felony trial since the one suspect I'd taken into custody all on my own had pled guilty. Good thing, since we'd managed to shoot holes through each other during our one and only encounter. Reuniting would have been awkward at best. Anyway, the prosecutors usually put the cops on the stand first to set the stage. They'd tell about the investigation and give us a framework for the rest of the evidence they planned to present.

I struggled to pay attention and wished I'd actually listened to yesterday's opening statements. The first cop was pretty green, and Rebecca, the hot prosecutor, took an edgy tone with him when he stumbled over the description of his initial investigation at the scene of the crime. Didn't help that the cop spoke only formal cop talk, using phrases like "secured the perimeter" and "ascertained the appropriate measures" instead of just talking like a regular human. I don't think I'd ever been that green. It took the better part of an hour for them to sketch out only a handful of pertinent facts. The initial report of the shooting came from a 911 call from the phone inside the bar where the murder occurred. Most of the patrons at the bar had scattered by the time the uniforms showed up, leaving only the bartender, the dead guy, and a single eyewitness. The dead guy, Manny Cruz, was shot in the parking lot behind the building, and he was toast by the time the first cops arrived.

Next up was the homicide detective who'd worked the case, Detective Tom Giraldi. He looked familiar, but I didn't dwell on it. Even after I'd left the force, I'd dropped by several of the substations a few times either to see Jess or one of my other friends still on the job, and then there were the times I got hauled in for questioning after engaging in some of the more shady practices my type of work often demanded. Chances were I'd run into this guy on one of those occasions.

It only took a couple of minutes for me to realize he was a pompous, know-it-all dick. He talked about how he and his partner had interviewed the bartender and the eyewitness, and they both confirmed that the defendant and the deceased had gotten into a heated argument shortly before the murder. The eyewitness had left the bar immediately before the defendant and was still in the back parking lot when the shooting went down. The bartender confirmed the time he'd heard the gunshots. No security footage, no other witnesses, no gun, but to Giraldi it was an open-and-shut case.

I took a minute to glance at my fellow jurors, certain they must be as annoyed as I was at this guy's bravado. Nope. They were glued to his testimony, as if he were the eyewitness himself. I shook my head and turned back to watch Giraldi as he described how they'd found the defendant at his home later that night. When they rolled up to his house and knocked on his door, they heard clattering in the house and the sound of a car roaring to life in the garage. They yelled "Police," busted through the front door, and made it to the garage in time to haul him out of his getaway car. In an amazing stroke of luck, the murder weapon was sitting in plain view, on a table in the entryway of the house.

I smelled bullshit. Was I the only one? But then I remembered Jess's words from last night about how she knew every last detail about the case and that it was a slam dunk for the state. She worked homicide, so it wasn't surprising she was familiar with another case within her department, but based on what I'd heard so far, I had some serious reservations. If I'd just murdered someone, I'm not going to go home, hang out, and wait for the cops to show up. Then, when they do show up, I botch my escape, and to top it off, I leave my gun behind? Not likely.

According to Giraldi, the defendant had been a member of the Texas Syndicate, a tough-guy prison gang and sworn rivals of the dead guy's gang, the Texas Mexican Mafia. Hard to believe he could survive that and turn into such a dope on the outside. Granted, plenty of criminals are stupid—a fact that keeps me and a whole lot of others in business—but if everything Giraldi said was spot-on, then this guy was the dumbest of the dumb.

I looked over at him. Rey Navarro was dressed in a suit that didn't quite fit and a tie that didn't quite match. He could barely look at Giraldi for more than a few seconds at a time, and his right leg bounced up and down under the table like he was about to launch out of his seat and run for the door. None of this was definitive. People got nervous about going to jail whether they were guilty or not, and anyone who says they can tell if someone's guilty by the way they react to a situation is a big fat liar. My only gauge at this point was my visceral distaste for Giraldi, and my gut told me he was either lying about something or, at a very minimum, had let his cocky desire to close this case in a hurry get in the way of investigating all the facts.

When the prosecutor spoke the magic words "I have no further questions for this witness," I looked at the clock. For normal people, eleven forty-five would be a perfect time to take a lunch break, but Judge Bowser could apparently subsist on justice alone. I held back a groan as I heard him say, "Ms. Watson, you may cross-examine the witness."

Bea Watson stayed seated and spent a couple of minutes shuffling through papers while everyone tried to pretend like the lingering silence wasn't awkward. When the judge cleared his throat, Bea looked up and offered an apologetic smile before she addressed Giraldi, whose own smile was starting to look a bit forced. "Detective, I'm sorry to keep you waiting, but for the life of me I can't find a copy of the report showing the gunshot residue you found on my client. I don't suppose you brought it with you today?"

Giraldi's expression turned sour and he shot a look at the prosecutor. Watson followed his glance, which caused everyone in the jury box to look her way as well, and the prosecutor squirmed under all the attention. Finally, Rebecca stood and asked the judge if they could approach. For the next few minutes we watched the attorneys' broad gestures and aggressive whispers, unable to hear exactly what was taking place. I had a hunch, though, and it was confirmed when Bea resumed her questioning with a more direct attack.

"Detective Giraldi, you do not have any evidence showing gunshot residue on my client's person, correct?"

"Well, the reason the test—"

"Stop right there." She turned to the judge. "I don't want to have to slow things down with another bench conference."

"Thank you, Counselor." Bowser frowned at Giraldi. "Detective, I'm going to ask you to just answer the question that's put to you."

"No, we don't have any such evidence." Giraldi practically spat the words, but Bea nodded her approval at his admission. She looked back down at her notes, but before she could get the next question out, Giraldi had a bout of Tourette's.

"But he probably washed his hands before we showed up to arrest him."

Bea hesitated only a second before meeting his smug grin with one of her own. "Did you see him wash his hands?"

"Well, no, but—"

"And there's nothing in your report about how you checked for evidence that he'd recently washed and dried his hands, correct?"

"Uh, I guess not."

"So, it's your conclusion that my client murdered Mr. Cruz, then drove home, washed away the gunshot residue, put the murder weapon on the coffee table right in the middle of the living room, and waited for you to come arrest him?"

While Giraldi tried to wrap his brain around the multi-part question, Bea shook her head and moved on to questions about the very first steps of the investigation. She was thorough and she'd scored some points with the whole residue thing, but it wasn't a slam dunk. When she finally wrapped up, I was about to eat my arm.

Bowser gave us one slim hour for lunch and warned us about being late. I'd hoped for longer since an hour wouldn't give me enough time to check out any of the spots still on my hunting-for-Perez list. It wasn't enough time to leave the courthouse at all, and as we filed out of court, I again wished I'd paid attention to Jess's suggestion that I bring along some food.

"Going to the cafeteria?"

I looked up to see Cris standing next to me. How did she manage to continually sneak up on me like that? "Uh, I guess. Judge sounds like he's going to keep us late."

"A few of us are planning to sit together. Want to join us?"

I willed my mind to switch gears and conjure up a reason I couldn't sit with Cris and the band of bland. "Thanks, but I have to take care of a few things. I'll probably just grab a burger and make some phone calls."

Her look told me she didn't believe me, but she didn't challenge my excuse. "Okay. If you change your mind, we'll be down there."

I gave her a halfhearted smile and walked away. I wouldn't be changing my mind. I grabbed a burger and fries from the grill and took the Styrofoam box of goodness outside into the sunny sixty-degree day.

For February, the weather was pretty much perfect, and I ate my lunch in the front seat of the Bronco with the windows down.

With the burger in one hand, I used the other to dump the contents of what I'd now dubbed the Perez Papers onto the passenger seat. I stared at all the pieces, willing a pattern to emerge. Most of the places I'd managed to identify so far were dives, but a couple were highbrow watering holes. The locations were scattered all over the city, so geography was out as a common link. Perez was up to something and these joints were the key. If I wasn't stuck at the courthouse, I'd be able to run these down in a couple of days, but no such luck. I divided the stuff into two piles: one for the places I still needed to check out and one for the places I'd managed to visit so far.

I picked up the coaster from Shorty's and started to toss it onto stack number two, but a twinge of doubt made me hang on. Fred's overreaction when I asked her about Perez told me she'd seen her, and she'd seen her recently. Shorty's was definitely worth a return trip.

I managed to make it back inside and to the jury room before everyone else and leaned back in one of the folding chairs to try to sneak in a nap, but before I could drift off to sleep, my phone rang. I didn't recognize the number, but on the off chance it was a lead about Perez, I answered. "Bennett."

"You find her yet?"

Cantoni. I looked around, but I was still alone in the room and decided it was safe to talk. "Why don't you ask the folks that've been following me?"

"I don't know anything about that, but I do know she's a popular gal."

Gal. I could think of many other choice words for Teresa Perez. "Did you call to give me a lead or give me a hard time?"

"Hey, Luca, just trying to pay back a debt. I don't know what kind of intel you got so far, but if a joint named Leroy's is on your list, you might want to bump it up to the top."

I opened the envelope and sifted through the paper. A matchbook from Leroy's was in stack number one. "Leroy's on Ledbetter. Got it. I'll check it out. Thanks."

"You're welcome. We square?"

"Yeah, we're square."

I hung up the phone and checked the time. The rest of the truth-finding crew should be back any minute. On cue, the door opened and Cris walked through, followed a few seconds later by the rest of the jurors. Their boisterous conversation died the second they saw me sitting alone in the room, and Cris's eyes shifted quickly away. I didn't really give a damn if they were talking about me, so long as they left me alone, but I was surprised when Cris sat down next to me and whispered, "Larry thinks you have secret information about the case."

I held back a snort. Barely. "Secret information? What does that even mean?"

She shifted in her seat. "I don't know. Maybe you have access to the full police report, things the rest of us aren't allowed to see."

"And how exactly do I get my hands on this 'secret' stuff?"

More shifting and the faint hint of a blush rose up her neck. "Didn't you say you lived with a cop?"

"And you assume she's the kind of person who leaks information about a case and I'm the kind of person who would use that information?"

Before she could answer, the bailiff appeared in the doorway. "They're ready. Let's go."

This time I was first in line to get back to the boring business of listening to lawyers and witnesses drone on. The sooner we were back in there, the quicker I could escape my annoying "peers."

The first witness of the afternoon was the medical examiner. I guess he was there to prove that the dead guy was indeed dead, because otherwise his testimony didn't add much. Two bullets from a .45 to the chest equaled homicide as the cause of death. The prosecutor spent a little extra time getting him to point out the trademark Mexican Mafia tattoo, MM, on Manny Cruz's shoulder as a way of emphasizing he and the defendant were fierce rivals. Bea asked him a few questions, but nobody really contested the manner of death, and she wisely realized there wasn't much point hashing out the gory details a second time.

When the ME stepped down, I watched the judge look at the clock on the wall and spend about five seconds scratching his head before he told the prosecutors to call their next witness. They had their investigator bring in a guy named Joe Donner. Joe was the bartender, and he'd heard the gunshots and called the cops. It was pretty clear this guy hadn't seen the crime and all he had to add was context. While the prosecutor drew out the questions, I could feel the burger and fries from earlier coursing through my system like an IV of sedatives. A hazy glance at the rest of the jurors told me I wasn't the only one who was suffering from a food coma.

"They argued?" the prosecutor asked.

"Yeah. They got pretty loud. That's when I told them to get out."

"Do you know what they were arguing about?"

He shook his head. "Nope. We get a lot of guys from different groups in the bar. I try to stay out of their business."

"By different groups, do you mean gangs?"

"You call 'em what you want. Texas Syndicate, Mexican Mafia. In my bar, they're all just customers."

Sounded to me like Mr. Bartender wasn't keen on being here today. Business had probably taken a dive right about the time he'd been subpoenaed as a witness, since ex-cons didn't usually hang out in places cops were crawling all over. But I perked up at the mention of the Mexican Mafia since that's who Teresa Perez had been in bed with when she'd traded being a homicide cop for a drug dealer. The spark of interest faded as it quickly became clear he didn't have much else to offer about the facts of the case. After he described the rest of the crowd at the bar in vague terms, Bea asked him a few pointed questions about the area behind the building to establish that the lighting was poor and it would have been difficult for the eyewitness to see anything. She also got out the fact that everyone in the bar had been drinking, which made it likely the eyewitness's eye-witnessing might have been compromised.

When they finally let the guy off the stand, the prosecutor announced she needed just a few minutes before her next witness would be available. Bowser shook his finger at the clock and told them they had fifteen minutes to call another witness, no exceptions. The bailiff ushered us out of the courtroom and warned us to stick close. I edged away from the rest of my group and went out into the hallway to call Jess. She answered on the first ring.

"You guys done deliberating?"

"Funny. But at this rate, we might be done a lot faster than you thought. I think Bowser wears a bag so he doesn't have to take pee breaks. I'm surprised he let us have lunch."

"He hasn't changed. So, he's keeping you late?"

"Yep. And then, you know…"

"Right. You have to work. Got it."

Her voice was flat and I detected a trace of pissed. I didn't feel the need to explain again that I was working and didn't really want to talk about it anymore since I was kinda sorta lying. Shit. She'd get over it or she wouldn't, but if she'd already decided she couldn't trust me to stay out late on a weeknight or that I would jump whenever her plans trumped mine, then we were in for years of fighting. "Okay. Well, then, I guess I'll see you later."

"Say hi to Bingo for me."

She hung up before I could respond. So that was it. She thought I was gambling. Like I had any money to gamble. Well, she could keep thinking that since she'd be really pissed if she knew I was hunting Perez on my lonesome.

I turned the phone off and stepped back into the jury room, where the rest of the jurors were huddled in their special little groups. I barely had time to down a cup of thick, scorched coffee before Sam appeared and drug us back into the courtroom. The next witness was already on the stand, and Bowser swore him in. Only took a couple of questions from the prosecutor to make it clear this was the eyewitness. Finally, maybe the testimony would be interesting.

While he answered the softball questions, I gave him a once-over. Dressed in an ill-fitting suit and a too-starched, high-collared shirt, he looked about as out of place in formal clothes as the defendant did, but unlike the defendant, he seemed to relish his place in the spotlight. He answered every question with more detail than was asked for, and he smiled after each answer like he was expecting a pat on the head. Dante Guzman. Age thirty. Lifetime resident of Dallas. Worked as a contractor. Wonder if the State of Texas had purchased his suit rather than have him show up looking like he'd been crawling around in the dirt, or whatever contractors do for a living.

His story was he'd been at the bar to grab a couple of beers after a hard day's work. He was barely into the second one when he heard the defendant and dead guy trading strong words. When the two started posturing, like they were going to exchange more than words, he slid a ten to the barkeep and slipped out. Before he could reach his truck, he heard loud voices and turned around in time to see the defendant pull a gun, fire three shots at the soon-to-be-dead guy, get in his car, and peel out of the parking lot. He shouted for someone to call 911, and then he ran to the dying guy and stayed with him until the police and paramedics arrived.

With only a few wrap-up questions, the prosecutor said the magic words, "pass the witness," and every eye in the courtroom looked from the clock on the wall to the judge and back to the clock again. It was six thirty, way past time for anyone to be able to retain any other facts that might come out during the defense's cross-examination, not to mention the fact that stomachs were rumbling all around me. All I could think about was where my next cheeseburger was coming from.

Apparently, Judge Bowser was hungry too and he adjourned for the day. I barely listened to his warnings not to watch the news or talk about the case as I ticked through my list of to-dos for the evening. When I was finally free and walking out the doors of the courthouse, I checked my phone and found a text from Jess.

Looks like you're not the only one working late. Your turn not to wait up.

I read the lines several times, certain she was still angry with me but uncertain about whether to respond. This shit was new. If a woman got pissed at me in the past, the solution was simple: steer clear of her until she either got over it or moved on. But life had changed and I could no longer rely on my gut reactions. I lived with Jess. The house was hers, but there were still traces of me in every room. It wasn't like I could just hole up in the apartment I no longer had and wait to see if she got over it. We shared stuff, including a dog.

Cash. Damn. If she was late, I needed to get home to feed him. I'd planned on heading directly to Leroy's, but I'd have to detour.

When I walked through the front door of the house, Cash stood up and placed his big paws on my chest. "Come on, boy." I opened the back door and followed him outside. While he did his business, I took in the view. Jess had bought this house when she'd been promoted to detective. She'd quickly moved up the ranks, which was good for her career but not so good for homesteading. She had a ton of plans for the backyard, but they'd stay plans for now: a deck here, a rock formation there.

Lately, she'd been asking me what I thought, and I didn't have a clue. The only backyard I'd ever had was the one at my parents' house, and it consisted of a balding patch of grass, a small grouping of aluminum chairs, and a rickety barbecue grill. And making plans seemed so damn permanent. Not like I didn't plan on being with Jess for the long haul, but planning wasn't my forte when it meant a change in my status quo.

All the planning I had in store for tonight consisted of feeding Cash and heading out the door. I shook some kibble into his bowl, and he skidded across the kitchen floor and wolfed it down like it was a hot dog lathered with cheese sauce. I was starving too, but I didn't find anything grab-and-go in the fridge, so I figured I'd pick up something on the road. Besides, Jess had a thing for keeping the kitchen clean, which didn't fit in with my schedule tonight. While Cash had his head buried in his bowl, I stepped my way to the front door, careful not to signal my departure, but the second I turned the doorknob, he was at my side, tail wagging his desire to join me. "I've got to work, but Jess will be home soon."

He offered a few deep howls to tell me the promise of another woman wasn't what he had in mind. To make his point clear, he stood and put a paw on the doorknob. I'm not usually one to fall victim to sentiment, but even I have my limits. Big blue pleading eyes and the sweet request of his begging tones did me in. I reached for his bright-red leash, and a minute later we were in the Bronco ready for adventure.

Chapter Six

I caught on to the tail a few blocks after I left the house. Another SUV, but not the same one as last time. Guess these guys had a fleet of big-ass vehicles ready to follow folks at a moment's notice. I did my damnedest to make out the license plate, but whoever it was stayed just out of range.

I debated my options: lose the shadow or let my stalker follow me directly to Perez and give her what she had coming. My big plan was to reserve the pleasure of revenge for myself, but another part of me was curious about what they had in store. I'd seen enough news coverage to know these cartel fuckers don't mess around. Hacked-off limbs, electric currents. Perez would be much better off in my custody, but I didn't expect her to come willingly. I glanced at Cash on the seat beside me and knew I'd made the right decision bringing him along.

Ultimately, I let geography decide my course. The driveway to Leroy's, the next bar on my list, was a narrow gravel road, and once I turned off the main drag, the SUV kept going, just like last time, but a second car appeared in its wake and turned right behind me. This time it was a Subaru—one of those station-wagon-looking things that cost as much as a Mercedes. Kind of a strange choice for drug dealers, but since I hadn't shopped for cars in the last twenty years, who was I to judge? I had no way of knowing if this car was actually following me or if it had turned in behind me by chance, but if I was going to have help in my hunt for Perez, I wanted to know who I was getting it from. The fact they'd have to pull up right behind me gave me an advantage, and I pulled into a space on the edge of the lot and waited for my shadow to reveal himself.

Ten minutes passed before Cash signaled he was over this whole waiting-around act. I spun the barrel of my Colt and shoved it into my shoulder holster, and then I opened the door of the Bronco and motioned for Cash to follow. The Subaru was parked about twenty feet away—lights off but the engine running. I didn't bother to hide my approach. I strode up to the driver's side and slapped my palm on the hood of the car. Next, I pulled back my jacket just enough to show the Colt and leaned down toward the window to get a face-to-face with my stalker. The window was slightly tinted, but I stared until a face came into view. The woman sitting in the driver's seat was the last person I expected to see. "Cris?"

I doubted she could hear me through the closed window, but Cris Perez-Soria did a semi-decent job of looking guilty. Guilty about what? Had she followed me on purpose, and if she hadn't, then why the hell was she here? I rapped my knuckles on the window until she finally lowered the glass a few cautious inches.

"What the hell are you doing here?" I growled.

She glanced from me to Cash, who at this point sensed my quest had taken a wrong turn. He weaved in and out of my legs, muttering. I snapped my fingers in her face to focus her attention back to me. "Speak. Now."

She pulled her eyes from Cash and shook her head. "I could ask the same thing."

I detected a trace of know-it-all in her tone, like she thought she'd caught me robbing a bank. I wasn't having any of it. "I'll ask the questions. Do you even know where you are?"

She wasn't quick enough to disguise the furtive sideways glance at the bar, and it didn't matter anyway, because I stepped up to block her view before she could make out the sign. She took my intervention like a champ. "You know where I am," she said with a confident shrug. "But the real question is what are *you* doing here?"

Verbal sparring isn't my thing. Besides, I had a job to do. Bad enough that jury duty had interfered with my pursuit of Perez during the day, but having this very concrete reminder of the interference was just too much. "It's time for you to leave. Go home and get a good night's sleep."

She shook her head and turned off the engine. "I'm not leaving here until you do."

She wanted me to ask her why, engage in whatever game she was playing, but I didn't have the energy. Best thing to do in these situations is walk away and hope the other party gives up. I didn't usually turn my back on someone set on provoking me, but I wasn't afraid of this chick. I snapped my fingers at Cash and started toward the bar. I made it about five steps before I realized he hadn't followed me, and when I turned to see what was up, his betrayal broke my heart. Cris had her hand on either side of his face and was fucking cooing into his ear. As if her crazy public display of affection wasn't bad enough, he was shoving his head into the palms of her hands in his classic don't-ever-stop-petting-me motion. Traitor.

"Cash, come here right now."

"That's a weird name for a dog."

"Buzz off."

"I'm serious," she said. "I'm not leaving here until you tell me what you're up to. If you don't have a good explanation, I'll report you to the judge."

"What the hell are you talking about?"

Her eyes closed into half slits and she shook her head again, but this time it was in that you're-a-moron kind of way. I so didn't have time for this. "Speak," I said. "You've got about five seconds before I lose my patience," I lied. I'd lost my patience the minute I'd seen her sitting in the parking lot.

"Don't you threaten me. I'm not the one violating the judge's orders. We're supposed to listen to the evidence that's presented in court. We're definitely not supposed to be investigating the crime on our own." She pointed at the door to the bar. "What exactly did you hope to find in there?"

Now I was completely confused. I followed the direction of her outstretched arm and squinted at the bar door. The neon sign above the entrance read Leroy's, but just below that, in ancient letters and numbers, was another sign with the address of the building. 3504 Ledbetter. It was the address on the matchbook in the packet from Cantoni's pals, but a faint spark of recognition told me I knew that address from some other source.

I looked from Cris to the door and back again. Her expression told me she was waiting for me to stop being stupid, and I was trying hard.

3504 Ledbetter...South Dallas...Seedy little bar. *Shit.* Memories from the testimony I'd heard earlier in the day slowly swam through the murky water of my mind. Suddenly I knew exactly where I was, but I still couldn't wrap my brain around it. "But the bar where the shooting happened was called Eddie's."

"That's what it used to be called," Cris said. "The place changed owners late last year, and they changed the name."

Either she'd done a little research of her own or I'd dozed during that part of the trial. I didn't bother to ask which. "Not that it's any of your business, but I'm meeting someone here."

She put her hands on her hips. "Right."

"Well, what's your excuse for being here, little miss professional juror?"

She looked around, her eyes darting like a scared rabbit, before she whispered, "I heard you. On the phone. Talking about checking things out here."

I had to give her points for being crafty because I didn't have a clue anyone had been spying on me. "And you just decided to follow me here? What was your endgame? Call the cops and tell them I was being a bad juror?" She opened her mouth to respond, but I held a palm up while I rubbed a mental itch until a better question popped into my head. "Wait a minute. Who was in the other car?"

"What other car?"

I waved her off while I cycled through the facts. Someone had followed me from my house but then ditched when they saw Cris's Subaru on my tail. The first car was probably full of folks thinking I was leading them to Perez. "Never mind."

"Well, what's your plan?" Cris asked, persistent little cuss.

"Like I'm going to tell you."

"Okay then." She puffed up big, which almost made me laugh, since at her normal height she was no taller than my chest. "I'll have to tell Judge Bowser you were here and you refused to answer any questions."

I'd had enough. I reached out and grabbed her car keys from her hand. Before she could react, I whistled to Cash, my formerly loyal dog, and we stalked off to the Subaru. As I slipped into the driver's seat, I yelled back to Cris. "You coming or what?"

Surprise didn't begin to describe her expression. She ran toward the car and jumped into the passenger side. "What do you think you're doing?"

"You want to investigate something, then you're coming with me." I started the faux station wagon and peeled out of the parking space. I'd come back here later when I didn't have a pesky peer in tow. In the meantime, I was headed back to Shorty's, but this time in a car no one would recognize. Fred's shifty behavior last night had festered, and I had a feeling she knew more than she was letting on about Perez's activities. After the sharp-pointed send-off I'd received when I was there last, I figured having company on this trip was the best way to disguise my real intent. Cash and Cris would make for a nice distraction.

I turned onto the main road and pointed the car toward Shorty's. As Cash leaned his head on my shoulder, his gentle panting told me he was excited, but a glance at Cris's sour face told me she thought she'd been hijacked. I mock-punched her shoulder. "Cheer up."

"Cheer up?" Her voice rose. "I don't have a clue where we're going. For all I know you're going to dump me on the side of the road and leave me for dead."

I couldn't help but laugh. "We're like five minutes from the city and I'm betting you have a cell phone. Even if I'm stealing your car, you can get help to respond pretty damn quick. Following me tonight was ballsy. What happened to your sense of adventure?"

"Please don't hurt me. I have a wife and a son."

"A wife, huh? Does she know you're out on the town, playing law and order? And why should I believe you were following me to Leroy's? Maybe you were there investigating the case for yourself."

She shook her head furiously, and I could tell by the bright light of denial in her eyes there was no way she would break the law on purpose. I held back a laugh. The night was young.

❖

Shorty's was busier tonight. Fred had a pal behind the bar, slinging ice into glasses and flipping the tops off beer bottles. I marched Cris and Cash past a different bouncer than the one who'd been here before and led them to a booth in the back of the room. The bouncer put a hand on my arm and pointed to Cash, but I didn't meet his eyes. "Seeing-eye dog," I said, barely raising my voice over the din. I didn't want Fred to notice me until I was ready.

While we waited for the skimpily dressed cocktail waitress to notice she had a new table, I looked around. At least two dozen folks were drowning their troubles at the bar, the majority of them sitting alone. A group at the pool table was having a lively debate about whether the shooter had scratched the alleged winning shot, and the air was thick with the threat of a fight.

"What are we doing here?" Cris mustered the courage to ask.

I ignored her question. "You want a beer?"

"No. I want to leave."

She did look out of place. What she likely considered casual probably cost more than a lot of folks make in a week. Before I could say just that, the waitress appeared and, between smacks of chewing gum, asked for our order. "Two drafts and a bowl of water for my guide dog."

She sighed and spun on her too-high-heel shoes. When she was out of earshot, I leaned across the table. "I'm working, and you're here because you decided to show up and get in the middle of my work. So you'll drink a beer and pet my dog and otherwise stay out of my way for the rest of the night. Okay?"

She nodded, but the act seemed almost involuntary. "Can I talk?"

I started to say no but decided we'd look more like normal bar-goers if we were at least pretending to have a real conversation. "I guess."

"Are you on the hunt?"

I closed my eyes and looked for patience. "On the hunt? What's that supposed to mean?"

She wriggled in her seat. "Well, I don't know what you call it. You're a bounty 'hunter,' aren't you?" She left her air quotes hanging until I nodded defeat.

"Look, this is going to go a lot better for both of us if we talk about something besides my work."

Not to be deterred, Cris charged in with her next question. "Are you married?"

I choked on my beer. "No."

"My wife and I've been together twenty-one years. We tied the knot in Provincetown. Couldn't be happier."

"Goody for you." The small talk was making me edgy, but something she'd said struck a chord. "Your last name, it's hyphenated, right?" She nodded yes. "Who's the Perez, you or her?"

"Me. Why?"

I paused before answering while I thought of a way to trick her into telling me the truth about whether she was kin to the Perez I was here to find. "I didn't notice them asking you about any cops in your family during jury selection. Is that because you lied on the questionnaire?"

Her whole face scrunched up, and she shook her head. "I don't know what you're talking about."

A big part of my job was listening to people lie: "I didn't get the notice about the court date"; "I was there, but they didn't check me in"; "You're looking for the other Jane Doe. People get us confused all the time." I've become a pro at figuring out when someone's lying to me. Cris Perez-Soria was telling the truth. "Never mind."

She settled back into the seat and was quiet for a few precious moments before her natural desire to irritate me resurfaced.

"Okay, so you're not married, but you have a girlfriend, right? She's a cop?"

I could keep shaking her off or I could engage just enough to keep her distracted while I cased the bar for signs of Perez. I settled on throwing a few crumbs her way. "She's a detective, homicide."

"Wow, that sounds like a cool job. I spend my days in meetings, planning more meetings, and having my eyes glaze over budgets. Bet the talk around your dinner table is pretty interesting."

"Uh-huh," I said, barely registering her comment. I was tracking a woman who'd just entered the bar. She had big blond hair and Jackie-O sunglasses that, while not real practical at nighttime, kind of fit in with the weird, anything-goes vibe of this place. What caught my attention was her dark skin. Didn't look like a tan job and sure wasn't soak-up-the-rays weather outside, so she was either wearing a wig or she colored her hair. She walked over to the bar and slid onto the stool closest to the back door. A few seconds later, Fred handed her a drink without a word exchanged between them, dubbing blondie a regular.

"...keep us late tomorrow night."

I looked up at my reluctant companion. She had leaned back in the booth and had one arm slung around Cash. "What?"

"I asked you what you're doing for Valentine's Day. Do you think Judge Bowser will keep us late tomorrow night?"

I recognized the individual words she spoke, but strung together they were gibberish. Valentine's Day was a made-up holiday all about dropping a bunch of bills on flowers that died within a week or candy you'd have to run for miles to work off. I'd never engaged in the sport as an adult, and my childhood memories of showing up at school with a sack of tiny cards in their tiny white envelopes were marred by the fact my mom made me take one for everyone in the class, even the kids I couldn't stand and who couldn't stand me.

"What do you have planned?" Cris asked.

Apparently, she took my silence for permission to grill me about my lack of romantic tendencies. I didn't care. I shouldn't care, anyway. Jess didn't expect anything from me.

Or did she? The second I thought the words, my memory dialed back to my conversations with Jess over the last twenty-four hours about her special plans for Wednesday night. Her rough reaction to my "I don't know if I'll be home any night this week" suddenly made sense.

But the Jess I knew had never expected candy and flowers from me. I'd watched her cycle through a few relationships over the years, and while she acted like she enjoyed the romantic attention she got from other women, I'd always assumed she was doing what I'd do—playing along to get laid. She didn't expect me to wine and dine her, did she?

A sick feeling twisted my gut. Surely she knew I wasn't going to change who I was just because I'd finally admitted I was in love with her? If she did, then I'd miscalculated this whole thing between us. I wanted to crawl out of my skin. "Nothing. I have nothing planned. And don't bother telling me all about how you're going to leave a trail of roses in your house for your wife to follow to the perfect gift, the perfect meal, the perfect flowers. I'm not interested."

I punctuated my declaration by pounding my fist on the table, which caused Cash to bark. The sharp sound caused several folks to turn our way, including the faux blonde at the bar. I ducked my head and cursed, certain that if it was Perez, she'd make me in a heartbeat. I counted to ten and risked a glance in her direction just in time to see her slip out the back door, holding a bag she hadn't had when she'd walked into the bar. I jumped up. "Stay here with Cash. Don't move until I get back."

Cash woofed something to Cris, and she stroked his chin and nodded at me before I took off toward the front door. When I hit the cool night air, I ducked around the side of the building, hoping to get a drop on whatever this chick who might be Perez was up to. When I reached the edge of the building, I could make her out, rooting through the bag she'd carried out of the bar and muttering. I hunkered down next to a drainpipe and watched.

A minute later, I realized she wasn't talking to herself. A guy was standing a few feet from her, his presence only revealed when a car drove past and its headlights hit just right. I couldn't see his face, but I was close enough to make out their conversation.

"It's all there."

"You better hope so." Definitely Perez's voice. "I won't be back for a while," she said, "and this has to last."

"Maybe you shouldn't have come back at all," the guy said. "Fred says folks have been asking about you." His voice sounded vaguely familiar, but I was way more interested in what Perez had to say.

"I'm not worried about Luca Bennett. She couldn't find her way out of a paper bag. The folks I'm worried about don't have a clue where I am."

Bitch. I vowed to give her something to worry about.

"Go ahead and count it if you don't trust me," he told her.

A few seconds passed with only the light sound of ruffling papers. I envisioned Perez stroking her fingers through a big sack of cash, and the idea she'd get away and have the means to stay gone pissed me off so much I drew my gun and started toward them. I'd made it two steps before a hand grabbed my arm. I twisted out of the grip and yanked the interloper close, shoving the Colt's muzzle up against his throat as I squinted to get a good look at the jackass who was getting in my way.

Shit. It was Cris, and standing next to her was Cash, who looked between us like he couldn't quite decide who needed protecting. To Cris's credit, she didn't cry out, but her eyes were wide and pleading. I put a finger on my lips and glared. She nodded, and I lowered the gun but kept her firmly in my grip and whispered, "What the hell part of stay-in-the-bar-and-wait didn't you understand?"

"I'm sorry, but I freaked out. The guy, the eyewitness. I saw him walking through the bar when you got up. I looked around inside, but I'm not sure where he went."

"What are you talking about?"

"From the trial. Dante. The eyewitness. If he sees us here, we'll both be in big trouble."

Cylinders starting clicking into place, and I motioned for Cris to stay put while I craned my head around the corner. Like magic, a big-ass truck with a line of lights on the roof drove by and shined its high beams directly on Perez, who was shoving the last stack of bills back into the bag, and the guy who waited for her to sign off on the deal.

Dante Guzman had lost his fancy courtroom suit and slicked-back hair. Tonight his hair was pulled back into one of those little ponytails that's hardly worth fooling with, and he was wearing jeans, boots, and an untucked gray T-shirt. Without the collared shirt and tie he'd sported in court, his true identity was revealed, but only for a split second before the truck moved on and darkness enveloped Dante and his pal, Teresa Perez.

"Luca, did you see that?"

I looked at Cris, made a zip-it motion, and ducked behind the wall. Any minute now, Perez would be on the run. My decision to drag Cris along on this expedition now seemed like one of the dumber things I'd done, and I wasn't about to compound it by taking her with me into what might turn into a gunfight. I came up with the best plan I could on the fly and tossed the car keys to her. "Get back in the bar. Now. Don't stop, don't look back. If I'm not there in thirty minutes, leave. If I don't show up tomorrow, tell the judge, tell someone, but until then keep your mouth shut."

I motioned to Cash and stepped out into the parking lot. Cris would leave or she wouldn't, but all my focus was on Perez. I slipped behind a row of cars and crept my way toward them, hunched down with Cash close behind. Assuming they were both armed, a little shock-and-awe would be my only chance at getting the drop on them, and Cash would fill the bill nicely. When I got as close as I could without alerting the crooks, I whispered in Cash's ear. We'd practiced this maneuver in the backyard at home until Jess had made us stop for fear the neighbors would call the cops. I howled first to get him going, but then he took over like a champion, crooning with every ounce of loud husky breath he could muster.

The eerie howling did its trick. Dante and Perez both looked like they'd wandered onto the set of a horror movie and their only concern was a route of escape. After a brief pause, they took off running, directly toward me, Dante in the lead. I stretched a leg into his path, and he hit the ground with a thud. Perez was following too close to stop in time, and she landed with her face in his ass. Perfection.

I placed a boot on Dante's back and ordered Cash to attack if he said a word, hoping he believed Cash would follow such a specific command. For all I knew, Cash thought I was telling him a story about hamburgers. Perez rolled off her pal, but before she could get her footing, I snatched her bag of cash and jammed my gun against her jaw.

"Say a word and you're dead."

She shook her head. "Your threats mean jack shit. If I don't get out of here now, I might as well be dead."

"Not my problem." I tossed her Cash's leash. "Let's put your special outlaw skills to work. Tie up your friend. Nice and tight."

She sat stubbornly still at first, but after a few shakes of my gun, she grudgingly complied. Memories surfaced of the last time I'd seen her and how she'd tied Jess to a chair and left us both to die. Red-hot rage almost made me pull the trigger. But that whole dead-or-alive thing was pretty much a myth in the bounty-hunting world. Killing Perez would mean lots of paperwork and a long interrogation, especially considering my record for run-ins with the law. Jess had intervened plenty of times in the past on my behalf, but after all she'd been through because of this bastard, no way would I call on her for help on this one.

Another option would be to deliver Perez to the folks who'd put me on her trail in the first place. No doubt they'd love the chance to deliver a slow, torturous death to the woman who'd double-crossed them. The idea of Perez in pain was pretty damn satisfying, but how much fun would it be if I could never tell anyone? Jess was cool, but she was a cop to the core. Besides, turning Perez over to the cartel would mean she'd never get the public shaming she absolutely deserved.

It was time for me to step up, and taking Perez in alive was the only way to close this episode of our lives. I thought back to my conversation with Cris in the bar. If I played my cards right, I might even be able to use Perez's capture for more than the bounty I'd collect.

Chapter Seven

"You're making a big mistake."

I glanced over at Perez in the passenger seat, hands cuffed behind her. I'd gotten Cris to drive me and my haul of felons back to Leroy's so I could get the Bronco, and then I sent her home for the night. Her wide-eyed expression when she drove away told me she was more than a little scared of what I might do next, but I had to admire her spunk for playing a role in my adventure.

Maybe I was making a big mistake, but not in the way Perez meant. My fantasy move was to push her out of the car while we were riding at top speed, then laugh while the semi behind us flattened her into the asphalt. Instead I just sighed and said, "Maybe I am."

She shot a look at Dante, who, guarded by Cash, was sacked out in the backseat, still out of it from his plunge into the concrete, and then she leaned across the seat. "I've got money. Lots of it. You'd never have to work again."

"Maybe I like to work. It's not that hard, you know. I just wait for stupid people to fuck up, and then I drag them in. You know, like cops do. You remember that, don't you?"

"I was a good cop."

"You were a bitch."

"Is that what this is about?"

Her gall blew me away. "Seriously? You're crazy. You kidnapped Jess and nearly got us both killed, not to mention, you totally ripped off your psycho Mexican Mafia buddies. They're still looking for your ass. Hell, I'm doing you a favor taking you in."

She huffed and made a big show of trying to get comfortable, which was damn near impossible considering how tightly I had her cuffed. My small foray into torture. We rode in silence for a few minutes before she started up again.

"What about him?" she asked, jerking her chin to the backseat. "Why did you bring him along?"

"I have some questions for him when his headache passes."

"He's not going to give me up."

"News flash, Perez. You're already up. Besides, what I have to ask him has zero to do with you." I caught a breath to consider how much I wanted to reveal. Perez didn't need to know I was currently serving on a jury. She didn't need to know my business at all, but she might know something more about Dante. I gave up a tiny bit of gossip, hoping for more. "He's an eyewitness in a case I'm investigating."

"Doubtful. Dante's not the type to see and tell."

"Shows what you know. He says he saw another guy get gunned down at Leroy's. Word is he even testified about it. What I didn't know until tonight is that he's Mexican Mafia." I'd seen the telltale tattoo in the parking lot and knew immediately something was off. Either the prosecutor or Dante had made a point of hiding the fact Dante was a fellow gang member of Manny Cruz, the dead guy. My guess was they didn't want to give the defense room to argue that Dante's testimony was colored by his affiliation with Cruz, but I sensed there was more to it than that. I decided to start by finding out how Perez fit in. "My big question is why an MM member is working with you at all after you double-crossed them."

She blew off my question and asked one of her own. "Who got shot?"

"Manny Cruz. Your pal Dante says a Texas Syndicate guy named Rey Navarro did the deed."

"That's not the whole story."

"I'm just telling you what he said." I slid a hand into my pocket and pulled out my phone. "Hang on a second." Perez was a freakin' know-it-all, and I planned to let her tell me everything she knew. I punched at the phone pretending to check a text, but instead I turned on the voice recorder and set the phone in the cup holder with the screen turned toward me.

"Are you late for dinner? Keeping the little woman waiting?" Perez asked with a smirk.

I resisted the urge to pop her in the jaw. It was my turn to goad her, not the other way around. "Dante seems like a pretty straight-up guy."

"You've got to be kidding. The only thing he's good at is playing both sides. If any of his buddies found out he was working with me, he'd be blood out in an instant."

I didn't have to ask what she meant. Anyone who worked in or around crime knew the Mexican Mafia had strict rules about membership: blood in, blood out. You gotta kill to get in and you gotta die to get out. "So why did he risk it?"

She laughed. "You've always underestimated me. You think when you and your girl Chance tried to bust me, you scared me away? I've got connections in the department you know nothing about. Dante and a few others were smart enough to realize revenge doesn't pay cash, but I do. I get the product and they spread it around."

I shook my head. "I don't get the connection. What does Dante have to do with Manny Cruz and Rey Navarro?"

She sighed like I was too stupid for words. When she opened her mouth to school me, I prayed the recorder was still on.

"Dante and Manny were both working with me, but Dante got tired of sharing his cut. He told Manny a Syndicate guy held up some of his dealers and stole his part of the take. So when Dante pointed out Navarro at the bar that night, Manny went nuts. He started shouting at Navarro, telling him to pay up or else. Bartender told them to take it outside, and next thing you know, Manny gets shot."

"I don't get it." I was legitimately confused. "That sounds exactly like what Dante said happened."

She smiled and lowered her voice to a whisper. "Dante had never met Navarro before. He just knew the guy was Texas Syndicate. He points him out to Manny and lets them duke it out. So, here's the deal. I was at Leroy's that night to meet Dante. I'd just pulled up in the parking lot when Navarro hightailed it out of there. He shot Manny, all right, but Dante finished him off."

I glanced at the backseat, but Dante was still out. For all I knew he might be dead. "Why the hell would he do that?"

"Think about it. He and Manny were splitting all the business I brought them. He doesn't want Manny to find out he's been double-crossing him. Along comes some other idiot and guns Manny down.

Manny's lying there bleeding out, and he suffocates him with his own jacket, then waits as long as possible before calling for help."

It was a lot to take in, and my first instinct was to write off Perez's wild story as a pack of lies. But she sure had a lot of details, and I couldn't figure why she'd lie. I did have another question, though. "You saw all this go down and didn't help Manny out? You with all your cop training couldn't try and save one of your own guys?"

"Too much at stake."

Classic Perez. We were about a block from the jail now. I pulled off the road into a warehouse parking lot, picked up my phone, and shut off the recorder.

"What are you doing?"

Her tone said she was hoping I was gonna let her go. Yeah, right.

I dug through the console and fished out a second pair of handcuffs. She asked me again what I was doing, but I ignored her. I stepped out of the Bronco and opened the rear door. Dante was starting to wake up, so I had to move fast. I cuffed his hands first, then loosened the knots in Cash's leash. Cash sniffed at it, but I nudged him away because I had other plans for the bright-red rope.

❖

A couple of stops on the way home meant it was after three in the morning when I finally pushed my way through the front door. Cash, who was usually up for anything, dragged behind me, a walking embodiment of the term *dog-tired*.

Normally, hauling a fugitive in and getting the paperwork I need to collect my money takes an hour, two tops, but tonight was different since I'd bagged a bonus prize. Booking Perez was easy. Her warrant was active, and the deputy at book-in processed her with just a few keystrokes.

Dante was special, though. He wasn't on any wanted lists, but after hearing Perez's story, I wasn't letting him go. Navarro might have shot Cruz, but the rest of the jury deserved to know the whole story about what went down that night.

I sweet-talked the deputy into listening to the tape I'd made on the drive to the jail and got her to roust the prosecutor, Rebecca Reeve, out of bed just before midnight. Rebecca wasn't very happy about any evidence that cast doubt on her case, but she did the right thing and called Bea Watson to the jail for a powwow.

By the time they finished grilling me about how I'd run into Dante and gotten Perez to talk, I was beginning to feel like I was the one on trial. But they both told me the judge would cut me loose from serving as a juror and might even order a mistrial. I didn't spill that Cris had followed me to Leroy's and was with me when we spotted Dante at Shorty's. If she wanted to rat on herself, fine. But no way would I get her blackballed from being a professional juror. She'd earned the right to sit in judgment.

I kicked off my boots in the entry and stepped softly through the house, careful not to rattle the bag in my hand, hoping Jess was up but not wanting to wake her. Cash crashed onto his bed in the corner of the living room and quickly snored his way to sleep, while I made my way to the kitchen. It was five o'clock somewhere and I needed a drink. I opened the door to the fridge and was pondering my choices when I heard Jess's voice directly behind me.

"Are you ever not hungry?"

I glanced back at her. Her eyes were bright, but her hair was smashed against her head and she was wearing only a robe, which told me she'd been in bed. I laughed. "I think you know the answer to that." I shut the door. "How late did you work? Did you get any sleep at all?"

She shrugged. "Not too late and not much. I hate to admit it, but I think I've gotten used to you being in bed with me."

"You say that like it's a bad thing." I used a joking tone, but part of me wondered if she was having regrets about what we'd become. It's one thing to be fuck buddies, but live-ins and I-love-yous are a whole other level. I set the bag in my hand on the counter and pulled her into my arms. "I get that you could do a lot better."

She whacked me on the ass. "Don't be a jerk. I want you. It's just that sometimes, I think you'd rather be on your own. You know, not have to account to anyone else."

She was right. Sometimes I did want that, probably because I didn't really know anything different. Not until the last couple of months anyway. I'd kinda gotten used to dinner at a table, a light left on late, and her gorgeous body next to me in bed every night. I tugged her back toward me and whispered in her ear. "You. Just you. That's all I want."

She kissed me, and her smile tingled against my lips. When we finally broke for air, she leaned against the counter and bumped into the orange-and-white Whataburger bag I'd set there. She pointed at it and said, "Why were you digging for food in the fridge if you had a sack of food already?"

I took a deep breath. I'd never done this before and wanted to get it right. "Well, actually, that's for you."

She looked from me to the bag and scrunched her brow. She reached in and pulled out a breakfast taquito wrapped in bright-orange paper with a sticker that read *Bacon*. Her smile was big and broad. "My favorite."

"I know. But there's more." I pointed at the bag and shifted from one foot to the other while she rooted through the napkins and salt and pepper packets.

Finally, she pulled out the cardboard envelope the guy at the all-night copy shop had said would keep the contents safe from taquito grease. She set the bag down, tugged the envelope open, and pulled out the photo. I held my breath while I watched and waited for her to figure out what she was looking at.

She pointed at the face in the photo. "Perez?"

"Yes."

"Tonight?"

"Yes."

"She's in jail?"

"Yes." I could say yes to her forever. "And she won't be getting out."

This time she pulled me close and held me hard against her. Slow, wet drops fell against my neck. I hated that she was crying, but I loved that they were tears of relief. We stood there, holding each other for a while, content just to be, before she looked into my eyes and said, "I have only one question."

"Shoot."

"Why is Cash's leash tied in a bow around Perez's neck?"

My turn to smile. "Because she's your present. Happy Valentine's Day, baby."

Hammersmith

Michelle Grubb

Chapter One

Belinda Reilly stared at the projector screen. Image upon image flashed before her. Every face filling the large screen was the face of a dead person. She was looking at dead people. Although she was an officer of the law, she'd only seen a handful of dead people in real life, all of them from vehicle accidents or natural deaths—gruesome, yes: mangled people crushed inside metal or decaying corpses rotting inside musty old houses. Death was never pleasant. This, though, was different. The people she was staring at had chosen to die, and they had chosen to take others with them. It was the first time she had deeply considered what the term "suicide bomber" *actually* meant. By design, it was a short-term occupation. By design it signified the end of your existence. Bel began to understand the enormity of the title, the calling, and the complete and utter waste of life.

Bel had recently joined the prestigious anti-terrorism unit in London, a division of the Security Service, operating out of MI5. Within the unit sat three specialist task forces. Charlatan was an above-ground response team trained to act quickly and efficiently following a terrorist or attempted terrorist attack. Orion consisted of the nerdy brains behind the outfit and the general all-round sneaky bunch. Orion heard and saw things in a super-spy way Bel had only ever imagined after watching Hollywood movies. The task force she was assigned to was called Hotstream—a description of the air that pumps through underground tunnels as a train approaches the platform in summer. Hotstream was the entry-level task force, designed to accomplish two results. First, it allowed new officers a chance to learn crucial aspects of counterterrorism while providing them with specialised negotiation and interrogation skills. The officers in Hotstream undertook constant education—beyond the initial induction—while patrolling the underground. Second, the skills learnt in Hotstream formed the basis for further training and advancement into Charlatan and Orion.

The original official title of the unit was the Underground Terror Alert Response Team. Whoever came up with that name must have been having a bad day because UTART was scrapped the moment Conrad Rush, the head of the unit, bothered to pen the acronym. The revised acronym, LUATRU (London and Underground Anti-Terrorist Response Unit), was the result of a swift name change, and the Charlatan, Orion, and Hotstream task forces were born. The unit was highly regarded and revered amongst its peers. Its purpose was simple: keep London safe.

Bel was one of only five new members on the Hotstream task force, and it was rumoured that over two hundred officers from all over Britain had applied for the positions. It was a welcome change from her last posting in Norfolk. Being the only female cop in a rural community was fraught with danger, usually in the over-consumption of tea and cake, so London would surely be the exciting change of pace she'd craved while gaining valuable experience in counterterrorism. She'd thought long and hard about her career progression, and when the opportunity arose to apply for this role, years of taking on every undercover job she had been offered—no matter how dreadful the conditions or boring the operation—were finally paying off.

Bel recalled the words of her superior upon being offered the job. "You have one of those faces, Belinda. You blend in."

He was right. She wasn't ordinary looking—her previous girlfriends had never complained—she simply had the ability to alter her look and blend in. "It's important not to draw attention to yourself," he had said. "Your short hair is perfect. It's more adaptable in disguise." He'd cocked his head to one side. "Be best if you lose the highlights, though. Plain brown is less distinguishable. The plainer the better."

Bel had taken a basement flat in Westbourne Green. It was surprisingly warm, airy, and spacious. *Nothing* like her dad had described when she first mentioned she'd applied for the promotion and would move to London if successful. His words of rising damp, mould spores, and pneumonia seemed a little dramatic in her middle-class neighbourhood with her trendy neighbours, fancy Italian delis, and traditionally British bars.

London was a great place to be in the height of summer, and

although you wouldn't think it was the best time of year to join Hotstream—stuck under the city in artificial light—when it came to suicide bombers, it was jokingly said to be off season. A considerable amount of clothing is required to hide the bulky explosives strapped to a bomber's body. In summer, a bomber was easier to spot.

Before Bel had taken up the position, she'd been reading *Gone Tomorrow* by Lee Child. It was hardly the prescribed text on the subject of suicide bombing, but it had made for compelling reading—well, the first few chapters had. She'd become too snowed under with real learning in real textbooks to finish the novel. Both fact *and* fiction texts shared alarming similarities, however. The telltale signs of a suicide bomber were well documented. Anyone could Google them, and just to make sure Mr. Child knew what he was talking about, Bel had checked it out for herself. He had been correct, of course. Depending on the sex of the bomber, the majority of them displayed either eleven or twelve signs that they might be on the verge of blowing themselves, and others, up. For ease of memory, the Hotstream team had condensed this list to eight.

Surprisingly, as well documented as it was and with the continuing advancement of explosive technology, the modus operandi of a suicide bomber had barely altered for several decades.

Suicide bombers killed people. The fact that they killed themselves in the process was of little concern to Bel; they needed to be stopped.

It was a highly debated topic that the average British police officer patrols unarmed. The debate for and against the use of firearms was a tired discussion, and Bel knew it would continue for years to come. For the officers on the task force, carrying a weapon was essential. It was difficult to reason with someone who had their hand grasped firmly to a detonator. Bel knew if she ever had to discharge her weapon, it would be a shoot-to-kill situation.

The very first time she held her Glock 17 pistol, a chill had rippled through her. Her days of wearing a uniform and popping into Mrs. Hudson's for a slice of Victoria sponge cake and a cup of Earl Grey tea were over.

The images flashing on the screen were a stark reminder that in her hand she held the power to stop a suicide bomber, the power to save lives. In her hand she held life and death. The possibility both frightened and exhilarated her.

Chapter Two

The first time Bel had entered the Wagon and Ox pub wasn't the first time she'd laid eyes on Esther. She would have loved to tell a story of lustful eyes locking across a crowded bar, but scrounging twenty pence at the laundrette nearing midnight just wasn't the same. It was the truth but hardly earth-shattering.

Esther was five foot, eight inches tall, two inches taller than Bel. When Bel looked in the mirror and saw a youthful-looking thirty-year-old—knowing full well she could pass as twenty-one—she saw the opposite in Esther. Esther was only five years her senior, but she had an older, wise, yet serene face. Her tanned skin and brown hair, which she always wore up, gave her the air of a traveller or an explorer—someone who'd seen a lot and experienced life. Bel was instantly drawn to her.

Esther looked like someone who practiced yoga for hours a day. She was lean, and somehow she just looked flexible. After the night at the laundrette, Bel returned to her flat intrigued and wondering how she could meet her again. She imagined Esther probably burned incense sticks, ate only organic produce, and probably sourced the most expensive cotton unbleached tampons.

She was wrong.

Esther behaved like a kid in a theme park. She pushed boundaries, she challenged everything about everyone, she lived to be alive, and when she wasn't on duty at the pub, she had sex like it was the last time she would ever feel the touch of a woman.

Esther was addictive and Bel was a willing addict.

"You're early." Esther pushed a gin and tonic toward Bel.

Esther's smile caught her unawares every time, but her reaction never changed. The wide mouth full of unblemished white teeth sent her brain into fuzzy mode. She loved that first smile. It was the first of many she would receive during the evening while she watched Esther at work, patiently waiting for her shift to end.

"My shift finished on time for once," said Bel.

Bel was a liar. Not about her shift, but about her occupation. She had lied to Esther from the very beginning, and although lying to someone she cared deeply about left her feeling guilty and nauseous, she wasn't sure when the lie should end.

"Well, I'm glad you could wind it up early." Esther reached over the expansive bar and squeezed her hand.

Bel immediately lowered her eyes and focused on Esther's cleavage. Tonight she wore a sleeveless low-cut black top and black bra. She rarely found tattoos attractive, but Esther's were different. They were words, not pictures, and, on her tanned skin, looked as sexy as hell.

"Hey you, up here, thanks." Esther pointed to her makeup-framed brown eyes.

Bel sighed. Waiting three hours for Esther's shift to finish was the last thing she felt like doing. Work had been intense, half her day spent in a briefing and half in the tunnels. Reliable and alarming intelligence was filtering through to her task force. Undercover operatives, those possibly performing the most dangerous and imperative role in the fight against terrorism, were hearing sniffs that something was about to happen, that a terrorist cell was primed and mobile. Her team was prepared for this possibility, and sitting in a briefing with the top dogs was one thing, but to walk among the thousands of innocent people commuting on the underground, well, that was another thing altogether. Hotstream could be the difference between life and death, the difference between catastrophe and calm. Bel had spent twelve weeks training to be part of a team who aimed to keep London safe. She knew the magnitude of her responsibilities.

"You need me tonight. I can see it in your face." Esther touched her cheek.

"I can't seem to remember a time when I haven't needed you." It sounded like a smooth line delivered by a well-seasoned player, but it was the truth. Bel struggled to remember anything romantic prior to Esther.

"That will help with your worry lines." Esther nodded toward the gin. "And later I promise to relieve you of every ounce of tension you're desperately trying to hide."

It had been only two months since they began their relationship, but Esther knew her so well—her moods, her facial expressions—and lately she seemed skilled at detecting high stress levels. Bel had told Esther she worked as a personal security guard. The moment she said it she knew it sounded ridiculous and cliché for a lesbian wearing skinny jeans, black boots, and a grey jacket, but she needed an excuse to be wherever she was for her real job and not look out of place. "I stay in the background, out of the way and out of sight," she had said. It was just enough information for Esther not to question her varied work outfits or irregular hours.

Esther was a carer, not of anyone in particular, just of the person she was with. Without asking, Bel would receive regular drinks and food throughout the night. When Esther went out back for her cigarette breaks, she would pour Bel a glass of water or make them both a cup of tea, and she'd gently take her by the hand and lead her outside before they kissed and before Esther lit her smoke.

That evening they walked arm in arm to Bel's place. Esther lived a train ride away—they rarely stayed at Esther's. She shared a flat with some weird free-love people, and it always stank of weed. Bel was drug-tested randomly, so she tended to avoid inhaling secondhand cannabis smoke. She knew it was difficult to suck in a measurable dose, but her job was too important to be jeopardised by some dope-smoking bludgers.

Bel was tired. Esther was never tired. She lived for the moment, and if she was awake, then she refused to be sleepy. The moment her head hit the pillow, however, she enjoyed a deep sleep until morning. As she stood at her kitchen bench sipping water, Bel felt Esther's arms encircle her. History suggested that from this moment, she was at Esther's mercy; her role required nothing more than to allow Esther to work her magic.

"You're tense." Esther edged her hand inside Bel's jeans.

"You can tell that just by touching my stomach?"

"No. I can tell that by the frown you've had plastered to your forehead all evening."

Bel laughed. Perhaps she overestimated Esther's guru-hippie-healing prowess. When it came to sex, Esther was a talker—a describer and a suggester. It wasn't a quality Bel usually admired in a lover, but something about the power of suggestion and the subsequent anticipation made Esther completely alluring.

"I can make that go away."

"You can, can you?"

"Uh-huh. That's what I do. I fix things." She blew hot air into Bel's ear. "When have I ever failed to fix you?" Her hand dipped lower.

It was true. Esther's touch was healing and hypnotic.

"I'm going to fix you right here in the kitchen."

Firmly but carefully, Esther pushed Bel over the end of the countertop.

The first thing Bel had learned about sex with Esther was that she was never in charge. For the first time in any of her relationships, this didn't bother her. Their relationship wasn't a dictatorship. Any time Bel fancied intimacy and became a little amorous, Esther's eyes would twinkle and she'd take things from there. It was her way, *their* way, and it suited them both.

"How long do you think it will take me to drag all that bad energy out of you?" Esther unbuttoned Bel's jeans and pushed them to the floor. She leant over and whispered in her ear, "How long before you'll want me to fuck you fast and hard?"

Bel squirmed. She'd always been a squirmer.

Esther pushed her knickers to the ground, and Bel waited patiently, naked from the waist down, bent over the kitchen counter for Esther to do anything to her that she pleased.

Esther was the kind of woman Bel had fantasised about as a youngster. She was soft and feminine, yet strong and confident. Everyone had their perfect combination and Esther was hers. Sexually, Esther was open and exploratory, and above everything else, they had fun in bed—or the kitchen or wherever the urge overtook them.

Bel spread her legs, an invitation to show she was ready.

Esther's hand appeared in front of Bel's face, and she gently pushed her thumb into her mouth. Bel sucked on it. She knew what was coming.

With her other hand, Esther separated her bottom cheeks moments before the moist thumb began to massage her asshole. Anal sex wasn't on the top of her list of the most satisfying of sexual activities, but she allowed Esther to continue because she knew this was only the beginning.

Esther had taught her that, in most cases, it was the sum of all parts that defined an experience as outstanding rather than simply mediocre if measured singularly.

"When I push my fingers inside you, all your toxins will release their hold." Esther found her opening and teetered on the edge.

Bel couldn't bring herself to call what they did to each other simply sex. Sadly, although she *felt* like Esther was making love to her—so tender was her touch, her attention—she couldn't guarantee Esther felt the same. Esther would refer to their intimacy as passionate and affectionate, even loving, but she never referred to what they did as *making love*. Without doubt, Esther gave one hundred percent—she fucked without limitation and inhibition, but Bel yearned for more. She wanted commitment, and although she knew Esther wasn't seeing anyone else, a part of Bel wanted Esther to grow out of her 1960s hippie-love stage. Marriage was a long way off, but she needed something more than Esther appeared willing to give.

Bel knew the thumb inside her was only inserted to the first knuckle, but she liked the idea of that small invasion. The fingers dancing at her opening were sending fireflies of anticipation throughout her body.

Esther entered her.

The moment of penetration was like a parachute opening. Until that time, Bel had been freefalling, desperate to be saved, desperate to be taken. Esther's fingers pressing against her G-spot signalled the best was yet to come. Besides orgasm, she treasured that first moment more than anything else during sex.

Esther worked to take Bel to the edge. As her fingers and thumb pulsed, Bel experienced simultaneous pressure inside her. Together they quickly established a rhythm before Esther removed her thumb from Bel's ass and slipped her hand around to the front, her index and middle finger surrounding her clit before gently massaging it.

Over the kitchen counter, the stimulation of senses was complete.

"Every thrust drives a piece of your shit day out of you." Esther put her entire body's weight into fucking Bel.

Orgasm was near.

Esther went deeper.

Bel felt herself slip into the zone where everything except Esther ceased to exist. She edged her legs wider to accommodate a third finger.

"You're divine. I worship every inch of you."

In her mind, Bel repeated the words *God, I love you* with every thrust. Each moment she edged nearer to orgasm, she was filled with unwavering gratitude to have found Esther and to have her free spirit light up her life in absolutely every way.

In the end, Bel couldn't distinguish where the pleasure originated between her legs. It was exactly how Esther described it, the sum of all parts. Everything felt amazing all at once.

Bel's first orgasm was rarely the most intense. It was usually the third or fourth that left her light-headed and seeing stars. Esther had a knack of talking her into holding on longer. The urge to feel the ultimate release only acquiesced long enough for Esther to milk every drop of obtainable passion from her.

"Not yet, I can go harder. Let me take you harder."

By harder, Esther meant faster and more intense. Inflicting pain wasn't her thing. Finding Bel's sweet spots and concentrating on them was what she meant. She didn't need permission, but her words always added another dimension to their already passionate sex. It was that timeless illusion of suggestion. Bel had learned about it in the police, not just in her current role, but when doing undercover work. To implant an idea into someone's psyche wasn't a new trick. Suggestion was powerful. Esther was powerful.

Bel was panting with every thrust. She could hear the squelching noise Esther's fingers made as they moved in and out of her. Esther's deep breaths steadily blew past her ear, and she could smell the faint aroma of brandy travelling in her direction with every exhalation.

The end was tantalisingly near.

"Come now."

It was hardly a pretty picture, but the best way Bel knew to describe her orgasm was like a vacuum pack. As the pleasure took hold, the orgasm literally took her breath away. In that moment, she felt it suck every ounce of oxygen from her body, and only when it released her could she again inflate with air. In the moments between breathing, everything went black and she floated away. It was the brief moment she described as pure bliss. The rippling aftermath of her orgasm was when she returned to herself.

"How do you feel?" Esther slowly extricated her fingers from inside her.

Bel wasn't sure if it was an original thought or the power of Esther's previous suggestion, but she felt cleansed from the inside out. She had indeed been detoxified.

"I feel pure."

Esther laughed. "You're far from pure, my darling." Her forefinger began encircling Bel's swollen clit.

"Not a truer word has been spoken." Bel glanced at the red lights on the microwave. It was nearly midnight, and she was on duty at six the following morning.

"We can't stop now." Esther's tone was neither solemn nor accusatory. The simple fact was she wouldn't stop now. Business was unfinished and tonight she was intense and passionate. Esther had sex like it was the last night before the apocalypse. If she wasn't fucking the very moment the world unexpectedly ended, she wanted her last thought to be of the night before. Tonight she was making every second count.

"Take me to bed and take me away from here."

Bel knew what that meant. She knew what Esther wanted. They had both fully undressed before they reached the bedroom.

Without hesitation Bel plugged her expensive headphones into her iPod and selected a playlist entitled *Esther*. She pressed play and gently put the headphones over Esther's ears. Garbage's first album and subsequent album 2.0 thumped loudly. With her woolly winter scarves, she tied Esther's hands to the bed head, and although Esther would prefer her feet restrained also, Bel's bed didn't accommodate that. Next, she lit a scented candle specially bought for use in such occasions.

The first time Esther talked her through this ritual, it took until the last request for Bel to realise what Esther was trying to achieve; when she had sex, she liked all her senses to be stimulated. The music was for her hearing, the candle for scent and also provided enough light to see, and what Bel would do between her legs was to fulfill the sense of touch. What remained was taste, and when Esther had asked Bel to sit on her face, she finally understood.

Tonight, Bel knew the ceremony by heart. She turned around and lay astride Esther, lowering herself onto her face.

Esther moaned at the taste.

Finally, Bel inserted two fingers and lowered her head to take Esther's clit in her mouth.

Like this, they would fuck for a long time.

Esther had the capacity to hold off orgasm for longer than any lover Bel had ever known. She entered a trance-like state and had told Bel she closed her eyes and allowed herself to be taken away from reality. Esther didn't need drugs; she just needed outstanding sex.

They moved as one, and although in the beginning Bel had struggled to concentrate on Esther while her tongue was inside her, she was slowly learning to stave off her own pleasure for the pleasure of another. It was a remarkably powerful experience. For many minutes their rhythm remained unchanged until Esther couldn't take it anymore. Bel fucked faster with her fingers and licked harder with her tongue. All the while Esther's tongue remained inside her.

On one occasion, they had come simultaneously, but not tonight. Tonight Esther came hard and long, leaving Bel behind.

She pushed Bel off her and removed the headphones. "I think I love you."

What?

Esther pulled the covers over them both and snuggled close to Bel.

Had she heard right?

"What did you just say?"

"You're an amazing woman and you deserve to be loved. If I could give you the world I would."

This was the first time Esther had shown any hint of sentimentality. She behaved lovingly—without question—but that was her nature. She was a healer, a nurturer, and the most tender person Bel had ever met, but they rarely shared loving sentimentality. Until now.

"I think I love you too." Bel matched Esther's words, frightened to create her own dialogue.

Esther laughed awkwardly, the sound laced with embarrassment. "But what is love anyway?"

"I honestly think the world of you. Don't tell me that doesn't count?"

"For tonight, my love, it means everything. Tonight you mean everything. I want you to remember tonight for the rest of your life. Promise me that?"

Bel nodded but realised Esther couldn't see her affirmation in the dark. "Maybe we can make things a little more…" She struggled to find the appropriate words. "I don't know, concrete, maybe?" The desperation in her voice annoyed her, but Esther deserved an honest appraisal of the situation.

"Right here, right now is the most uncontaminated we will ever feel."

Bel saddened. Esther wasn't answering her question.

"I can't be owned, Bel."

"I'm not asking if I can own you, just be with you."

"I have a spirit even I can't contain or control."

"So you're saying you don't want to be tied down?"

"No. I'm saying I'm not in control of my own destiny."

Bel didn't understand. "Then who is?"

"Tonight I'm yours. You feel that, right? Tonight I gave myself to you wholly and unconditionally. Tonight is all that matters. Tonight we became one."

Bel sighed. "And tomorrow? What do we become tomorrow?"

"Tomorrow is a brand-new day. Unstained and pure. Tomorrow we start again."

It was no use. Esther always spoke in riddles when the conversation became too difficult.

They were both exhausted, and soon Bel succumbed to the soothing swirling motions Esther was tracing on her leg. In no time at all, sleep took her.

Chapter Three

If you wanted good coffee in London, you looked for a place that served only one size—preferably nothing resembling the size of a washing-up basin—and you avoided the places where lanky sixteen-year-olds hollered your name to gain your attention before delivering a bucket of coffee to you without so much as a sideways glance.

Bel needed coffee. The first sip of one's first morning coffee was a private moment to savour.

Esther had left the flat early, around five, and Bel had rolled over and gone back to sleep for another fifteen minutes before her day officially began. Everyone knew your day didn't *really* begin until your alarm went off. Every precious second counted. Before then was your time. Bel chose to sleep.

Yesterday's briefing had been the first official one she'd attended where they had received direct information from other agencies that required a tightening of security around key London stations. The more experienced officers in Hotstream took it in their stride. This information was provided with alarming regularity, and the culprits had been thwarted well before they could get near the underground or, alternatively, the threats never amounted to anything substantial. Hotstream wasn't in the business of taking calculated risks or hedging their bets. They acted on every piece of credible information.

Bel was assigned to Hammersmith all day. Other than her loaded gun, which remained out of sight, she hid in the open. Her earpiece—her link to her superiors at Control—looked like earphones, and her radio pack sat in her breast pocket as a phone might. Her small but powerful torch was lodged in her front jeans pocket. On her first day, she'd stared in the mirror and immediately thought she stood out like dogs' bollocks. She was convinced she would be spotted immediately, but when she stepped foot on the train for the first time, she realised just about *everyone* looked suspicious: the guy with the backpack, the lady with nervous eyes and an oversized handbag—the list was endless. Everyone looked suspicious, and this is why Bel knew she blended in; she did too.

The one thing that annoyed her was her inability to switch off her suspicions while travelling on the train; before she'd even clocked in at work, she was alert. Would she ever be able to ride the underground like a normal person? Regardless of how she tried to preoccupy herself, she automatically assessed each passenger in her line of vision. The signs of a suicide bomber clicked through her mind in sequence like a slideshow on repeat. There was no prescribed sequence, only the order in which she'd memorised them. Shutting her eyes didn't work; she couldn't bear not to see everything that was going on around her. Everyone in Hotstream was the same. They all admitted over-vigilance. In that respect, her lack of normality made her feel normal.

Until now, Bel had never had to travel on the underground as part of her daily routine. How did people cope every day? From the moment some commuters stepped on the train, they read from their tablet or listened to the news on their phone or read the paper. Those lucky enough to have a seat appeared relatively comfortable, but even those standing weren't deterred; the coordination and balance of some passengers who read and fiddled with electronic devices impressed her. If it wasn't for the mad dash to jump onto an overcrowded carriage, the entire experience could have been relaxing. Few people barely batted an eyelid when announcements were made regarding delays or when a train stopped unexpectedly mid-tunnel. As a sample of the population, given the volume of people and rather stressful timings, Bel concluded that London commuters were a chilled-out bunch.

At exactly five fifty-five her earpiece crackled into action. "Hey, Bel." It was Charlie from Control. After her shift commenced, she would be known as five-seven-oh-nine. Until then, she was Bel.

She glanced up toward the nearest security camera. She knew Charlie had her in her sights. She casually spoke into the mouthpiece as if on the phone. "Morning, Charlie. What have you got for me?"

Charlie was a great lady and an accomplished police officer. She was in her forties—Bel had no idea of the exact number—and she lived alone with her cats. Had every word of their conversations not been recorded, she knew Charlie's reply would have been cheeky, but they always kept it professional for the tape.

Every morning, time was dedicated to a briefing. Because Bel was always armed, unless there was a requirement for her to attend the office, she commenced work in the field.

"Nothing new since yesterday," Charlie said. "Let's hope it stays quiet."

On the surface, Charlie's job at Control was less than glamorous. In reality, it was one of the most stressful assignments on the Hotstream task force. Under pressure, Charlie was like an air-traffic controller at London's Heathrow Airport with only one runway open and every other airport in the entire United Kingdom closed. Charlie was so cool and focused, she'd have all those planes down without incident and as efficient as you like.

For the duration of her shift, Charlie and the five other Control officers would view the underground on dozens of monitors showing images from any camera on the underground they selected. Those on duty had direct radio communication to every Hotstream officer. Charlie and her colleagues were authorised to stop trains, evacuate trains, and even evacuate entire stations. One visit to Waterloo station—with twenty-three escalators and approximately fifty-seven thousand commuters entering during the morning rush hours—and it didn't take much to understand the enormous responsibility they carried and the gravity of even considering evacuating the bigger stations. Charlie was unflappable. Bel liked the security of her presence on the other end of the line.

"You armed and loaded, Bel?" It was part of their procedures to have this question and corresponding answer recorded.

"Yes."

"Excellent, 5709, I'll leave you to it." The line crackled into silence. Bel looked at her watch. It was one minute past six. She was officially on duty.

"Thank you, ma'am."

On duty and hungry. The best thing about blending in and looking like everyone else was that Bel could act like everyone else. Her allocated home-base station was Paddington, and she knew exactly where to find breakfast.

Ten minutes later, armed with a bacon sandwich, yet another coffee, and a pink iced doughnut for later, Bel rejoined the throngs of commuters and headed down to the next available train on the Hammersmith line. At this hour of the morning, the flow was steady. She listened to the public-address-system announcement that there were delays on the Bakerloo, Jubilee, and Victoria lines. This would mean an influx at Baker Street station in approximately twenty minutes when passengers looked for alternative routes; these two lines intersected Hammersmith at Baker Street, so this was where she would disembark and hang around for a while.

At this hour, Bel rarely sat down. If a seat became available, she tended to offer it to older passengers. Standing gave her a better vantage point of the passengers. If the train was packed, she could barely see past the passengers immediately surrounding her.

Exactly as she was trained to do, she immediately began scanning for the obvious visible signs of a bomber and resumed clicking through the traits.

The first thing Bel looked for was thick, bulky jackets or clothing that looked too large for the wearer. *Click!* She blinked and cleared her mind, systematically commencing a scan of the passengers in her vicinity. Unseasonably thick jackets were number one on her list. It was summer, after all. Not exactly warm at that hour of the morning, but certainly not cold enough to wear a jacket that could be hiding explosives strapped to your body. She wore a jacket herself, but it was cotton and only just thick enough to help conceal her weapon. She concluded her scan. No one near her was overdressed.

Not dissimilar to airports, train stations were one of the last places you would want to see an unattended bag or package, and part of Bel's brief was also to scan for anything suspicious, unattended, or simply out of place. She scanned her immediate area, and all bags appeared to have owners.

Second on her list for a suicide-bomber trait were hands, or hand, in a bag or in the bulky jacket pockets. Because no one was overdressed, she focused on hands in bags. The bag usually contained a detonator, and because a suicide bomber was a novice—it was, after all, their first and only day on the job—they were reluctant to let go of the detonator. Having your finger on the detonator made for a very nervous bomber.

During training, Bel was asked to think about a time when she had participated in something that frightened her but was ultimately out of her hands. She immediately thought of the time when her close friend and colleague, Sam, beat her in the police charity fun run. Her loss resulted in a tandem skydive. Terrified of heights, she was violently ill the entire morning until the midday jump. Had the decision of when to jump been left in her hands, the plane probably would have circled until it ran out of fuel and jumping was her only option. Because someone else made the decision to jump at the optimum time, she was absolved of all responsibility.

Making the choice, or having someone decide for you in difficult situations, was not a luxury suicide bombers were afforded. Making the decision to press a button and blow others up was one thing, but making the choice to press a button and blow *yourself* up also, now that was enough to make anyone a nervous, terrified mess.

Suicide bombers were often a nervous wreck. They were trained to press the button at the first sign of trouble. If the bomber was forced to deviate from the plan or if they were identified and the authorities attempted communication or negotiation, they were to immediately blow themselves up. The hand in the bag was an unavoidable giveaway for a suicide bomber.

Click! She saw plenty of hands in pockets, but none in bags. So far, so good.

Characteristic number three, the bomber will most likely be chanting or praying. When Bel was eleven, her family dog, Tom Jones, was hit by a car. Her mum rushed him to the animal hospital, and because of his extensive injuries he underwent surgery and remained in care overnight. Bel had never been to church; she only really knew about Jesus because of Christmas and Easter, but that night in bed she found herself praying. Regardless of your beliefs, it's not unusual to pray in times of extreme stress.

For a suicide bomber, imminent death is understandably rather stressful. For those extremists of the Muslim faith, they believe their death will deliver them to paradise. It's well reported that those about to be received in paradise are often praying.

Click! A few passengers were grinning as they stared at their phones, but no one appeared to be chanting or praying. Bel's ride was smooth so far.

The trait Bel looked for next was ambiguous at the best of times.

It involved someone on drugs. Suicide bombers were reportedly high before they blew themselves up. And why not? You were about to die, why not take the edge off with a good dose of happy pills? She was hit-and-miss at telling if a person was high at the best of times, unless they were behaving like a stoned-out idiot. If she could see them walking she had a better chance because they tended to walk erratically, and with the extra weight of a bomb strapped to their body, they stood out. But if they were sitting down, her strike rate was fifty/fifty or less. Someone with a good dose of the flu or a severe head cold looked high to Bel. People rarely looked at you long enough for you to peer into their eyes and check for dilated pupils.

Click! She slowly scanned the faces in her line of vision. Everyone seemed normal in that respect, even the skinny teenage boy whose grey track pants sported a yellowing stain on the crotch. He certainly wasn't a suicide bomber. He was probably smelly and a complete crap ride for the people sitting next to him, but at least he'd stay intact for the duration of the journey.

Next on Bel's list was sweat. It's not difficult to imagine that, sitting on a train enduring your last moments on earth, possibly high as a kite, before you press a trigger that ends your life, you might work up a little sweat. Couple this with the fact that you're wearing bulky warm clothes and are weighed down with explosives, one would expect the bomber to be dripping. Bel laughed to herself. She invariably worked up a decent lather just going for her smear test, so it was little wonder a suicide bomber might be a little clammy and shiny.

Click! She didn't see any excessively sweaty passengers near her. Everyone appeared to have the appropriate complexion.

This led to her next characteristic. Many male suicide bombers of extremist faiths often shaved all visible body hair before blowing themselves up. It also helped to detract attention from them. A Middle Eastern man with dark hair, olive-toned skin, and sporting a dark beard often fit the public profile of the stereotypical suicide bomber. One of Bel's close friends, Frank (his mother loved Frank Sinatra), was of Syrian descent. He was a handsome, well-dressed architect with about as much knack for bomb building as a gay man is for cage fighting. Every year their mutual friends held a themed New Year's Eve party, and one year the theme was Bad Taste. Frank grew a beard and attended the party as a Bin Laden; (he wore a garbage bag to cover the Bin aspect). Given the theme, it was a clever costume, but in the weeks leading up to the party, as his fashionable stubble grew into a full beard, Frank became a target for abuse and threats. Extremists, regardless of their country of origin, made it difficult for ordinary people like Frank to live a trouble-free life. As usual, the minority of bad eggs screwed it up for the good people of the world.

Click. No man near her was sporting a two-toned face where his beard had protected his face from the sun, nor could she see anyone with the orange glow of fake tan trying to hide a recently shaved beard.

Characteristic number seven was staring or being fixated on a specific spot or object. An inordinate number of bombers captured on cameras or CCTV before death show a face with eyes staring straight ahead. It's not clear why this is the case, but a bomber rarely makes eye contact with anyone, nor do they look about themselves smiling or gazing happily at the people they intend to kill.

During training, Bel constantly reminded herself that these people behaved as they did because they were only minutes from death, minutes from meeting their maker, and minutes away from ever seeing anybody they knew or cared about ever again. If it was so easy to train a person to blow themselves up, why couldn't a bomber be trained not to look so stereotypically like a bomber? Every time Bel's mind wandered into this dangerous territory, she reminded herself they were going to die. It was always a sobering thought.

Click! Loads of people stared into space on trains. Their thoughts and daydreams often consumed them, and based on this trait alone, over half the commuters on the London underground could be suicide bombers. But as Bel noticed someone staring, she clicked through her list and eliminated them. Systematically, she looked at the people in her vicinity and discounted them all; no one staring into space possessed any other suspicious traits.

In reality, this process took Bel only minutes and, in some cases, seconds to complete. By the time the train had reached its next stop, she would have analysed all the passengers in her sight.

The Hotstream task force fluctuated in numbers depending on intelligence. When the terror alert was categorised as low or moderate, officer numbers were reduced to a minimum, a fact that certainly wasn't shared with the public for obvious reasons. The categories of substantial and severe threat saw more officers deployed underground, and when the status reached critical, intelligence suggested that a terror attack was imminent. In the case of a critical status, the unit usually knew names and places. For the officers working in Hotstream, when intelligence suggested an attack on the underground was likely and the terrorists hadn't been thwarted before they reached their domain, it was a race against time and a shoot-to-kill situation. Hotstream were the last line of defence and all the officers took the responsibility seriously.

Bel was no fool. Monitoring the underground on a daily basis when the alert was low or moderate would reap little, if any, rewards. The chances of one of her team being near a bomber at any given time were slim at best. However, since the July bombings in 2005, the British government had made promises to the people, and an effective terrorist-response team had to know its battleground inside out. The Hotstream team knew its stuff.

Bel exited the train at Marylebone station and pushed her way through the commuters to stand with her back to the station wall. She automatically scanned the area for unattended bags and for the final telltale sign of a suicide bomber, a robotic walk. Unless she was off the train or it wasn't busy, it was near impossible to tell if someone was struggling with an extra twenty kilograms of weighty explosives attached to their torso.

A normal police vest, carrying radio, baton, etc., weighed approximately five kilograms, and although it didn't affect your gait, Bel's first few weeks on the job saw her return home after shift to a hot bath and a heat pack on her back. During training, they were all strapped into various replica explosive vests and homemade devices. Some of them were filled with nuts, bolts, screws, and nails to cause maximum damage upon detonation, and these alone could be weighty. The training officers had analysed each other's gaits, and it was true that an average-framed person walked differently with explosive strapped around their middle. Of course there was always an exception to the rule. One of the tutors was a strapping six feet six inches tall, and his gait didn't alter at all wearing the fake bombs. However, had he been staring into space and chanting, wearing an oversized jacket while sweating profusely, he'd have gained Bel's attention. Detecting a suicide bomber was like constructing a jigsaw puzzle; all the pieces had to fit together in the right place to form the correct picture.

Click! Bel watched the hordes of people struggle through the crowds to board the train. Everyone walked swiftly, even the elderly couple dressed up for a day out in London.

"Control, this is 5709, I'm at Marylebone. I'll perform a sweep of the bathrooms on ground level." Bel spoke casually and softly into her microphone. She needed a pee.

Every moment in the station or on the train required complete concentration. The only time Bel could relax was the moment she closed and locked the cubicle door behind her.

She took the opportunity to check her phone. One message from Esther.

Last night was amazing, unforgettable. I'll dream about you forever xx.

Bel smiled. She was wearing Esther down—in a good way—and hopefully soon they would formalise their relationship somehow. It was probably too soon to move in together; Bel hated the reputation of lesbians who shacked up on date number two, but she would at least attempt a conversation and suggest a city break when she next had a few days off. Somewhere like Amsterdam or Paris or even Prague might be nice. Upon reflection, Bel dismissed Paris. She didn't want to go anywhere with an underground rail system.

Bel had often imagined what it was like to become "one" during lovemaking. Until last night she thought that feeling must happen only to other people. Experiencing it for herself certainly reaffirmed her feelings for Esther.

She checked her watch. She'd been in the toilet one minute and thirteen seconds.

Esther was like a force field of energy, and no matter how tiring Bel's day or how disturbing her tutorials had been, Esther had an uncanny knack of drawing every bubble of energy from her and bringing them together. It was a beautiful thing and something Bel wasn't willing to give up.

When she first met Esther, she knew they shared something special. She fell in love faster than ever before, and even when she tried to fight the feeling or at least approach the issue with a level head, she found it was utterly useless. Bel knew what love was at seventeen, then again at twenty-three, twenty-five, and twenty-nine. The concept was nothing new to her, but the instantaneousness of love, and in truth passion, with Esther was what astounded her. After that first night in the laundrette she couldn't shake her from her mind, and after last night, thoughts of Esther remained at the forefront of her brain.

She looked at her watch. Two minutes, six seconds.

Bel finished in the toilet and stepped out into her office. "Back on, Control."

"Copy that, 5709."

CHAPTER FOUR

The underground was heaving with people and it was noisy, but the voice in her ear was silent, just the way Bel liked it. She had just departed the Whitechapel station, westbound, when her earpiece cracked into action.

"All officers on platform. I repeat, all officers on platform."

It had been too good to last.

Automatically, Bel stood, ready to disembark at the next station, Aldgate East. Her pulse quickened, and she instinctively opened her mouth to inhale more oxygen while at the same time slowing her breathing. She hadn't forgotten any of the basics learnt in the twelve-week induction training.

"Platform" was the order to disembark at the next available station. It could be nothing or it could be everything. The platform order had been given just last week, and it had been a drill. You didn't know until it was over. Other officers spoke of a recent platform order when a suspicious package was found in South Kensington station. All Hotstream officers were to make their way to South Kensington while Transport staff performed a sweep of all other stations in the event that the parcel was a decoy for a different device in a different location.

You had to be fit to work in Hotstream. At first glance it hardly appeared that way: sitting on a train half the day watching people and then attending training of some description during the other half. On the surface it appeared barely enough to raise a sweat, but when there was a bomb threat you had to be able to rush to the right place at the right time, to climb stairs, to run through stations and into the daylight, knowing exactly where you were and how to find your next destination. An intimate knowledge of London was essential.

As the train pulled into the station, Bel caught sight of a familiar face standing motionless on the platform. Although obscured by passengers after that fleeting first glance, she was sure it had been Esther. But what was Esther doing in Aldgate East station? That morning, after a passionate kiss good-bye, she'd told Bel she was going home to sleep for another few hours. Besides the kiss, she'd touched Bel's cheek and whispered, "Good-bye, my love," before disappearing into the dusky morning light.

During training, the officers were advised not to actively seek out people they knew whilst on duty, but if you knew someone and they sat next to you, or began talking to you, it was preferable to be polite, find out where they intended to disembark, and rearrange your travel. If they were travelling more than one stop, it was best to make up an excuse why you had to get off at the next stop. It was easy when you knew the underground system as intricately as they did.

At this time of day, work was Bel's priority, but if she could squeeze in just one stop with Esther, or chat for a moment or two on the platform, surely Control wouldn't detect her. What a pity they were under a platform order. If Esther remained in sight she would wait for the platform order to end before making a move toward her. Seeing Esther, although only fleetingly, sent her spirits soaring.

A platform order simultaneously scared the hell out of Bel and left her exhilarated. It could be seen as a chance to put into practice everything you'd learned, and it could also be the prelude to the most frightening and career-defining day of your life. Bel relished the sensations it sparked within her. Every police officer wanted to be a hero on some level.

The doors opened and she disembarked the train to stand amongst the hordes of people already assembled in chaotic order on the platform. She announced her location to Control. "This is 5709. I'm at Aldgate East."

She waited at least ten seconds before she heard a reply. "Copy that, 5709."

Everything was running as per procedure. Bel's heart raced as she began to check the platform, all the while trying to see if Esther remained at the station. It was likely Esther had jumped on the train she had just left. She shook her head and refocused on her training.

"Officers remain on standby." Charlie was loud and clear in her earpiece.

The platform order remained in place. She was half hoping Charlie might have been delivering a message to stand down but apparently not. Bel concentrated on slowly pushing the air from her lungs before deeply drawing it back in. She feared this might not be a drill. She remained calm and kept her movements to a steady pace as she checked the platform. She was careful not to do anything that could draw attention or create panic amongst passengers.

Aldgate East was an average-sized platform, and another train was due within the minute. Bel needed to catch a visual of as many passengers as she could before they jumped on the incoming train. To visually sweep so many people, she focused on the three standout traits: hefty jacket, unnatural gait, and hands in bag. Her eyes darted back and forth as she weaved in and out of people, trying to take in as much as she could in the little time she had. Not by coincidence, she was moving in the direction she'd seen Esther.

A solid tap on her shoulder caused her to swing round.

"Are you all right, madam? Can I help you with any trains?"

She stopped and turned.

The metropolitan transport employee appeared nervous. He was nervous because she had appeared abnormal.

She had failed.

She hadn't been subtle enough. She'd appeared like she was looking for something and caught his attention immediately. If a bomber had been on the platform and saw her behaving like that, he'd be long gone. A brief memory flashed in her mind of a time she'd been running late for a flight at Heathrow Airport. She'd reached the end of the substantial queue looking agitated, out of breath, and clearly sweating. Within seconds after she joined the queue, a security officer asked would she be willing to be x-rayed. The officer explained that her selection had been random, and the plus side of this security measure was that she would advance to the front of the queue. At the time, she saw it as a blessing; queue-jumping at least fifty people was a great result. Of course, the X-ray was clear. She wasn't a drug smuggler, just an idiot who'd misjudged traffic. It wasn't until she relayed the story to a friend that she realised why she'd been selected. Nervous, sweaty, and agitated people are at the top of airport security personnel lists. They are at the top of Metropolitan Transport employees' lists too.

She smiled at the man. "Yes, I'm fine, thank you. I'm running late for a doctor's appointment. I usually avoid the underground at this hour of the morning. It's so busy."

The man nodded and rolled his eyes knowingly. "I just thought I'd check. You looked a little lost."

"Thank you, but I'm okay. Twelve-week scan and I'm as anxious as hell."

In a gesture that left her feeling guilty that it was a lie, the man briefly touched her arm. "I'm sure you'll do great." He moved on down the platform.

Bel's earpiece hissed briefly before Charlie's voice came through, clear, slow, and deliberate. "We have a cleaner. I repeat, we have a cleaner. All officers remain on standby and remain on platform until further instructions."

Bel's legs began to shake.

Cleaner was the code word for suicide bomber. Stupidly, Bel had only really thought this was a drill. She felt far from on her game.

Hotstream officers were trained to respond identically regardless of a real or manufactured situation, but when the radio crackled into action again and Charlie announced firmly that it wasn't a drill, Bel momentarily forgot to breathe.

She reminded herself to calm down and then thought of Esther. If there was danger on the underground, she had to warn her.

Bel advanced toward the area of the platform where Esther had been standing. The silence in her earpiece was uncomfortable. When it was necessary, Control would provide her with audio of operational orders, some of which might be directed at her, but regardless, everyone in Hotstream would hear the operation unfold. Anything was better than the silence.

Bel clicked through her traits: hefty jacket, unusual gait, and hands in bag. As she weaved in and out of unsuspecting commuters, she silently repeated those words.

While all Hotstream officers remained on the platforms, or were at least on their way to the platforms, the activity in the control room would be frantic. Control would have received intelligence that suggested a suicide bomber was possibly already in the underground network or en route.

The code for a package bomb or a planted bomb was "cat in the cradle." History suggested that the police, or in some cases the head office of Transport for London, would likely receive a tip-off when a bomb was planted, but history was changing. In the past, bombs were planted to make a point, to have the government of the day stand up and listen, and to demonstrate that some organisations could bring the underground, and London, to a standstill after one simple phone call. Nowadays, a bomb threat usually had a very different motive. A bomb was set, not to gain attention and never go off, but to explode and kill and maim as many innocent people as possible. The world had certainly changed, and this was no planted-bomb scenario.

Finding a suicide bomber was like finding a needle in a haystack without reliable intelligence. The task for Control now was to locate the bomber if the undercovers didn't already have him in their sights. Given the lack of communication between the call of cleaner until now, Bel concluded they'd lost their target and were frantically searching the monitors to find him or at least provide a helpful description to the Hotstream team so they could begin their search also.

A train arrived at the platform. Bel continued her search for the hefty jacket, the unusual walking gait, and hands in bags, all the while trying to make her way to Esther to warn her.

"Officer 5709. Board that train."

Bel automatically diverted and leapt through the closing door of the carriage just seconds before it began to move. A few passengers took offence at her abrupt arrival, glaring at her disdainfully—she'd knocked into them to clear the closing doors—but other than an apologetic grin, she had nothing to offer. She was on one of the newer trains with walk-through carriages. She liked these because she could see better, but she found she drew attention to herself walking through for no obvious reason, and when the train was near capacity, pushing your way through was the quickest way to an ear full of frustrated abuse.

Adrenaline surged through her. She had to be on the train with the bomber, or at least be the closest officer to them; otherwise, why was she there? She reminded herself repeatedly to remain calm and to act cool. Her intense training flooded back. "You don't want to alert a potential bomber that you're after them," her instructor had said. "One look at you, and if they know you're trying to stop them, they'll detonate." She focused on looking nonchalant, but the fact that she'd only managed to appear flustered on the platform just now didn't fill her with any real confidence.

She spotted Esther two carriages away as the train took a wide bend coming into Liverpool Street station. She pulled out her mobile and began to dial Esther's number but stopped. She had a microphone on her that went directly to the control room, and she was being recorded. She knew full well she wasn't permitted to make that call, or any call, during a cleaner-coded operation unless it was fake or unless it was the only means of communication. Calling her lover to warn her would not make the grade. She pushed the phone back in her pocket.

Esther was now out of sight due to the train straightening. There was nothing she could do.

"Bel, is everything okay?"

She was being watched.

"All good." Her voice was quiet.

"Stand by for further details."

Suddenly her earpiece filled her ears with information. "Jason, confirm you're at Liverpool?"

So sophisticated was the communication hardware, Jason sounded like he was in the next carriage when he replied. "Confirm that."

"Hammersmith westbound incoming less than one minute. That's your train." Charlie spoke quickly but concisely.

"Copy that," replied Jason.

"Moorgate, stand by," said Charlie.

"This is Sean at Moorgate. Confirm standby."

"Piccadilly and Northern, are you near King's Cross?"

"Control, this is Max on Piccadilly, currently at Leicester Square, train to Cockfosters inbound in one minute."

"Negative, Max, you won't make it in time. Stand by."

Bel immediately registered that Covent Garden, Holborn, and Russell Square stations were between Leicester Square and King's Cross. Max was too far away.

"Copy that."

"Control, this is Jean on Northern at Euston, train on platform."

"Take it," Charlie rushed to say.

Less than ten seconds later Jean replied, "Made it."

Bel knew what she was listening to was Charlie coordinating those nearest to the Hammersmith line to be in a position to jump on her train or be in the vicinity if the bomber either remained on that line or jumped ship.

If only Bel knew who the damn bomber was.

She had completed a scan within her immediate area, and under the proviso of wanting to look at an eastbound map, she moved ten feet toward the front of the train. Liverpool Street station was approaching so she didn't have much time.

Click. No bulky coats or clothing.

Click. No one had their hands in their bag.

The train began to slow.

Click. No one looked nervous or sweaty or was chanting or staring into space.

The train stopped.

She was doing all she could with the little information she had received.

The noise level rose as commuters left the train and more arrived. "I need more," she said efficiently into her microphone. "What the hell am I looking for here?"

"No description yet, Bel."

She felt blind.

"Moorgate, not this train but the next from Liverpool. That's your train," said Charlie.

"Copy that." Sean's voice raised an octave and Bel knew hers probably had too. Action was imminent, it was only natural. Sean had been told not to take the train that was at his platform now, but to wait for her train. The knowledge that backup was on the way eased her stress levels, if only slightly.

"The cleaner is female. All officers take note, the cleaner is female." Charlie spoke loudly and slowly.

Female? It certainly wasn't impossible, and in the current climate, it was becoming increasingly popular, but a female suicide bomber threw her. Statistically it should have been a male, and she was disappointed her predisposed image had been that of a male, roughly between the ages of twenty and thirty-five and of Middle Eastern origin.

"Description, do we have a description?" Bel jumped from the train and moved down the platform only to leap on another carriage. She was now on the carriage Esther had been on, but she was nowhere to be seen.

The relief that filled Bel was fleeting yet satisfying. Either way, Esther had gotten off this train and was hopefully well on her way to another, or better still, she was exiting the underground system completely.

Knowledge of the gender of the bomber was a good start. She could immediately discount half the people on the train.

Suddenly a woman of Asian origin caught her eye. She could have been from Pakistan or India, but Bel had no real way of telling. She was pleasant looking, with fine facial features, and she was staring into space. What caught Bel's attention first was her clothing; she wore a large camel-coloured jacket, and although she was visible only on one side, Bel could tell her hand was in her bag. The size of her body seemed out of proportion to her head, and her lips were moving though she wasn't talking to anyone.

Bel's heart pounded so hard deep within her chest, she swore Control could have heard it.

"I need a description," Bel whispered impatiently.

"Stand by, Bel."

Communication between Control and the other officers filled her ear again, and she did her best to shut it out. She took in her surroundings and subconsciously felt for her weapon. It was loaded, she knew it was loaded. It felt heavy.

Chapter Five

Jason from Liverpool was on the train.

As far as Bel could tell, he was a good operator, and the times she'd encountered him, he'd been helpful, sincere, and switched on. She was glad she was no longer alone.

"Bel, your position, please?" asked Charlie.

"Carriage three."

"Jason?"

"Carriage seven, Control."

Before Bel called in the woman, she ran through her characteristics once more as she positioned herself closer: jacket, hands, staring, and muttering. Four traits out of seven for a female. Those remaining undetermined were an unusual walk due to the weight of the explosives, sweating, and the possibility of drug inducement. Four out of seven.

She was possibly only metres away from someone intent on blowing the train, and themselves, into next week.

Bel edged closer.

In her ear she heard Charlie coordinating other officers, but she remained focused on the partly obscured woman who was possibly a suicide bomber.

"Control, this is 570—" She began calling it in.

Her message was overridden. "All officers note: the cleaner is a white female wearing a black jacket."

"What? Can you repeat that, Control?"

Charlie repeated her previous message, and Bel stared at the woman on the train. They were approaching Moorgate station. The suspected bomber didn't move. *You've got this wrong, Charlie.*

Protocol told her she should regroup and concentrate on locating the suspect described by Control, but Bel couldn't take her eyes off the seated woman. What were the chances of two bombers on the train?

"Control, this is 5709. Could there be a decoy?"

The train was slowing and the woman hadn't moved; she continued to stare at an unknown object. Regardless of whether or not you're disembarking at a station, most people look about themselves when a train comes to a halt. Was an explosion at the station a possibility?

"Bel, the intelligence is a lone cleaner, female, white, black jacket. Confirm you have an alternative target?"

Bel's ass was on the line. "Confirm. Third carriage, left-hand side, seat seven. Asian female, brown coat, hands in black leather-look bag."

"Stand by, Bel."

The train came to a halt and the woman didn't move. It occurred to Bel she might be about to die. Fleetingly she thought she should just shoot the woman, save them all. But what if she wasn't a bomber? Bel suppressed a sudden urge to run away. She lost sight of the woman as hordes of people moved on and off the train.

"Officer 5709, step off the train."

Bel was right, she was a bomber.

"Sean, this is your train."

"Copy that," said Sean.

As ordered, Bel immediately pushed through people and leapt onto the platform, sucking in stale, warm underground air. Her suspect was the bomber, and she was being ordered off the train to save her life.

Fuck!

She immediately knew her summation was flawed.

She stood with her hands in her hair, watching the train disappear into the tunnel. She'd made a terrible mistake.

Her earpiece hissed quietly and it sounded different. A male voice startled her. "Bel, this is Scott." Scott was one of Charlie's counterparts. They were on a different channel now. "Your suspect was sitting with a child. She was sharing earphones with a small boy, and she removed her hands from her bag to feed the child sweets of some description."

Fuck, fuck, fuck! Bel stumbled back against the tiled wall at the station for support. She knew a suicide bomber would hardly take her child with her to blow up a train. She hadn't seen him; the woman's large body had obscured her vision, a body she was sure was oversized and packed with explosives.

"You're off your game today, Bel. I'm calling you back in. Get a coffee and some fresh air and return to base."

"But surely you need as many officers on this as possible. I'm right here!" Desperation gripped her.

"Not today, Bel. See you soon."

"Scott, I mean, sir, please. I can do this."

"Base, 5709. Now."

"Yes, sir."

When Bel was eleven, she watched her dad push their boat from the jetty as she ran from the rented beach house trying to catch him in time. She had been excited for weeks at the prospect of fishing with her dad, but that morning she'd been so engrossed with the cartoons on the television she'd ignored warning after warning to hurry up. She had glanced at the clock on the old VCR and thought she had plenty of time, but the clock had been wrong, and when her mum came to tell her that her father had left already, she'd initially thought he was mean for not waiting for her. It wasn't until then that she realised the clock on the VCR was twenty minutes slow. Tears streamed down her face as she ran after her dad, but by the time she arrived he'd pushed the boat away from the jetty and was heading down the estuary. He didn't hear her screaming for him, and he didn't turn to see her on her knees, crying on the worn wood. She hated that feeling, and she'd never been late for anything since.

As the train pulled from the station, it was like watching her dad sail away all over again. She was left behind and there was nothing she could do.

She couldn't stop the moisture developing in her eyes and wasn't sure she could control it, so she put her head down and headed to the nearest bathroom. Already she was going over in her mind what went wrong. She would take her time returning to base; she had to have in her mind a clear analysis of the entire situation before she even considered entering a debrief. Her superiors would want her to identify the problem and come up with a solution. Nothing in MI5 was ever handed to you on a platter.

Not many things motivated Bel more than failure. In fact, the desire to avoid failure drove her to achieve such high standards. In golf, you gave yourself five steps to berate your last poor shot, the one that landed in the water or the bunker. Then it was best to move on or else the next shot would be affected. She gave herself five minutes to get a grip.

The bathroom smelled of cheap perfume and cheap bleach. Her tears never came, just an annoyance that she'd cracked under the pressure of her first real suicide-bomber threat and that she'd fallen victim to a severe case of tunnel vision. All she could do was learn from the experience and perform better next time. She hoped there would be a next time—not necessarily a suicide bomber, she wouldn't wish that on anyone—but a chance to prove her worth on the team. The repercussions from this incident could be severe. Other members of the task force had no reason to doubt her abilities, until now. The coming weeks were imperative to regain her colleagues' trust. She had to show them she could hold her own and cover their backs at the same time. Right now, she had let herself and her entire team down.

Her earpiece was eerily silent, and she hated not knowing what was going on—especially when she knew *everything* was going on. It was probably switched off—she assumed by Scott—but she left it dangling from her ear regardless. She wasn't in the mood for idle chitchat with strangers, and it always worked as a deterrent. Annoyed to be excluded from the chase, she switched off her microphone; it was the only way she knew how to feel alone in a heaving underground-train network with surveillance cameras covering every inch.

Reluctant to return to the real world, she pushed through waiting teenagers intent on blocking the toilet door and held her head high as she made her way toward the escalators in a bid to reach fresh air aboveground before continuing her journey in the belly of London. She wondered about the fate of those entering the station.

Headquarters was in Southwark, and from Moorgate, Bel intended to take the Northern line southward to London Bridge station and then the Jubilee line to Southwark station. From there, headquarters was only a short walk.

Terrorist intelligence-gathering was an unpredictable beast at the best of times, and MI5, not unlike other government security agencies around the world, set parameters and guidelines when dealing with sensitive information. Risk assessments were complicated and certainly not foolproof. They involved analysing economic damage, property damage, and of course, casualties. Bel knew that because the underground system hadn't yet been evacuated, it was likely the terror threat was not linked to any of the well-known extremist groups active in the United Kingdom and the rest of the world. She also knew that the information they had received was yet to be verified to an acceptable level or else they would know if the threat was imminent and who exactly was making it.

The London underground system was vast and could bring London to a standstill if it was obstructed in any substantial way. Consequently, systems were in place to minimise hoax threats. Before Bel had commenced in Hotstream, she'd imagined one phone call with a bomb threat would shut down the entire system. This obviously wasn't the case, although the police often received bomb threats—mostly from disgruntled commuters and the occasional mentally ill person—but they were swiftly contained without the need for evacuation or any real disruption of services.

Most people had little cause to notice, but there were small things in place to assist underground security. Of particular note was the obvious lack of rubbish bins in many of the underground stations. Extra bins had been installed for the 2012 Olympic Games, but when they were broken or damaged, they weren't replaced. If there was a bin in a station, it was strategically placed, was filmed at all times, and consisted of a clear plastic bag suspended over a hoop. The London underground was a difficult place to leave a bomb, and it was specifically designed that way.

This current threat must be genuine, but it was obviously unclear by whom the threat was made. Bel never liked to guess how high-level anti-terrorism undercover officers gathered their information. They were often a law unto themselves, and after having met a few, she knew she didn't have the balls for the level of undercover work that ran to the deepest lowlife places on earth, full of dangerous people with even more dangerous ideals.

Bel stopped to watch a busker performing a great impression of Neil Diamond when something familiar caught her eye. Esther walked right by her.

"Hey, Esther." Esther continued without noticing. Bel jogged after her, weaving through a handful of strangers. "Esther!"

Esther turned, wearing an unreadable expression. "Oh, hi, Bel."

"Didn't you hear me calling you?"

"Must have been a million miles away." Her smile was brief and appeared forced. "You're not at work today?"

Bel registered that Esther's voice was higher in pitch than normal, as if she was nervous. She had no time to dwell on that observation because she had to think quickly. "Just on my way to a job. Got a bit of time, though." This wasn't exactly a lie. She *was* on her way back to base and certainly wasn't in any hurry.

She was delighted to see Esther, but their meeting left her feeling uneasy, guilty, really. She couldn't hug her because any bodily contact would reveal she had a weapon in a holster beneath her jacket, and how would she explain that? Unless she was guarding a foreign diplomat, she'd hardly be armed—it wasn't America. Then there was the feeling that Esther wasn't as pleased to see her as she'd have hoped. Esther seemed distracted, even keen to just move on and return to her day. Bel felt deflated.

Luckily Esther didn't seem to notice that they hadn't hugged in greeting, and the awkward moment passed.

"So where's your job?" Esther visibly inhaled deeply and smiled directly at Bel, her shoulders dropping slightly. "Minding anyone important today?"

Shit! Never mind Esther's odd behaviour, she really should have thought this through more—lying wasn't second nature to her and she wasn't all that good at it. When she undertook undercover work in the past, she'd found that being herself was a dead giveaway. What ultimately worked was to invent a completely different person, a character for her to play, and it was only then she could be convincing.

She'd not thought through talking to Esther in advance, and now she was left wanting. It just wasn't her day.

"Not today." She wanted to avoid telling a direct lie. Not to Esther. It felt so wrong.

Esther raised her eyebrow, waiting.

Bel looked around and saw a poster of a touring band on the wall. They were playing at the London O2 Arena that evening. "I'm just providing numbers for the afternoon shift for them." She cocked her head toward the poster and shrugged. Esther barely registered the famous band and simply nodded. "It's just while their A-team rest up for the evening and it's only rehearsals." *Liar, liar.* Bel was failing miserably.

She really wanted to be able to tell Esther about her disastrous morning. Being a member of the Hotstream task force was a prestigious posting, but there was nothing prestigious about having no one to talk to about your job, especially when, by not even eight o'clock, you were having the worst day possible.

"Who on earth would hassle them at rehearsal?" asked Esther.

"What?"

Esther pointed to the poster. "Do they really need minders during rehearsal?"

Bel had no idea. Did they? *Think, you idiot.* "The O2 is a big complex, and loads of people work there. It's just precautionary. That's why the real minders take the afternoon off." It was possible her story sounded plausible, but it was equally possible that it sounded like the load of old shite it was. Bel shrugged. "Beats me, but I get paid, so I'm not complaining."

"What's the going rate for a minder like you these days?" Esther shifted weight from one foot to the other.

Was she nervous?

Since when had Esther shown the slightest hint of interest in her work? She had no idea what a pretend bodyguard earned. She racked her brain before, thankfully, a Hollywood movie entered her head. She halved the amount quoted in the movie and, before she spoke, halved it again—this was far from Hollywood.

"Three hundred."

Esther thought about this.

Bel waited. Maybe three hundred was too low.

"Not bad for an afternoon's work, I don't suppose," said Esther.

"Yeah, well, that's what I think."

"Sounds a bit boring, though."

Bel couldn't agree more, especially after the morning she'd had. But then, most days came and went with little or no action. Today had been remarkable and unique, and she'd fucked it up.

"Easy money."

"Well, not exactly. Easy money is drug dealing or being an assassin or something like that," said Esther.

"I guess I was off school the day Mr. Hughes suggested we

consider illegal activity for a career." It certainly hadn't been Bel's first thought for easy money.

"You've seen those shows, though, right? You know, the ones where good people do stupid things for a good cause?"

Of course Bel had seen those shows; she hated them. Right was right and wrong was wrong. Producing methamphetamine and selling it to build a stash of cash for your family to live comfortably on after you died from terminal cancer was still illegal and morally corrupt. If there was one thing Bel knew, it was right from wrong.

"I'm not about to get arrested for ensuring the safety of a bunch of overpaid and under-talented musicians, though, am I?"

"No, but you're not about to make thousands of pounds either."

Bel was tired of talking about the pros and cons of her imaginary job. Where the hell had all this stuff Esther was on about come from?

"Money isn't everything," said Bel.

"It is to some people."

"Who?" Esther was the last person Bel expected to be money focused.

"What?"

"Who?" Bel repeated. "Who are we talking about specifically?"

"No one." Esther shrugged. "I was just thinking out loud."

Bel eyed her warily. "Are you trying to tell me something? You're not laundering money through the bar or something dodgy like that, are you?"

She was expecting a laugh or a playful punch on her shoulder, but Esther offered nothing more than a shake of her head.

"Fancy a coffee? My shout." More caffeine was far from what Bel needed, but hanging out with Esther was delaying her return to base, and it was all she could think of. Esther was acting weird. She just wanted to do something normal with her.

"I don't know if I've got time for coffee."

"Where exactly *are* you going?"

"Nowhere important."

"So, one coffee won't hurt?" Bel was struggling with Esther's secrecy.

Esther looked around her. Her eyes darted back and forth as if she were expecting someone else, but before Bel could probe further, she said, "Oh, come on, then."

They walked in silence, dodging the crowd until Bel returned to a previous subject, not willing to chance her luck again about Esther's destination. "*Is* there something illegal going on at the bar?" she asked.

"We sell alcohol to underage people and sometimes don't pay the kitchen workers minimum wage. Of course there's something illegal going on at the bar."

"Why don't you do something?"

"I do."

Bel's earpiece crackled, dragging her back to the present. She was probably being watched as she and Esther leaned against the far wall on the upper level of Moorgate station. They reached a coffee vendor and Esther ordered them each a latte, directing the young man to keep the change. Bel only noticed because she used a twenty-pound note to pay for two coffees worth barely five pound.

"I feed them a healthy dinner and give them the leftovers to take home to their friends or family."

Bel smiled. That was exactly what she knew Esther would do. Most of the people that worked in the kitchens were migrants, and to buy even a burger at some of these bars cost more than an hour's wage, maybe two.

"Do you wish you could do more?"

"I wish the people who have everything could just see how much difference giving a little could make. If every above-average earner in London accidentally dropped a ten-pound note one day and an underpaid person picked it up, who do you think it would make the most difference to?"

Bel knew the answer, and she knew this compassionate side of Esther was one of her most endearing qualities. "The rich wouldn't even notice it was missing."

"Exactly. But that struggling person who picked it up could feed their kids for a week with that."

"Yeah." Bel scoffed. "And spend the tenner they saved on a cheap bottle of wine or a packet of smokes."

"No, Bel, and that's precisely the narrow-minded mentality I'd expect from those that have more than enough. You think like that because it justifies you doing nothing. In reality, they'd buy their kids some shoes or a warm hat and gloves. The sacrifices some of these parents make for their kids are astounding."

"I'm sorry. I was being flippant. I see your point."

Esther looked disappointed.

"I do, honestly. I was being an idiot."

Esther's questions about her job had distracted her from what was going on in the tunnels. She needed to craftily encourage Esther out of the underground system.

"So where was it you said you were going today?" She fully focused on Esther. "And are you cold?" She eyed the thick black coat Esther was wearing.

Esther looked down at herself. "I guess I was feeling a little under the weather."

Bel pressed the back of her hand against Esther's forehead. "You're burning up." Tenderly she tucked a wayward strand of hair behind Esther's ear. "And you're a bit clammy. Should you see a doctor?"

"A doctor?" Bel knew Esther wasn't a fan of western medicine. "It's the doctors in this country that do their best to keep us all ill."

Bel humoured her. "Okay then. Perhaps you need some chicken soup and a day in bed." She saw an opening. "And some vitamin D. How about you catch the bus to wherever you're going? Get some fresh air and sunshine." She thought for a moment. "Honestly, Esther, where *are* you going?"

Bel's earpiece crackled again, only this time the channel remained open and her ear filled with commands and discussion about the operation. She yanked out the earpiece. She was no longer involved in the operation, and getting Esther aboveground was her priority.

"Honey?" She waved her hand in front of Esther. "Earth to Esther. Where are you going?"

"Oh." Esther shook her head. She'd been a million miles away. "I've got an appointment."

Sometimes Esther's vagueness made Bel want to scream. She gave up with the questions and tried a different approach. "Come on. I'll walk you out. I was just on the way to get some fresh air myself."

"Why don't you go ahead?" Esther cupped Bel's face. "I'm not in a rush. I've got all the time in the world."

"What time is your appointment?"

"It's not 'til later. You'll be long gone by the time I get to where I'm going."

Bel cursed. She should be better at this kind of thing. Today just wasn't her day. She racked her brain to come up with something better. "I've got time to kill, Esther. Can't we do something together just for a while?" If in doubt, whine like a child and go for the sympathy vote.

Esther frowned awkwardly.

If she hadn't known better, Bel could have sworn Esther just wanted her to bugger off and let her get on with her day.

Bel's phone rang. How difficult could it be for a MI5 operative to get one woman, just the one, out of the underground? She pulled her phone from her breast pocket and frowned at the number. Poised to decline the call, she recognised the last four digits. *Oh shit!* It was her office number. Her desk phone. "Fuck. I have to take this."

Esther smiled and shrugged.

How were you supposed to answer a call from your own phone? She went with a safe bet. "Hello."

"Where the fuck are you?" Charlie's tone was far from bubbly.

Bel turned to face the wall. If she was about to get her arse kicked, she wasn't keen for Esther to bear witness. "I'm just leaving Moorgate now." It wasn't exactly a lie. She heard Charlie relay her location to others in Control. She was out of the hunt. Why did they care where she was? She perked up. Perhaps they needed her back.

"And why the fuck isn't your mike on?"

"I'm on—"

"And on whose damn authority did you decide not to answer when Control called you?"

"I was—"

"Shut up and listen to me, Bel. You've been seen with a woman. Who is she?"

Fuck, fuck, and even more fuck! The day was turning out to be horrendous. She couldn't do a thing right, but then she wasn't convinced she'd done anything wrong, not by the umpteen policies and procedures that had been drilled into her in the past few months. "I've been chatting to a friend, Esther." Bel turned to give Esther the obligatory eye roll at mentioning her name, but she was gone.

"Is she with you now?"

Brown hair, black jacket—she scanned the immediate area, but every second person wore a black jacket and had brown hair.

"No."

"No? What do you mean no?"

"She was here and now she's not."

"Where is she?"

"I don't know." Bel finally remembered she was a trained operative and not in kindergarten. "What the hell's going on?"

"The woman you were with, Esther, do you know her well?"

"Charlie, where is this—"

"Answer me! Do you know her well?"

"We're friends." She opted for the truth. "Close friends."

"You sleep with her?"

"Well, that's one—"

"Do you sleep with her?"

"Yes. I sleep with her."

"What's her last name?"

"Come on, you can't be serious. I was just chatting to a friend."

"Bel, answer the question."

Bel couldn't think straight. Why all the interest in Esther? Do they check out your partners to make sure you aren't leaking information to the Russians? *The cold war is over, you idiot!* She was never told she had to inform anyone she was in a relationship. "Banks. Her last name is Banks."

"Is that her real name?"

"What the fuck? Of course it's her real name."

"We had vision of you both until our system glitched for no more than five seconds. We weren't able to find you again, and now you can't see her?"

"No." Bel didn't know whether to stay put or go searching. Why had Esther suddenly disappeared?

"No, us neither." Charlie barely took a breath. "You're to return to HQ immediately. Conrad is waiting to speak to you."

"Rush?" She really must be in all sorts of trouble if Conrad Rush wanted to see her. In fact, she'd thought he was an imaginary boss for the first month she worked there. He showed his face eventually and she immediately wished he'd stayed away. He was the single most intimidating man she'd ever met.

"Charlie, I was on my way back. I ran into a friend, that's all." Unless she'd shot the PM himself, she wasn't sure why Rush would even know of her existence, let alone be waiting to speak to her. "How come Conrad is involved in all this?"

"Turn on your mike, replace your earpiece or connect it or fix whatever you've done to become off-line, and get your arse back here now. If you see Esther again, call it in."

"What has she got to do—"

"That's an order, 5709. Over."

Why had Esther disappeared and why was she in so much trouble? Bel struggled to compute what had just happened. Charlie, Esther, and bloody Conrad Rush. What the hell was going on?

As ordered, Bel replaced her earpiece and the line crackled into action, but it wasn't on the main channel because she couldn't hear anything regarding the ongoing incident.

Although she knew exactly what she should do next—hightail it back to the office—something stalled her: Esther. Beautiful, tender Esther. But there'd been something else. Something she couldn't put her finger on, something distant. Yes, that was it, Esther had been distant. So distant in fact, she'd disappeared. Bel couldn't stand the mystery a moment longer. She jumped on the next southbound train on the Northern line, toward HQ.

Chapter Six

Come with me, Bel." Charlie met her the moment she shoved her swipe card into her breast pocket after entering the secure main offices of the task force.

"Charlie, you're scaring the hell out of me here. Am I about to get fired?"

"Not now. We don't have time for this."

Bel was expecting a direct route to Conrad's office, but they were marching swiftly in the opposite direction. They were heading toward one of the incident rooms.

Hotstream's incident rooms were state of the art. Without the trendy television-set lighting and excessive, if not completely useless, props, they looked nothing like the shows she used to watch religiously. The equipment inside was imperative once you knew what you could access and how quickly you could access it. The information at your fingertips was mind-blowing.

She stepped inside, and the images she saw displayed on the monitors hit her like a truck. She swallowed hard to counteract the reflex of vomiting.

"Clear the room," Conrad bellowed.

Apart from her and Charlie, everyone obeyed the order immediately.

"Do you know this woman?" Conrad waited until the last person left before he directed his question to her.

The woman he was referring to was Esther, and pictures of her were plastered all over an entire board. Bel was in some of them—the ones taken from the underground CCTV system that morning. Many, however, were older pictures. Bel could tell by the length of Esther's hair, the less prominent wrinkles on her face, and the tattoos missing on her arms.

Conrad waited for an answer.

"I know her. That's my…um…that's Esther."

"Actually, no, it isn't." Conrad hadn't seemed to notice that Bel's world was swiftly falling apart before his eyes. "The woman you know as Esther is actually Esmeralda Gaffney. Does that name ring a bell?"

Gaffney, Gaffney, Gaffney. Bel shook her head, and then it hit her. "Brian Gaffney's daughter." She said the words to herself as the little minions in her brain ran off to fetch all the information she knew about Brian and Esmeralda Gaffney.

Turns out she knew enough to put the pieces together. Brian Gaffney had been a decorated police officer in Dublin, but he'd poked his nose into the IRA or, more accurately, the corrupt English politicians and high-ranking police who saw personal benefit and wealth in sustaining a volatile relationship between England and Ireland. Esther, or Esme as she was known at the time, was rumoured to have been forced to witness the cruel and inhumane torture and subsequent death of her father. Esme disappeared off the face of the earth. Some stubborn yet skilful detectives had uncovered the truth eventually—Brian Gaffney left a solid trail of evidence, so he must have known what he was getting involved in—but no one knew what really happened to five-year-old Esme. The criminals denied killing her, at the time coming up with what appeared to be a bullshit story about how she escaped. It was assumed she had been killed, but without a body, there was no evidence.

For all intents and purposes, Esmeralda Gaffney had been dead for nearly thirty years.

Until now.

"Esther is Esme Gaffney?" She already knew the answer.

"We're almost one hundred percent sure."

"But I don't understand. It's not a crime to be Esme Gaffney, surely?"

"It is when we think you've got thirty kilograms of explosives strapped to your body."

This time she couldn't stop the vomit but at least found a rubbish bin.

Esther's odd behaviour that morning came flooding back. The

coffee without change, the big jacket, and the bizarre questions: it all seemed suspicious now. Then there was last night: the intense sex, the sentimental words, and Esther declaring her love. She couldn't bring herself to believe it, but it was textbook stuff. The indicators were that Esther was a suicide bomber.

"Why'd you switch off your mike today?" Conrad was relentless.

Bel at least turned away to spit the chunky bits of her breakfast into the bin. She wiped her mouth. "You must have heard what I did this morning?"

"Oh, I heard about it all right. Nice attempt at a decoy."

"A what?"

"Do you expect me to believe your little fuck buddy there is working alone?" He pointed to Esther on the screens.

"I didn't see the kid with the woman this morning."

"How convenient. What are you, blind? Your screw is walking around ready to go off while you try your best to set up a decoy."

"Fuck you!" The insult was out before she could engage her filter. Then, in light of having said the worst possible thing to the head of LUATRU besides "I fucked your wife," Bel kept going. "Esther is my girlfriend, not my fuck buddy or my screw, and I'll be damned if I'll sit here and let you tell me she's a terrorist."

Chapter Seven

The saliva that induced her vomiting had disappeared. Bel's mouth was dry with fear.

The look on Rush's face indicated that she had gone too far. "Do you know what I've got Thompson working on right now?" The veins in his neck grew larger.

She didn't really like Nicolas Thompson and couldn't have given a damn what he was working on. She shrugged.

"He's at your apartment, Reilly, so if you've got something you want to say, now might be the best time to say it, because it looks to me like I've got one terrorist out there preparing to blow up a train and another one standing here fucking with me!"

Her own stupidity slapped her in the face. Until that very moment, she thought Conrad Rush was just pissed at her because she'd been too stupid to realise she was sleeping with someone they now suspected to be a terrorist. "There must be some kind of mistake. Esther isn't a terrorist and neither am I." Her policing instincts kicked in. "You must have had me under surveillance for months now? I've done nothing to indicate to you that I'm a terrorist. Surely Esther's done nothing either. She works in a bar and gives free meals to the underpaid workers. She's a good person."

Conrad sat down. He indicated she do the same.

Bel kept her life simple. She had one phone, one computer, and one bank account. "It's not difficult to poke into my life. Thompson should be done by now. He didn't find anything, did he?"

Conrad shook his head. "I had to be sure."

She gave him the benefit of his doubt. If she ever reached a position of authority, she imagined she would have done the same thing.

"If what you're saying is true, I just don't understand the purpose of her bombing the underground. What's her motive? What is she trying to achieve? So what if she's Esme Gaffney? It means she's had a shit life, a fucking terrible childhood, and Christ knows how she survived, but how does that make her a bomber?"

"We have the intelligence, Reilly."

"But *what* intelligence? Who's she targeting?"

"Terrorists don't need a target. They want to destroy, kill and make a point."

"Then what's her point?" None of it was making sense. "Who's she working with or for?"

"As far as we can tell, she's working alone."

"Alone? You're fucking kidding me?" Something was missing. "How did the undercovers get onto someone with no previous record or involvement in terrorist activities and who by all accounts is working alone?"

Conrad shrugged. "I don't know and I don't care. But thank God they did."

It was too difficult to put the puzzle together without all the pieces. Bel couldn't imagine that any grudge Esther held was worth killing innocent people to settle. She lost control of her emotions. "I love her. I don't want her to be Esme Gaffney." She stood and walked away. The fact that she'd said the words aloud was enough; for Conrad Rush to see her cry was unbearable.

"Look, Reilly, she's pissed off at someone for reasons only she can know. But she needs to be stopped."

Charlie spoke for the first time. "We need your help to find her before she does something she might regret."

Bel pulled out her phone. "I can call her. That's all I can offer. She didn't say where she was going. I was supposed to meet her at the bar tonight." She looked at her watch. She would meet her in eleven hours. It seemed so distant. She wanted to fast-forward until then so she could walk into the bar and see Esther flirting with a customer or frowning as she concentrated on pulling the perfect beer. She had to endure an entire day to reach a time where that scenario might be possible, except it was probably impossible. Whatever happened that day would shape the rest of her life. With the exception of the day her mother died, never before had Bel wanted to start the day again as much as she wanted to now.

"Bel?" Charlie raised her voice.

"Sorry, yes. I'll try her now." She dialled the number and placed the phone on speaker before resting it on the table in front of them.

"Hi, you've reached Esther. Leave a message and I'll call you back."

It didn't ring, just went directly to message bank.

"It was Esther you were after this morning, wasn't it?"

Conrad nodded. "We had her, but then we lost her. It was Scott, wondering where the hell you were, that spotted you both chatting. Then the system surged and we lost you."

"We only went to get coffee. I was trying to walk Esther in the direction of the exit. I wanted her out of danger." Esther was the danger.

Charlie and Conrad exchanged glances. "We had to consider you were working together. We directed our attention to the platforms. We didn't look near the stairs," said Charlie.

"There'll be severe repercussions for switching off your mike, Reilly."

Bel knew her career was probably over.

"You wanna hope she doesn't get a chance to blow anything up, or that error might haunt you for the rest of your life."

Bel cringed.

"No, not a pleasant thought, is it, knowing you had a hand in the deaths of countless innocent people?"

Charlie intervened. "Let's get back to Control." She stared at Bel, who was staring at Conrad. Bel looked away, reluctantly backing down from defending the accusation that it was her fault. Charlie continued. "We need to find her before she does anything stupid." She nodded encouragement to Bel and eyed Rush warily.

He nodded. "You know her better than any of us. You'll recognise her immediately. I want your eyes on every screen in there. Find her."

Bel wanted to find Esther, but when she did, what was she to do? The faint hope that this was all a mistake had settled in the pit of her stomach, but weighing heavily on top of that was all the evidence that suggested otherwise. She was, after all, part of a team that specialised in this area, and if she were a betting person she'd wager that Hotstream had it correct. If she saw her on the CCTV, should she tell Rush where she was and risk her being shot? If she didn't tell him and Esther detonated the bomb, she'd have to live with her death and the death of scores of innocent people for the rest of her life. She knew the drill. Shoot to kill. It seemed that either way she went, Esther was dead.

Chapter Eight

Control was a buzz of well-rehearsed action. Everyone had a job to do with a defined outcome. At the moment, everyone was searching for Esther.

Bel sat tentatively at her assigned desk. Several monitors beamed at her, and she manoeuvred the mouse that controlled the cameras she could select to view at intervals she chose. It was the only thing that even hinted toward her having some control over the situation.

Unfortunately, nothing sprang to mind that might lead her to look in any particular place. She had no romantic memory of a moment shared on the underground, no station or location that was special between them. Nothing. In any case, it was doubtful Esther would deliberately bomb a special place, but because they shared no special place, there wasn't one single location she could discount. She knew Esther intimately, but it was becoming painfully obvious she barely knew her at all.

"Chances are she'll still be wearing the same coat, but you have a better chance of recognising her in any outfit, so keep your mind open as well as your eyes," said Charlie.

Bel didn't know where to begin. Even her comprehensive knowledge of the underground left her jittery with confusion; she had too many options. She inhaled deeply and pushed her hair off her forehead. She commenced looking on the Northern line and concentrated her search around central London. She systematically clicked through the images on the screen, station by station, carriage by carriage, train by train. The task was enormous. She could click on one camera, only to have Esther walk into a shot moments after she clicked off. She could be chasing her all day. Except she didn't have all day. She wished she knew how long she *did* have, but there was no answer to that question. There were no answers at all, just more questions.

Women wearing black coats were everywhere. After barely fifteen minutes her eyes were nearly stuck closed from squinting, and her nerves were frayed from listening to her colleagues' attempts at hunting Esther down. Bel wanted to be looking in the tunnels, but when she gave that choice due consideration, she knew if she were down there, she'd probably want to be where she had unlimited access to the entire system. She was in the place statistically offering the highest chance for a result, but it didn't seem like enough.

Bel understood the psychology behind panic, she knew that the empty sense of helplessness eating away at her insides was a natural response, and she realized the increasing tempo of her thumping heart was inevitable. What would never be written in any textbook was the way it would make *her* feel. She wanted to scream, run, punch, fight, and explode. She slammed her fist hard on the desk before pushing her chair away and fleeing the room.

She ignored Conrad calling her name.

In the sanctuary of the toilet, Bel sat on the closed lid and forced her throbbing head between her legs. She had nothing left to throw up and honestly feared if she dry-retched, her insides would come away, like a boat breaking its tether in a storm. She might be forced to flush her intestines, and indeed her life, down the toilet.

It briefly occurred to her that for a boat to have its tether broken was a chance at freedom. The owner mourned the loss and the boat rejoiced in the open sea. Bel's beliefs were being challenged, and she honestly didn't know what to think anymore.

She rested the side of her head on the toilet roll as her fear and panic subsided. *Boats don't think.*

She regained valuable focus.

She knew what she had to do.

Bel returned to the control room purposeful and calm. The chances of finding Esther were akin to winning the lottery, but you had to be in it to win it, and to find her she had to look and she had to make it count. Recalling her training, she concentrated on shutting out all external noise and distractions. Within a minute, it was just her, the screens, and the hundreds of thousands of people using the London underground system.

Every moment that passed was another moment Esther was alive, another moment she could be saved, and another moment the people of London were safe. If Esther really was the bomber, Bel wasn't naive enough to misunderstand that it was also another moment closer to detonation.

Although she refused to absorb the noise around her, she sensed Conrad was beginning to panic. The busy morning rush of commuters would soon be ending. If Esther was going to detonate a bomb causing supreme devastation, the window of opportunity was closing.

Precious minutes passed and Bel remained focused on the screens. She looked carefully and deliberately at everyone resembling Esther. She had to find her before the others did. Brown hair, possible ponytail, black coat, and denim jeans. Such was the quality of the cameras that unless you had a specific target to zoom in on, it was all she could go on.

Click, click, click. She searched the District line: White City, Shepherd's Bush, Holland Park, Notting Hill Gate, Queensgate, Lancaster Gate, Marble Arch, Bond Street. Her eyes remained wide and alert. Time was ticking.

"She might have thought twice about going through with it after seeing me this morning." Bel offered the comment when a natural lull in the control room saw the volume decrease. She never removed her eyes from the screens.

"She won't have." Conrad was quick to squash the notion.

"She could have." Charlie was giving it serious thought.

Bel wanted to ask Conrad who he'd slept with to get to the top, but then men didn't need to sleep with anyone to advance. They just needed to be good suck-ups, mediocre golfers, and loyal members of the boys' club. His narrow-mindedness had surely hindered him his entire career. Charlie could easily make him look incompetent if she wanted to, and he was too stupid to see it. But then, he was the boss. Maybe Charlie was exactly where he wanted her.

"Is someone at her place?" Again, Bel spoke without looking away from the monitors.

"Her place has been searched, Reilly." Conrad's temper was fraying. "I can't afford to have people wandering off all over the place when I need them here."

"I'll get the local police to wait at her flat and her work," said

Charlie. She immediately picked up the telephone. "We'll keep our specialised resources here. I should have thought about that before."

Charlie was covering for him, and if Bel knew it, everyone else did too.

"So, for all we know, she's back home cooking an omelette with her feet up watching *Good Morning, Britain.*" Bel couldn't hide the contempt for him in her voice.

Conrad pounded the wall with a balled-up hand. "She's here!"

For the first time, Bel looked up, but it wasn't to glare at Conrad. It was to eye Charlie. Bel thought she might hold the clue as to why the idiot in charge was so damn sure Esther was still a threat.

Bel returned her full attention to the screens, and after only seconds, she glared at an image that caused her heart to race and her head to burn hot with anticipation, relief, and pure terror. To cover her tracks, she clicked from the image of Oxford Circus to a camera view of Wimbledon station. In her mind, even as she was rising from her chair, she was calculating the fastest route to her destination. Without a word she walked from the control room.

"Where the hell are you going now?" Conrad shouted after her.

"The bathroom." Bel kept her tone low and unagitated to avoid raising unnecessary suspicion.

Tick, tock.

The moment he was out of sight, she ran down the dull beige corridor and slammed through the fire-escape door into the stairwell. Taking the steps two at a time and using the handrail to corner as quickly as she could, Bel reached the ground floor. It had taken her eleven seconds. She slowed herself enough to walk at a reasonable pace on the approach to the security desk. How long would it take them to realise she wasn't in the toilet, and when they realised that she was missing, how long before someone offered the useful suggestion that she'd fled the building?

She saw nothing unusual about the activity on the security desk; the two civilian contractors manning the station constantly eyed everyone with suspicion. It was their job. Should she smile at them and risk drawing attention to herself, or should she act nonchalant and saunter past like she owned the place? The latter worked in expensive hotels if you needed an urgent pee stop, but she wasn't sure if she could pull that off now.

She took a deep breath. She walked past this desk every day, more than once a day at times, and unless they had already been alerted, why would security care whether she was coming or going? She was an agent with MI5, highly paid and well trained, and she concluded the best action to take was to act like it.

Holding her head high, Bel marched tenaciously past the security desk, drawing her sunglasses from her breast pocket and placing them firmly on her head. As if starring in a blockbuster spy movie, she stepped through the sliding entrance doors as a gentle breath of wind caught her hair and propelled it back from her forehead. The similarities to a Hollywood spy movie ended there.

The moment the fresh air hit her she burst into a full sprint toward Southwark station. She was agile and moved through the familiar London population with ease. Her phone rang. It was an unknown number, but she knew it was Charlie, or perhaps Conrad was calling to fire her himself. Without a second thought, she declined the call and made one of her own.

"Esther, it's me." She wasn't surprised the call diverted directly to voice mail. "If you get this, I need you to stay where you are. Please let me help you." She couldn't think of anything else to say so she hung up.

Her phone rang again, and this time she recognised her own work number. Predictably, Charlie and Conrad were persistent, but again, she declined the call and returned her focus to Esther. Suddenly, a jolt of panic tore through her insides, and as she was poised to descend into the abyss of the underground network, she paused on the dank stairs and called Esther again.

"Look, I don't know what today will bring, but I want you to know I love you." She hung up feeling neither stupid for loving a potential bomber nor frightened that life as she knew it was ending that day.

She disappeared into the station.

Chapter Nine

Bel was an accurate judge of space and time; it was one of her most useful qualities. Of course, it was something you could learn or practice, but she required nothing other than her instincts. She could pack a suitcase, small bag, car boot, or anything really with an unfathomable amount of objects. It was like a game of Tetris. Shapes, spaces, and at times stubborn brute force would see her succeed. When it came to time, she possessed an uncanny knack of running a scenario through her mind in fast-forward and translating that scene to normal time. She calculated that if everything went to plan and the trains ran on time, she would be in Esther's vicinity within fifteen minutes.

It seemed like such an agonisingly long time to reach her destination, and if she were to run between trains the time would be halved, but running and drawing attention to herself was not a viable option. If Control spotted her running they could track her easily. In fact, if she were to remain wearing the same outfit, she'd be apprehended in no time. She paused to look around. Two doors down from a specialty cupcake cart was a vendor selling London souvenirs. The locals knew the goods were cheap crap made in China, but she made a beeline for the little stall, selecting a cap and a flimsy black zip-up hooded jacket emblazoned with the Union Jack and the words, In London, I Am the King.

With only the stall holder as her audience, she quickly transferred everything from her jacket pockets to her jeans and took it off. Her holster and weapon were in full view. The man's eyes bulged from his head like those of a character in a cartoon.

"Oh, don't worry. It's not real." She sounded relatively convincing, even to herself. She pulled on the black jacket. "I'm an extra on *Scott and Bailey*. Have you seen that cop show?" He looked relieved but clueless. "You should watch it. It's great." *Scott and Bailey* was filmed miles away in Manchester. It was the best she could manage under the circumstances.

She pulled on the cap and resumed her journey to reach Esther. It was a long shot. Esther was probably on the move, but this was Bel's only chance. Sitting and waiting for something to happen wasn't a viable plan. Conrad Rush finding Esther first wasn't viable either. Bel had one chance and she was taking it.

She walked briskly toward the westbound platform. When a group of people rushed by her, she tagged onto the end of their pack, inconspicuously gaining ground. As the train arrived, she leapt on it and stood by the door. She needed an escape route.

If Control located her, the odds of reaching Esther were slim. Her knowledge of the underground network was not superior to others in Hotstream, and once Control agents were tracking her on camera, it was unlikely they'd lose her. Although they'd lost Esther once already that morning. She prayed Esther stayed lost until she found her.

The next station was Waterloo and it was always busy. It was imperative she leave the Jubilee line as soon as possible. The Jubilee line was the only one that serviced the Southwark station. It left her exposed to remain on Jubilee one moment longer than necessary.

Waterloo station was extensive, and although CCTV cameras more than adequately surveyed every nook and cranny, the masses of commuters using the station relieved some of her tension.

Bel swiftly made her way to catch a northbound train on the Northern line. Heading directly into the city, the Northern line was busier than Jubilee and was a good place to blend in. As she took up position in the doorway of the carriage, she looked at her phone. She'd had another seven missed calls, but nothing from Esther. She had no service now, so there was no use trying Esther.

Bel appraised her plan. It required little consideration until she reached her destination. If Esther was there, she had to talk to her. As if on cue, the pointer finger on her right hand, her trigger finger, twitched. If Esther wouldn't talk to her she knew what she was trained to do. She shook her head. Who was she kidding? She looked at her watch. She'd set the stopwatch running the moment she'd entered the stairwell at HQ. It now said five minutes and thirty-six seconds. Training or no training, within ten minutes, she might be faced with the real possibility of aiming a loaded gun at her lover. The pressure was immense. The situation was impossible. Although Bel was slowly soaking layers of clothing with sweat, the thought sent a ripple of cold shiver through her.

The train stopped at Embankment, Charing Cross, and Leicester Square. She looked again at her watch. Nearly nine minutes had passed, and as the train slowed, easing into Tottenham Court Road station, she prepared to disembark.

The platform at Tottenham Court Road was busy. She stared out of the glazed upper half of the door, first in line to leave the Northern line and change to the Central line. It hadn't occurred to her until now, but people stood dangerously close to the edge of the platform as the train approached. She stared into the faces of people staring back. It was hardly surprising that, although she looked, she never really saw anyone.

That was until she saw Abby Wandsworth.

Agent Abigail Wandsworth was a senior trainer in the Hotstream team and had mentored Bel in her first four weeks. The look of surprise followed immediately by horror on Abby's face was probably a mirror image of her own. She watched as Abby called it in. Bel couldn't read lips, nor could she hear a word she was saying, but as Abby advanced down the platform, never taking her eyes off Bel, she knew she was informing Control of Bel's exact location.

Any agents in the nearby vicinity would be called to apprehend her.

Shit!

Bel quickly searched her section of the train. No one paid her particular interest, and she had to assume that so far Abby was the only agent nearby.

She turned back and saw Abby weave her way through the crowd, gaining ground as the train prepared to stop completely. Bel scanned her memory for an escape route.

She had deliberately placed herself in a middle carriage, and it was just as well she did. When the train stopped, she leapt through the barely open doors and crashed through a mass of people pushing to get on the train. Bel scampered for the stairs that ascended from the middle of the platform. Seeing a train pull up on the other side, heading south on the Northern line, she rushed to jump through the doors. The whistle blew just as she saw Abby launch herself from mid-platform onto the same train, only three carriages away.

The doors began to close. Bel had no idea what to do. Abby was on the same train. She was at risk of being arrested before she had a chance to reach Esther. Suddenly, it occurred to her that they might use her to find Esther. She needed time alone with Esther before the cavalry arrived. She had no control over other agents and knew a shoot-to-kill order would be in place for a suspected suicide bomber whether Bel was there trying to talk her down or not.

Through the smallest of gaps, Bel jumped back through the doors and onto the platform. She tripped over a small Superman suitcase on wheels and scrambled to her knees just as the train pulled away. Abby Wandsworth stared helplessly as her fist pounded the glass door.

Bel had to get out of the underground.

She dashed for the exit stairs and took them two at a time. Only aboveground could she give herself the best possible chance of reaching Esther. Aboveground she couldn't be hunted by Control via the CCTV, and aboveground she had more options to hide.

Hiding in the open was what Bel did best.

Chapter Ten

At the entrance of Tottenham Court Road station, Bel was greeted with glaring sunlight. Normally ascending from the underground into bright sunshine was one of her favourite things, but today she squinted at the glare, pulled the sunglasses down from her head, and burst into a steady run down Oxford Street. If her calculations were correct and her pace remained constant, she would reach her destination, and hopefully Esther, within four minutes.

People stared at her. Who wouldn't? Her only saving grace was that no one was chasing her. She muttered "sorry" as she knocked into dawdling tourists and window-shoppers. Oxford Street was notoriously busy. As one of London's premier shopping locations, it was rarely quiet. The masses of people were so dense on the footpath, it was easy enough to lose a friend just walking out of a shop together. While a busy street had its advantages, she was forced to alternate between the gutter and the footpath to maintain a steady pace. Taxis and buses beeped her but she carried on relentlessly.

A rickshaw with loud dance music pulled alongside her. "Hop in, baby. You're sure in a hurry."

The words were laced with an Eastern European accent that didn't seem to fit. On any other day, Bel would have smiled at his attempt to be a suave Jamaican; however, this lean, pale, bearded man was far from Jamaican. He was a godsend. She jumped in.

"Oxford Circus, please," said Bel.

Obviously sensing the urgency of the situation, the man nodded and said, "Yes, ma'am." The muscles in his legs tightened as he rose from his seat and began pedalling, forcing the contraption to gain momentum.

Bel scrummaged in her jean pockets for money. She pulled out a five-pound and a ten-pound note. The earlier conversation with Esther came flooding back. She pushed the five back into her jeans, then pulled out her phone. It had beeped the moment it came back into range, but it was just a text message from Charlie urging her to return to HQ. She dialled voice mail and found three voice messages.

"Hey, can you turn that down, please." She raised her voice over the throbbing dance beat, and the driver immediately flicked a switch on his makeshift dashboard that held a sat nav and an iPhone.

She could at least hear herself think now.

The first message was from Charlie. *"Bel. You're making a career-destroying mistake. Call me and we can sort this out."*

The second message was from Esther. Her heart faltered. She held her breath in anticipation.

"I'll be waiting for you."

That was it. *I'll be waiting for you.*

Bel was so elated to hear from Esther she nearly didn't bother to listen to the third message. The tone of Charlie's voice immediately demanded her attention. *"It's a setup."* Charlie was speaking in a panicked whisper. *"You won't have long—"* After a few moments when it sounded like the phone was being covered somehow, the call ended.

Although it was difficult to hear details with all the activity on Oxford Street, Bel was almost certain Charlie had cut the call short because someone was listening, or perhaps she'd been interrupted. Either way, it was a warning, and the tone in Charlie's voice from one message to the other was so dramatically different that it demanded serious consideration.

Bel reviewed the information. It was sketchy at best. Esther was probably waiting for her at Oxford Circus station, and something about the current situation was a setup. Charlie was warning Bel, so the setup had something to do with her. Or more likely, Esther. But whose side was Esther on? Esther was being hunted, she was a suspected suicide bomber, and she was Esme Gaffney. Who was setting up whom, and what could Bel do to protect herself?

She began with the obvious: remove the clothing Abby would have reported she was wearing. She jerked her gun from her holster, untucked her T-shirt, and pushed the gun down the front of her jeans, pulling her T-shirt over the top. She loosened her belt. It was uncomfortable as hell, and she adjusted the weapon as a man would his appendage in uncomfortable underpants. She removed her new hat, jacket, and the gun holster, stuffing them down the side of the seat. It briefly occurred to her that work would be pissed off that she needed a new holster until she remembered she'd probably need a new career. The thought saddened her, but right now, it was the least of her worries.

As the rickshaw pulled up onto the curb at one of the entrances of Oxford Circus station, she decided to trust no one. Not Charlie, and until she knew more, not even Esther, but especially not Conrad Rush. Bel was on her own.

The driver was clearly surprised to have a ten-pound note thrust in his hand, but he smiled his thanks. Beyond that, Bel had no idea what he did; she was already down the stairs inside the station.

She tried to think what Rush would do, knowing Abby had spotted her at Tottenham Court Road station. How far would he be expecting her to travel beyond there? Would his calculated guess presume she was close to Esther? It was useless trying to second-guess someone trying to second-guess you. She gave up and focused on expecting every outcome. Every bad outcome. She wanted to be prepared for the worst.

Oxford Circus station was under the intersection of Oxford and Regent Streets. Three lines intersected at Oxford Circus: Bakerloo, Central, and Victoria lines. Oxford Circus had six platforms; it was the busiest train station in the whole of the United Kingdom.

If Esther had stayed where she was when Bel spotted her on the cameras at Control, she'd know exactly where to find her, but a woman wearing a bulky black jacket in the middle of summer, sitting stationary while trains came and went, would draw attention to herself. So, even though Bel would commence her search where she'd first spotted Esther, she didn't for one moment expect to find her there.

Bel descended the escalators to platform three, the southbound Bakerloo line. She walked the entire length of the platform, relieved not to find Esther. She performed the same sweep of the northbound Bakerloo line on platform four with the same result.

The Victoria line was the latest addition to services at Oxford Circus, being added in 1969. The northbound and southbound lines ran from platforms not adjacent to each other; they were separated by the two Bakerloo lines. The northbound Victoria line was the closest, so she rushed there next.

It was nearing the end of the three-hour peak period on the underground from six to nine a.m., and the seconds were ticking for Esther. She scanned constantly for any signs of other Hotstream agents. In the back of her mind she knew at least one must be there, but with so many stations and walkways and ticket offices, Control must have known they were looking for another needle in a haystack. Bel prayed that just for a few minutes longer she remained undetected. She was close. She could sense it.

It was a mind fuck, trying to remain undetected while simultaneously trying to determine if she had been detected, if she was being followed, and if someone was scanning the faces of everybody they encountered, trying to find her. She forced herself to look at the people surrounding her while at the same time hoping no one was looking her way.

A train was arriving on the southbound Victoria-line platform when she turned right into a crowd of people edging forward. Everyone stood staring expectantly as the train slowed, eyes forward attempting to locate the carriage with the most available seats. Some people shuffled right, some left, but one set of eyes wasn't looking forward, was oblivious to the incoming train, and harboured pure fear.

Esther's eyes were fixed on Bel. She was barely twenty metres away.

Bel was so relieved, she held her breath and stumbled into a suited lady when she finally exhaled. "I'm so sorry." The woman didn't acknowledge her, just pushed forward to board the train.

When Bel looked up, Esther was gone.

Bel pushed through the crowd, but now the platform was full of people who had just disembarked the train. She couldn't win with these crowds. She jumped up and down trying to spot Esther, but gave up when she realised she might draw unnecessary attention to herself. She spied a set of seats. On the London underground, seats, usually in sets of fours, were sparsely scattered along the back wall of most tunnels. It was a risk, riskier than bobbing up and down in a mass of people, but the reward was probably greater. She could stand well above everybody on the platform and spot Esther immediately.

Oh, fuck it! She pushed her way to the rear of the platform, stepped up, and scanned the area where Esther had been. She was almost upon that spot now, but there was no Esther. She glanced back to where she had come from, on the off chance they had unknowingly passed each other. Nope. No Esther. Finally, before stepping down she looked to the far end of the platform. The train began to move, and as the final carriage disappeared into the black tunnel, so did Esther.

"Esther, no!"

Bel leapt from the seat and barged her way to the far end of the platform. "Esther!"

What the hell was Esther doing? She had to get to her before she killed herself or blew up the damn tunnel.

The commotion behind her gained momentum, and she turned to see a Metropolitan Transport employee and a couple of eager members of the public rushing in her direction. It was now or never.

Bel leapt onto the train tracks. Wafts of black sooty dust rose as she disturbed the sediment with every step. She quickly found her stride and chased Esther, calling her name. A residual glow from the platform provided enough light for her to proceed at speed. A quick glance around her and she knew she'd have to maintain a decent pace because there was certainly nowhere to hide in the tunnel yet. Most tunnels had alcoves and doors leading to staircases and passages only accessible on foot, but if another train came now, she'd have nowhere to go but to lie down in the suicide pit. She would fit in the pit, she knew that based on the dimensions she'd studied during training, but the thought of a train hurtling over the top of her wasn't an attractive prospect.

"Esther," she called. "Wait, please, just wait." She couldn't see Esther, but she knew she could be heard. She also knew the Hotstream team would be on its way. If there had been an agent at Oxford Circus, it would only be a matter of minutes before Control would have the train on that line stalled while the agent accessed the tunnel. Bel was now a terrorist suspect, along with Esther, and she would not be afforded special treatment.

Something caught her eye on the left hand side of the tunnel. Esther's bag. It sat atop a large metal hatch. She pulled on the hatch. It was unlocked. Of course it was unlocked. Bel had to think and it had to be quickly.

She grabbed the bag, opened the hatch, and disappeared. Bel found herself in a small tunnel. She quickly flashed her torch in the immediate vicinity. She couldn't see Esther. A quick look around and she knew she was in the disused Royal Mail tunnel, out of service since 2003. How did Esther know how to access the tunnel? She paused, crouching low, and gathered her thoughts.

For the imminent future, by slipping under the Hotstream radar, Bel had limited herself to two options. Option one was to find out Conrad was wrong and this was all one big mistake. In Bel's experience, mistakes rarely end up in a disused tunnel under London, so she wasn't holding out much hope. The second option was causing her the most distress. If her worst fears were correct, in the Royal Mail tunnel now were one bomber and one armed Hotstream officer.

Bel drew her gun, flashed her torch left, then right, and chose to go right because the tunnel followed a path away from Oxford Circus station. More access doors or hatches were likely inside the station, increasing the chance of interception by her team. She lowered her torch to illuminate the immediate space in front of her and set off at a steady pace.

The only sound she heard was the crunching of heavy blue metal stones under her feet. She shined the torch on her watch. It had been over four minutes since she'd followed the train on the northbound Victoria line into the tunnel, and she'd not heard or felt a train since. It was too long. She had seen that the next train had been due three minutes ago. Service on the line was surely suspended. It was likely the platform had been evacuated, and it was possible the whole station was in the process of evacuation.

Bel had studied cross-section diagrams and maps of the entire underground system. She forced her brain to recall a three-dimensional diagram of Oxford Circus. In the picture in her mind, she removed all commuters and tried to think where the Hotstream officers would come from and where they would go. Given that it was now almost five minutes since she had disappeared into blackness chasing Esther, she placed at least two officers in the tunnel and another five arriving at the scene. It was only a matter of time before either someone saw the hatch or Control directed an officer to it.

Bel longed to breathe fresh air. Her heart was racing, and she deeply inhaled the stale, dusty air in the oppressive tunnel. She'd never been claustrophobic, even after the time she was accidentally locked in the cupboard under the stairs as a small child, but the Royal Mail tunnel was barely over two meters in diameter, and the thought of sharing the space with Esther and a wad of explosives left her on the verge of panic. She concentrated on the rhythm of her steps and attempted to focus in preparation for what might transpire next.

"Bel, stop there." Esther's voice echoed through the tunnel.

Bel thought she would be relieved when she caught up with Esther, but her voice was different. Esther sounded empty. Bel stalled and immediately shone her torch in the direction of the voice. The powerful light beam illuminated Esther no more than thirty metres away. Bel trained her Glock onto Esther before switching off the light. Charlie's warning reverberated in her mind. She let her finger rest heavily on the trigger. At this distance, in such a small tunnel, Bel was sure she wouldn't survive the blast if Esther detonated. Her only solace was that no one else would get hurt. If Esther detonated, the whole purpose of killing scores of people in a suicide bomb attack was a failure.

Just the two of them would perish.

"What's going on, Esther?"

"Don't shoot me."

Bel felt nauseous at hearing Esther, the woman she loved, asking her not to shoot her. The enormity of the situation finally hit her. How had they arrived here? The facts were simple. Right now, Bel was the *only* one that might shoot her. She kept her gun and torch aloft and ready.

"Whatever's going on, Esther, we can talk about it."

"This isn't the afternoon shift at the O2 Arena, Bel. Who are you?"

"I lied to you. I'm sorry."

"Are you a cop?"

The charade was over. "I work for MI5. I'm in anti-terrorism."

"This morning, I had no idea," said Esther. "But you did, didn't you? You knew who I was."

"This morning I fucked up my job and stumbled upon you. When I saw you I wanted to warn you there was danger on the underground. I wanted you to make me feel better about my shitty job, but then you disappeared."

"What did you fuck up?"

"I wrongly suspected a mother with a child of being a suicide bomber. I'd been ordered back to base when I ran into you."

"You were searching for a bomber?"

"Yes."

"How?"

Bel didn't understand the question. This wasn't the conversation she imagined having with Esther. Had Charlie been lying? Who was setting up whom? "How do we search for a bomber?"

"No, how did you know there *was* a bomber?"

"We had intelligence. We had a description."

"Of me?"

"Yes. And then you disappeared."

"You need to listen to me carefully, Bel. Please keep an open mind."

Bel held her breath. "Whatever you've done, we can walk away from it. Together. I promise," said Bel.

"You don't understand. I don't have the power to make that decision."

"Yes, you do." Bel wanted to run to Esther and hold her, assure her that whoever was putting her up to this could be caught, *would* be stopped. Bel refused to consider that Esther was working alone. She took one step toward her but didn't advance further. She closed her eyes in the oppressive darkness and regrouped her thoughts.

"To my knowledge, I have approximately fifteen kilograms of explosive in a jacket around my torso. There's other stuff in with them too, I can tell that. Pieces of metal or nails maybe."

To your knowledge? There were others. She knew Esther didn't have it in her to make a bomb jacket. It was a slight relief to realise for certain she wasn't working alone. Bel instantly hated the asshole who'd brainwashed Esther and talked her into this. How had he, or they, convinced Esther to hate so much that she wanted to kill for them and kill herself in the process?

"Please, just while we're down here, just while it's you and me, please put the detonator down. Maybe just rest it gently on the ground while we talk."

A wry laugh came from Esther. "I don't have the detonator."

"What?" Bel couldn't believe Esther was stupid enough to leave the detonation to someone else.

"I'm not a suicide bomber. I've been set up. Do you know a police officer called Conrad Rush?"

"Rush?" How the hell did Esther know who Conrad Rush was? "Rush isn't a police officer, Esther. He's the head of the London and Underground Anti-Terrorist Response Unit."

"It's all the same. You're all the same."

"How do you know Rush?"

"I realise all this might be difficult to comprehend, but the name I was born with wasn't Esther Banks."

"I know who you are. You're Esmeralda Gaffney."

"So you'll know enough to understand the implications when I tell you Conrad Rush's father killed my dad."

It was all happening too fast for Bel. She shook her head, trying to jiggle the information into some sense of order. "MI5 pokes around in your past and in your life. How could it go unnoticed that Rush's father was a convicted criminal?"

"His father's name is Alan McGory. He was a creep of a man, by all accounts, and was never named on his birth certificate. I imagine his mother lived in fear of him, but when he was charged with murder, she fled to Scotland. I suppose she saw a chance to escape and begin a new life. Conrad resents his mother for not standing by his father."

"How do you know all this?" asked Bel.

"He told me when he was strapping explosives to my body and setting the detonator."

"Fucking hell." Bel lowered her gun and switched on her torch. Esther shielded the bright light from her eyes. "Sorry." She directed the light at the side of the tunnel, and it remained strong enough to see Esther. She walked toward her.

"No. Don't come any closer. I honestly don't know if this will go off or not."

Bel instinctively stepped back after the warning, but everything in her wanted to go to Esther. "So, Alan McGory was IRA?"

"Yes. My father's investigation put Alan McGory in prison for life. According to Conrad Rush, he died there."

It all made sense now. Rush had said Esther was working alone. Bel now knew the tip-off for the undercover officers came from him. He knew Esther wouldn't have been back at her place when they were looking for her. "I'm glad you listened to my message. I'm glad you stayed put until I found you."

"What?"

"I left a voice message for you. I found you on the CCTV footage at Control. I came here to find you as soon as I saw you. I left you a message."

Esther lowered her head and her voice failed. "I meant in heaven. I thought you were on your way to work. By the time you listened to the message, I thought I'd be dead. I wanted you to know I was waiting for you."

Oh hell.

"I was supposed to be on the Hammersmith line, and my target was the son of one of the officers who investigated my father's death and who helped put McGory in prison."

It didn't make sense. The Hotstream team was trained to shoot a suspected bomber. The way Rush had run the investigation and hunted Esther down, she'd likely have been shot before she had a chance to find the target. Then it dawned on her.

"You didn't do as you were told, did you?"

"No. He said he had you and would kill you if I didn't do what I was supposed to. But then I saw you at the station and knew he didn't have you. I knew you had no idea what was going on. I went aboveground to get here."

"He lost you. That's why he had to tell us you were the bomber. All morning he sent us on a wild-goose chase as a decoy, but then he lost you and needed to find you. He needed us to find you." The pieces were beginning to fit.

"Why here? And I saw you fifteen minutes ago, sitting in the same spot on the platform."

"I made my way here after I left you. I knew about the Royal Mail tunnel from a school project. God knows how I remembered it. I was moving between here and the southbound line, trying to remember where I should jump on the line and trying to calculate a safe distance before the next train came. I can't hurt anybody down here, and I don't know if he can get a signal to blow this thing up. He said it's booby-trapped. If I try to take it off, it'll explode."

"Can you remember what he did when he put it on you?" Bel's brain switched into Hotstream mode.

"It's like a vest with a zip. He said my body heat was keeping it from exploding. As soon as I take it off and the temperature drops, it'll go off."

Bel ran through the scenario in her head. She hadn't heard of a device set to explode after a drop in body temperature. She seriously wondered if it were a load of shite.

"He switched a button and a red light came on," said Esther. "He showed me an old Nokia mobile phone, said it was more stable than the new ones. He said he would set it off with that phone." Esther began to cry. "He said he had you and would kill you if I didn't do what I was told."

"We'll work something out, I promise." Bel began to pace. Three steps forward, three steps back.

"He said I was already dead. He said the only person I could save was you."

Bel stopped. "But you had to kill dozens of innocent people to do that."

"Then I saw you and I knew it was a lie."

Bel made a decision. "I want you to listen to me carefully. I need you to take off both jackets simultaneously. Unzip them both and take them off together."

"I can't."

"Why?"

"The bomb vest is zipped at the back."

Of course it is.

Bel advanced down the tunnel.

"Don't, Bel. Stay back. It's not safe."

"I have an idea. We have to work a way out of this." Bel continued to walk at a brisk pace. She bounced a light beam off the wall and onto Esther's face. "Trust me, okay?"

When she stood before Esther, she gently touched her face. "Hey, you."

"Hey, you too." Esther was crying.

A loud clanking noise stopped them both dead.

"We don't have much time." Bel recognised the sound of the hatch opening and closing. She turned her head, and even at the distance she estimated they were from the hatch, she could see faint beams of light back down the tunnel. "Take your coat off and put it on backward." Esther did as she was told. The bomb vest underneath was grey and stitched neatly. It was a professional job. "I'm going to unzip the vest, and on the count of three, we're going to push both jackets off you, trying to keep as much heat in as possible."

"And then what?"

Bel shrugged. "And then we run for our lives."

"That's your plan?"

"Got a better one?"

"No, but aren't you a bomb expert? Can't you disarm it or something?"

"Honey, I shoot people with bombs. I usually don't get close enough to have a fiddle with it." Bel glanced down the tunnel. The light beams were becoming larger.

Esther put her jacket on backward. "Incidentally, how many people have you shot?"

Bel took up position behind her, ready to unzip the vest. "None."

Esther turned and kissed her. "I love you."

Bel smiled. "Tell me again when we're out of this mess, and I promise I'll say it back."

"What if…"

"We will. I promise." She switched her torch on. "Now, on my count. One, two, three."

In a remarkably smooth motion, Bel unzipped the vest and pushed both jackets from Esther's shoulders.

"Run!"

Bel was sure she'd grabbed Esther and turned to run before the jacket and vest hit the ground. The gravel beneath their feet crunched as they ran for their lives.

Bel braced herself for the explosion. Esther was bracing herself too, if the bone-crushing hold she had of Bel's hand was anything to go by.

The air was thick with dust, but she pushed her lungs to inhale deeply, forcing oxygen to the spent muscles in her legs. She could hear Esther's laboured breathing, and it was only when she began to gasp and stumble that Bel realised the jacket hadn't exploded.

Bel stopped running. "We're far enough. It didn't blow."

Esther doubled over puffing, unable to offer more than a grunt.

"He lied. He fucking put you through hell, and he fucking lied about it."

"Us." Esther flung her arms above her head, expanding her chest to suck in valuable air. "He put *us* through hell."

"Oh, you think that's hell?" A familiar voice echoed through the tunnel from in front of them.

Bel drew her gun. She knew the Hotstream team was behind her, so Rush must have entered the tunnel through a different hatch. It stood to reason that he was trying to tidy up his mess before the others found them.

Esther gasped.

When Bel trained the beam of light on Conrad Rush, it wasn't to see who it was, but to blind him with the strong light. When she caught a glimpse of his gun, pointing right at them, instinct took over.

Bel deliberately lowered her gun an inch or two and discharged her firearm. She shot Conrad in the thigh.

"You fucking shot me, you bitch." He hit the ground after the bullet—shot from a range of approximately fifteen metres—propelled him backward.

Bel's heart pounded, and she was convinced it would thump right out of her chest. Her aim was perfect. She was briefly surprised by her hidden talents, but then Conrad Rush had pissed her off today. The sensation of a firearm in her hand, freshly smoking from the bullet, was exhilarating. In reality, she knew her Glock wasn't smoking, those theatrics were for the television, but the smell of a bullet exiting a gun she'd successfully discharged, landing Rush flat on his arse, was a job well done in her book.

"And I'll shoot you again if you even think about using that." She aimed her torch and her gun toward Rush's right hand and his own service weapon, just centimetres from his fingers.

His fingers twitched.

"Go ahead. Really, *sir*, I enjoyed the first one so much, I'd welcome another excuse to have a second go," said Bel.

"Okay, okay." He moved his hand to press on his wound.

Bel walked toward him.

"Christ, I can't believe you shot me." He winced. A bullet through your thigh would be agony.

Bel picked up his weapon and tucked it in the back of her jeans. She went and stood by Esther. "It's not the fucking movies, Rush. What were you expecting, a witty dialogue of banter before we both drew our weapons, mine on you, yours on Esther? Or were we going to walk back ten paces and have a good old-fashioned shootout?"

He groaned.

"Nope, not the way I roll. I'm into time management. By shooting you now, I've saved us all a rather uncomfortable few minutes."

"Don't ever write a book, Reilly. It'll have a shit ending."

"How about I write the ending?" Esther's voice was cold.

From the corner of her eye, Bel could see Esther was pointing something at Rush. She immediately felt the back of her jeans. Esther had Rush's gun.

"Esther, put the gun down."

Esther wasn't listening. "How about I do to you what your father did to my father?"

"Your father cried like a girl, cried for his dear old mammy. My father put him out of his miserable existence."

"Your father put him down like a dog." Esther was crying. "I was there, remember? I saw it all. Your father was an evil man, and I can see the apple didn't fall far from the tree."

"My father had a vision for Ireland. You wouldn't know a damn thing about that. You have no pride, no sense of place, no sense of patriotism. It's people like you who let the English divide Ireland, and it's idiots like your father who should have shut their mouth and let the real men fight."

Esther laughed. "Like you fought the gallant fight this morning? You strapped a fucking bomb to a woman, to me, you asshole, and you were going to watch me blow up myself and innocent others. You know nothing about real men. You're a castrated version of your father. You're impotent because you lack courage. Give me one good reason why I shouldn't shoot you."

"I can think of one," said Bel.

"Stay out of this, Bel. This is between me and the gutless prick who tried to kill me today."

Bel touched Esther's shoulder. "And if you shoot him, you'll be no better than he is."

Esther began to shake.

"Please, Esther."

Bel turned as the cavalry finally arrived. She stood between them and Esther. After all, it was her they were hunting. "I'm Officer Belinda Reilly with the Hotstream team. I have this situation under control."

"Officer Reilly, you have no authority here. You are an enemy of the state. Please put your weapon down."

Bel recognised the voice as Jason's from Liverpool. She knew he would shoot her if he had to, if he'd been ordered to do so.

"I can't do that, Jason." Bel worked to keep her voice even. "The vest of explosives you're hopefully dealing with back there was placed on a woman called Esther Banks this morning."

"Officer Reilly, stand down immediately."

"The man who made Esther wear that vest is right here. It's Conrad Rush."

"What?" Nothing could disguise the surprise in Jason's voice.

"He's been shot. He's alive, but his leg is pretty bad." She remembered the message Charlie left her. "Where's Charlie, Jason? You need to talk to her. She can explain." Bel hoped she was right. She hoped Charlie had worked it out.

"Charlie's on her way to Guys and St Thomas, Reilly. She was mugged just outside base."

Bel detected that Jason's explanation lacked conviction. She pounced on the opportunity. "I'm standing here with Esther Banks, who was born as Esmeralda Gaffney. Her father was killed by Alan McGory in Dublin. Alan McGory's son is Conrad Rush, but he's not listed on the birth certificate, so it'll take longer for you to check that out than he's got to live."

Bel knew by Jason's hesitation that she had him thinking.

Suddenly, a massive explosion rocked the tunnel. The noise was deafening, and the blast propelled them against the grimy walls. Bel's ears rang, and a plume of dust engulfed them.

"Jason!" Bel stumbled to her feet. She checked Esther first, who was dusting herself off but seemed otherwise okay. "Jason!"

She could hear panicked voices, and in the commotion she heard the Hotstream officers call each of their names. The dust was thick and suffocating.

"We're all right back here," called Jason. His coughing and spluttering echoed toward her.

Bel turned to see Esther standing over Conrad. "We need to get out of here, Esther. The tunnel may not be stable."

Esther wasn't listening to her. When Bel arrived, the gun Esther was holding was pointing directly at Conrad's head. "Come on, Esther. It's over."

"I watched your father beat my dad, I watched him rape him with a gun, and I watched him fire a bullet into both his knees so he didn't stand a chance of escape."

Esther bent down and rested the gun on Rush's knee. "This one's for my dad." She pulled the trigger, and the recoil of firing the gun sent her backward.

Rush screamed in agony.

Bel couldn't believe what was happening. Before she had a chance to intervene, Esther advanced again, this time with the gun against the other kneecap. "And this one's for me." She pulled the trigger.

Epilogue

"You were lucky today." Bel poured two glasses of champagne to kick off the celebration. Until the judge handed down his sentence, she hadn't been convinced Esther would be a free woman.

"Luck had nothing to do with it."

"How do you figure that?"

"It was justice. A vindictive asshole put me through hell and tried to kill me. He'd have shot us both, you know that. The fact that I lost my shit and ensured he'd never walk properly again doesn't change that." Esther grinned.

Bel's sense of right and wrong wavered, but only a little. "You shot an unarmed man."

"I disagree. He had been armed. He was just stupid enough to put down his weapon."

Bel and Esther had bounced this conversation around for nearly a year, and on every occasion they agreed to disagree, until now. Now Bel had to concede that Esther was right. She'd been found not guilty of grievous bodily harm on the grounds of self-defence, and although the judge was never able to voice his opinion, Bel had heard that he'd implied in chambers that justice would not be served by incarcerating the victim of such a heinous crime.

The result was certainly worth celebrating.

"Come and celebrate over here," said Esther.

Bel looked into the lounge room and smiled. Esther sat seductively on the couch, a cheeky grin creasing her face. For the first time in a year, she looked relaxed, almost content. It had been a long and exhausting road for them both. Esther had conceded to seeking help with the ordeal, but naturally, it had uncovered deep wounds from her childhood. With Bel's support, they were slowly working to heal the past.

Although Bel was cleared of any wrongdoing for her part in what happened to Conrad Rush, she resigned from MI5 against all protests from her superiors. In the end it had been an easy decision. One day after all the fuss had died down, Charlie, still sporting a yellowish shadow around her eyes after the beating from Conrad Rush, had showed up on her doorstep. Three hours and a bottle of brandy later, Salt and Reilly Protection and Investigations was conceived. Their first client was a wealthy MP left in a precarious position, through no fault of his own, due to foreign policy and tough decisions regarding corrupt activity in the Middle East. Salt and Reilly worked with his government-agency protection team to offer that extra level of security. As far as first gigs went, it was a lucrative contract that would lead to many more.

Bel stood before Esther and held aloft her champagne. "Here's to us."

"Here's to you taking your clothes off."

"Why, Miss Banks, how very forward of you."

"It's been a long time."

It had been a very long time. Bel had given Esther all the space she'd needed, and for the past seven months that included space in the bedroom. Bel flushed at the thought of how much she wanted Esther.

"Have you forgotten what to do?" asked Esther.

"Surely it's just like riding a bike."

"Are you implying I'm like a push bike?" Esther hooked a finger over the top of Bel's jeans and pulled her nearer.

"Not at all, but I've memorised every inch of you. There's no way I'd forget what to do."

Esther slowly unbuttoned Bel's jeans.

"I've missed your body." Esther pushed the jeans to the floor, revealing black lace pants. She raised her eyebrows. "These aren't usually your style."

"I'm trying a new look."

"All posh now you're minding an MP." Esther pushed the pants in the same direction as the jeans.

Bel's heart raced in anticipation. "I wear Armani now, what can I say?" She'd been naked with Esther on dozens of occasions since they stopped having sex, but all of those moments were nothing like now.

The moisture between her legs was just the physical sign of how she was feeling inside. Inside she was on fire, and she knew exactly how to put out the flames.

"Step out of them, please."

Bel complied.

Esther ran the back of her index finger from under the bottom of Bel's shirt to her clit. "Open your legs, please."

Bel squirmed and the hairs on the back of her neck stood to attention. When Esther pushed her fingers toward Bel's opening, her legs weakened, and the champagne instantly caused her to become giddy. "God, I need you."

"I'm sorry it's been a while."

Esther massaged her clit with her thumb.

"I would have waited longer. Much longer."

Esther pulled her hand away. "I can make you wait all night if that's what you'd like."

Bel was quick to grab her wrist. "I don't think that's necessary."

Esther smiled. It was one of those million-dollar smiles, and it melted Bel to the very core. She shuffled forward, encouraging Esther's hand to explore farther. Bel couldn't remember physically wanting anyone as much as she wanted Esther now. Without invitation, she straddled Esther's lap and slid a hand around the back of her neck. They kissed deeply and intensely. For a moment, Bel could have sworn they became one being, one entity, and the only thing that drew her away from the sensation was the feeling of Esther's fingers dancing around her opening.

"Please." It was the only word Bel could mutter and, apparently, the only word Esther needed to hear.

In one smooth movement, Esther pushed two fingers inside Bel.

So powerful was the sensation, Bel broke their kiss and grasped Esther firmly as she began to rock up and down. Esther found her G-spot immediately, and although Bel knew she would come quickly, she wasn't prepared to ask Esther to stop or slow down. She reached the edge of orgasm in no time.

"I've missed you," said Bel.

Esther added a third finger. "I'm sorry I went missing for so long."

Bel shook her head, although Esther couldn't have seen her. "Just promise when you go, you'll always come back to me."

"I promise. Right now we have all night, so you don't need to hold back. Come for me, Bel. Come for me now."

Bel released immediately. She closed her eyes so tightly, she feared her head might explode. She felt the most satisfying and warm sensation between her legs.

Esther pulsed her fingers gently inside. It was exactly what Bel liked after her first orgasm.

"Welcome back, baby," said Bel.

Esther's fingers gained momentum. "It's good to be back."

Hell Fire

Ali Vali

Chapter One

Abbott, get your ass in here," Captain Brock Howard yelled as he stood in the doorway of his office. The Bronx precinct station had been freezing since their shift change that morning, when the boiler blew up, making so much racket everyone carrying had drawn their weapons.

Detective Finley Abbott glanced up from her computer screen and flipped her middle finger at her pseudo partner Roberta Schumer when she let out a long "ooh."

"What the hell did you do now?" Roberta asked.

"I'll tell you after I recover from the shock that Howard actually knows my name," Finley said. The captain had never talked to her directly. "Do you think he's finally realized he's got a computer sitting on his desk and it's not really a paperweight slash sticky-note holder?"

Finley pushed her bangs back, cursing her mother lovingly for giving her the straightest blackest hair known to man. It was impossible to style and grew faster than she could keep up with. At least she'd inherited her family's height.

"I wouldn't hold my breath, and the vein in his forehead's bulging, so move it," Roberta said.

When Howard opened his mouth as if to scream again, Finley walked into his office. "Yes, sir."

"Sit," he said, as if she were a cocker spaniel, and pointed to the only empty chair except his. "You and your pal out there find anything yet?"

"Not yet. The traffic we've been following is coming out of this area, but they're bouncing all over the globe, and the transmission cuts out before we can figure out who they're communicating with."

Howard nodded but appeared confused. "I heard 'not yet,' then blah blah blah."

Finley laughed and was glad Howard joined in. "Think of when you were a kid and played with two tin cans and a long string. It was easy to trace who you were talking to and where they were. These guys start here and the string goes to London, Moscow, China, but before it gets to the end, someone cuts the string."

"That I can understand," Howard said as he leaned back so far Finley was afraid he'd land on his head when the chair snapped. "So I take it you and your sidekick aren't going anywhere anytime soon?"

"I promise we'll be out of here as soon as we've got something."

He waved her off. "I'm not rushing you, but why you're working from here still rubs me the wrong way."

"I don't blame you, and I'm trying my best to clear up that first trace. There can be two reasons it originated from here and why it hasn't happened since." She didn't like talking about ongoing investigations, but she had to keep Howard happy so she wouldn't blow her cover. The agency had vetted him enough for her to trust him a little, but Howard also thought the police commissioner had sent her and Roberta. "Either it was run through your system as a joke, or someone out there isn't happy with the pension they're working toward."

"What's your take?"

"Whoever it is," she glanced out to see if anyone was overly interested in their conversation, "is smart, and you've got plenty of smart people out there."

"So they're out there?"

"Smart people are also sitting in dark rooms moving girls all over the country with a few keystrokes." An old-appearing picture of two girls in shorts and bright-colored blouses on Howard's credenza was starting to yellow and fade. "If those are your girls you should understand the importance of why I'm here, and you'll be happy to know I'm persistent."

"They sent me your record so I believe you, but it still pisses me off that someone under your command might be leaking our advantage to the scum on the streets. It's not like we have that much of an edge, you know."

She nodded and understood his frustration, but she also understood Howard might be full of shit. That's why she was willing to share only so much. At times police work included some give-and-take, but you never gave away more than you got from the scum, as Howard had said. "If that's the case here, believe me, I'll weed them out for you. And neither the DA nor the feds will cut them any slack."

"Don't kid yourself, Abbott. The feds cut more deals than the DA's office even considers. No one wants bad press smearing the police department." Howard stood and hiked his pants up, most likely to signal their meeting was over. "Let me know if I can do anything to clear the way for you."

"Thank you, sir." She closed his door and signaled to Roberta that she was heading out.

She'd finished here for the day, but she still had to report her total lack of progress to her real boss, FBI Special Agent Russell Welsh. Russell had recruited her six months before she'd graduated from LSU in Baton Rouge, after she'd hacked into the secure servers of two major banks. She hadn't stolen anything; she'd done it simply to prove to herself she could. Russell and his team, as well as the bank, had been pissed that after all their investigations they couldn't prove it was her.

Though she'd worked for him over three years, he still asked on occasion how she'd done it, but she was never in a sharing mood since she technically could still be charged with the crime. Not that she thought Russell would do that, but she wasn't the gambling type. In reality she was more the nerdy, introverted type who enjoyed her job more than probably ninety-nine percent of the world's population.

The Bronx job was her first undercover assignment, and it certainly was different than sitting in an office all day monitoring six computer screens to find perverts who trolled chat sites for unsuspecting twelve-year-olds. She wished she could believe that the level of some people's depravity surprised her, but she'd crossed that scummy bridge a long time before. When pretending to be a young boy, she interacted only about twice with the creeps before they dropped their pants to show her their idea of *candy*.

"Let the inquisition begin," she said to herself when she got on the subway headed uptown after she triple-checked that no one had followed her.

❖

"Mama, can we go in there?" six-year-old Victoria Eaton asked, pointing to the M&M store in Times Square. The colorful window displays, along with the large digital monitors, made Victoria want to stop and stare every time they passed the place.

"We can, but not right now, okay?" Abigail Eaton said as she settled her three-year-old son on her hip. He was heavy, but carrying him was better than keeping track of him and her two girls in this crowd. "Remember, we're meeting your grandparents for lunch, so after that we'll go again."

Abigail's eight-year-old daughter said, "Why can't we go somewhere else? We've been in the M&M store like a gazillion times already," her tone quickly becoming whiny. The girls were two years apart, but to the older girl, Victoria was the definition of an annoying evil spawn.

"We've got two more days, so after we visit the candy store for the gazillion and first time, we'll go wherever you want to," Abigail said, not wanting any meltdowns before they reached the restaurant her in-laws had picked. With any luck it'd be more casual than the last place, where everyone had glared at them the entire time because her children had the audacity to act like children.

This was the second year Abigail had made this trip alone since her longtime partner Nicola Eaton and her brother Frederick had died. Their private plane had gone down somewhere over the Atlantic, leaving her alone with three children.

Her in-laws' only remaining link to Nicola and Frederick were the three children she and Nicola had brought into the world, with Frederick's help. Her kids were now the heirs to the considerable Eaton estate, so this yearly trip wasn't necessarily voluntary. The Eatons wanted her to visit them in the city so they could introduce their grandchildren to the culture only available in New York. In fact, Nicola had stayed in New Orleans solely because of business, but had warned Abigail that eventually she and the children would have to move to New York to be near her parents.

Because Abigail was close to her parents and extended family, she didn't want to leave New Orleans. Her parents weren't jetsetters, but they loved her kids. Nicola's death had not only saved Abigail from that decision, but also from having to end a relationship that wasn't working for either her or Nicola. When Abigail had chosen to stay home with the kids, Nicola's opinion of her had plummeted, since her mother had worked until the day she went into labor and was back at her desk two weeks later. Abigail had pointed out that Nicola and Frederick knew their nanny better than their parents, but that hadn't gone over well.

That argument seemed like it had happened a decade before, but unfortunately it had occurred only a few days before the Eatons' chartered plane had vanished. Abigail had lost more than one night of sleep because of guilt, but they'd had so much more bad than good for so long, one big blowup really hadn't made things worse. They'd already been at the end; she'd just never imagined it'd be Nicola's death that ended their relationship permanently.

"Where we going, Mama?" Victoria asked as they crossed another street with what seemed like a sea of humanity. Abigail regretted not taking a cab, as her son's weight was making the small of her back ache, but they were too close now to try to hail one.

"A place called Sarabeth's," she said, smiling at the way her eight-year-old, Sadie, kept a tight grip on her sister despite their constant battles.

"Can I get peanut butter?" Victoria asked, swinging her free hand back and forth.

"We'll ask first thing."

They finally reached the street that bordered Central Park and took a right, like her phone's GPS instructed, at Central Park South. The restaurant wasn't that much farther, and she looked forward to putting her son down more than getting anything to eat.

"Mom, look," Sadie said as she pulled both her and Victoria to a sudden stop, surprising Abigail with her show of strength.

She'd seen numerous limo buses on their walks, so it wasn't until Sadie pointed to the one stopped in traffic less than fifty feet from them that Abigail noticed it. This one definitely stood out since four men with what appeared to be small machine guns were surrounding the vehicle. She barely had time to register what was going on before gunfire that went on for what seemed like forever shattered the winter day.

Abigail tightened her hold on Sadie's hand and clutched her son to her chest, then ran in the opposite direction, praying the entire time that both her daughters could keep up. If these guys decided not to leave witnesses, they were in deep trouble. After they rounded the corner she slowed down and tried to calm her breathing so she could deal with her three hysterical children. "Are you okay?" she asked both girls. They were still crying but appeared unharmed.

"What was that?" Sadie asked as she hugged Victoria.

"Probably a movie or television show, so it's nothing to worry about." She was lying but saw no sense in jacking up the hysteria. Sirens were blaring from what sounded like every direction, and all she could think to do was get out of there.

After four taxis passed them by, they started the walk back to their hotel. The Eatons would have to understand them canceling. She was prepared to tell them just that when her phone rang and her mother-in-law Valerie's name appeared on it. However, Valerie did most of the talking.

"Abigail, sorry to call so late, but David and I have to cancel today and everything else we had planned. You need to catch a flight home as soon as you can, and we'll see you next month for our regular visit."

Valerie's tone was firm, but she also made no sense. The Eatons weren't especially fond of her, but they found it important to spend time with the children and paint a totally unrealistic picture of Nicola and their equally brilliant Uncle Frederick. Cutting the visit short on their turf was incredibly out of the ordinary.

"We're running late," she said, her gut telling her to lie. "Are you sure you don't want to reschedule?"

"It's business, which I won't bother you with, but no. Leave today and I'll be in touch."

Abigail stood holding the phone, but Valerie had already hung up. "How about pizza instead?" The girls nodded but were still sniffling, so she stopped at the first spot she could find to sit down. After a few minutes of hugs and reassurances everyone seemed fine, but she guessed Sadie would have a lot of questions later.

Victoria was completely okay after two bags of bright-purple M&M's and a stuffed candy character for her and one for her little brother Liam. Victoria carried the plush toy under her arm, and it got its own seat at the pizza place their hotel valet recommended. Abigail tried to remain upbeat, hoping the children would forget what they'd seen. She could just imagine what the people in that vehicle looked like after the hail of bullets hit it from all sides.

"Where'd you want to go, Sadie?" she asked as Sadie picked at her second slice of lunch.

"The big toy store Nan took us to before. Do you think we'll be okay to go?" Sadie asked, using the term she and Victoria had called Nicola.

"That's a good idea, and we'll take a cab. I promise we'll be fine. Think you can wait until after naptime?"

"Yeah. Then we can stay longer if no one's cranky," Sadie said and laughed when Victoria punched her in the arm with a greasy hand. Abigail guessed it was for the cranky comment.

"No hitting your sister. Now let's go back to our room so *I* won't be too cranky to buy treats."

Chapter Two

"Is that all the cameras we've got in the area?" Russell Welsh asked the guys manning the terminals in their main conference room.

No one would forget a mass killing in the heart of the city anytime soon, and he'd been on the phone with more politicians and self-described important people from the time the last bullet was fired than he had all year. All of them demanded answers and results, but none of them realized he couldn't do anything if he was on the damn phone.

"We're subpoenaing the businesses in the area for their footage, so this is all we've got so far," one of the techs said.

"Call every one of them back and tell them cooperation will help *not* dry up their business if people are too scared to go out."

"But ask nicely," Finley said when she stepped next to Russell. "Politeness goes over better than threats."

"Can you find anything while we wait?" Russell asked her. "You know, work your magic through the back door."

"I could, but if we find something it'll be inadmissible in court. Give it a few hours, but until then let me take a look." One of the guys gladly moved when she arrived, and they all watched as she pulled up footage from all the police cameras within a one-mile radius.

With a little tweaking, two of the shooters' faces became clearer, but the stockings over their heads still made a positive ID impossible. Finley widened the search in small increments, then stopped when she reached the blond woman with three children.

"Who's that?" Russell asked.

"Innocent bystander who thinks quick on her feet, and because she did, she saved those three cute kids. We need to track her down."

Russell placed his hand on her shoulder and turned her around.

"The police commissioner was one of the first to call after this shit. He wants our cooperation and resources, but he also wants the NYPD to handle the investigation. Right now you're the best bet going for all sides. Since technically you're currently a NYPD detective, he doesn't mind you working the case. That'll keep us in the loop."

"Sir, Agent Abbott is a computer geek, not an investigator," one of the guys in the room said, obviously not happy with Russell's decision.

"Who was in the bus?" Finley asked before Russell could answer.

"I was wondering when someone would ask," Russell said with a touch of sarcasm, even though they were a little over an hour into their investigation. "We've got nine dead inside."

"All due respect, sir, but the police that responded provided that count as part of their initial call-in," the same guy said.

"Finley, pull up the pictures."

Two of the women's faces were unrecognizable because of the carnage, but Finley recognized three of the women lying dead at odd angles on the floor. These women, from Honduras, had managed to contact her and her team about their circumstances, which in each case began with a familiar story about the promise of a new life in the States. The job they'd been offered, though, had nothing to do with cleaning services or taking care of rich people's kids. It had everything to do with the growing sex trade. Once the women arrived, very few of them ever found a way out until they were so broken the monsters who'd exploited them threw them away to the streets or unmarked graves.

Very few of them even made it to the streets, where they might be able to call for help.

"Damn." Finley exhaled loudly and fell back in her seat. She'd spoken to these women and given them her word she'd do everything she could to find them and help them. Deportation back to poverty, they'd told her, was better than their life now. That was one of the reasons she was working out of the Bronx. An NYPD informant had infiltrated one of the sex rings and talked to a woman named Gloria, leaving a phone number and a throwaway phone with her. "That was our only lead."

"If you couldn't locate them, how would you know it's them?" one of the agents not working the case asked.

"This girl..." Finley pointed to the young woman on the left with the bleached hair. “Her name’s Gloria Sanchez, and her only communication with me wasn’t a call. It was a text, including selfies, to the cell number I was able to get to her through the informant. She wanted me and the team to recognize her and her friends when we found them. I was able to triangulate the signal of the phone she used to a three-block radius, but these bastards are good.”

“Why do you say that?” the agent asked.

“It took us a few weeks, but we checked every building and found nothing. If they were there, they’d been moved.”

“Abbott’s right,” Russell said. “They move regularly and so far have left very few clues. The traffic coming through the Bronx precinct has been the most prolonged we’ve gotten, but it’s turned into squat.”

“All these girls,” she pointed to the van, “are seeing on average ten guys a night, for maybe fifty to a hundred bucks, depending on what the john was in the market for. Low overhead and quantity are the secrets to this business’s success.” She stared at everything around the bus, trying to find what didn’t belong. “Nothing fits that scenario. Any clientele around here is looking for a different level of professional.”

“There’s no one left to question, and the shooters fled in the chaos,” Russell said.

“Where’s the driver?” she asked.

“Seat was empty, and he or she managed to slip every camera with a well-placed hoodie,” one of her team said. “The bus was reported stolen three days ago.”

“That’s bullshit. Lean on the livery people. Somebody drove that off the lot and got paid well to do it.” Something didn’t fit and Finley couldn’t figure out what.

Russell sent a couple of guys to talk to the company that owned the bus, while she followed the path the woman and her children had taken. She guessed the valet the woman had talked to had to be a clue as to where she was staying. Russell called the police commissioner and got the green light for her and Roberta to find the woman for questioning.

“Hunt these bastards down,” Russell said as she got ready to go.

“That’s what motivates me to get up every morning, boss.”

❖

Abigail flagged a cab and sat in the middle of the backseat with Liam on her lap. She wanted to follow Valerie's advice to fly home, but she didn't want her children to fear coming to the city. There was no telling how involved in their lives the Eatons wanted to be, but these trips seemed to be important to them. She wanted to avoid making any future treks with three terrified kids.

FAO Schwarz had been a yearly happening with Nicola, and the only Sadie thing really remembered about those trips. Abigail loved to reminisce about it because she remembered Sadie's complete joy at having Nicola's total attention. Business usually didn't allow that type of free time, but her late partner had seemed to enjoy one of her own happy memories with their children.

"Look at the man, Mama," Victoria said excitedly as she pointed at the guy dressed like a soldier outside the store.

"I see," she said, and choked up. They might've not been getting along, but she still missed Nicola at times.

"Come on, Mama," Sadie said and grabbed her hand, ready to go.

She paid the driver and glanced toward the Plaza, not seeing anything out of the ordinary. Not that she'd know what to look for. "Hold Victoria's hand," she said as she allowed Sadie to open the door.

They started for the front entrance, and she figured it was too late when she saw the guy separate from the crowd. In that instant she knew her gut had been right. Something was very wrong, and the morning's incident was more than what it seemed. This time she didn't have anywhere to run, and she prayed he was there only for her.

"Mom," Sadie said, and the panic in her voice was hard to miss.

Chapter Three

"How'd you swing this?" Roberta asked as they headed to the toy store after speaking to the cab company and finding out where Abigail Eaton had been dropped off.

Finley drove through the heavy traffic, not wanting to miss this woman who might've seen their shooters sans masks. She had one of the team finding out about Mrs. Eaton, but so far all they had was that she and the children were visiting from New Orleans.

"The people in the limo bus are connected to our investigation, so the big boys agreed to our help. There's general confusion as to why, and why there."

"You think they're moving these women to places we wouldn't think to look? The only two spots we've come close to were in industrial parks in mobile trailers with shitty partitions and no paper trail as to who owned them," Roberta said as she placed her hand on the dash to brace herself when Finley had to slam on the brakes.

She had to tense as well when a cab cut her off, but that wasn't what held her attention. People were always in front of FAO Schwarz, but now people seemed to be running in the opposite direction too fast to not signal something was wrong.

"What the hell?" Roberta said as traffic ground to a halt.

Finley slapped the blue light on the roof and got out. She and Roberta weaved through the crowd, and at the corner she saw a man with a gun pointed at the woman who appeared to be her witness. The guy shot, and Eaton went down with the little kid in her arms and the other two started screaming. Without hesitation she drew her weapon as she ran. "NYPD, drop your weapon," she yelled, knowing he wouldn't, so she pulled the trigger when he turned the gun on her.

The guy went down, but she hadn't aimed to kill him, only to disable him. She needed him alive to start connecting her very scattered dots. "Cuff him," she said to Roberta as she headed to Eaton. Abigail was alive, but the arm of her coat was covered in blood. "Stay down, you're okay," she said as she knelt next to Abigail, her badge hanging around her neck.

"What happened—who was that guy?" Abigail asked, her face a mask of pain.

"We'll find out soon enough," she said as she took her phone out to call for an ambulance. "Are you hit anywhere else?"

"Just my arm, and I'm pretty sure it's only a flesh wound." Abigail held pressure on her arm and tried to smile, Finley guessed for her children's sake.

"Do you have a compact X-ray machine in your purse?"

"I'm guessing, but I'm also a pediatrician, so I have some medical experience to draw from. Not that I get a lot of gunshot victims in my practice, but I'm from New Orleans, so it's not impossible."

"Think you can walk?" Finley didn't get up but was glad to see the number of police bearing down on them.

"I think so."

"Good. I'll drive you to the hospital so you'll get there sooner. Give me a minute, okay? You guys all right?" she asked, looking at the little girls, who nodded. "Good, and your mom will be fine."

"Make sure you stick to this guy and try to persuade whatever precinct gets him to hold off questioning until I get there," she said to Roberta. "When they check him out at the hospital, make sure they photograph all tattoos or other markings and text them to me."

"I'll try, but I can't promise one of these guys won't beat you to talking to him."

"I'm taking Abigail Eaton in for treatment, so I'll check up with you as soon as I can." She made another call to Russell as she headed back to Abigail. "It came at a cost, but we might've caught a break."

"We're watching, so what do you need?"

She gave him a list of calls to make and hoped the commissioner would agree to have an FBI interrogator join in. "I'll call you as soon as I'm sure Mrs. Eaton is okay and in a safe place. Right now none of this makes sense. Are they after her because they're afraid she saw something she shouldn't have or for something else?"

"Whatever the reason, keep your head down."

"No wonder my mother loves you."

❖

David Eaton sat in his home office staring at a picture of his children taken at the party he and his wife had hosted for their twenty-first birthday. Over three hundred guests had come to the spot where Studio 54 once reigned supreme. He'd had it opened for the party, wanting Nicola and Frederick to have great memories of that night.

"Did she go?" he asked, not swiveling around to face the door. He knew it was Valerie since no one on the household staff was allowed without him or Valerie being with them.

"Abigail is nothing if not predictable, so of course not."

Neither of them had welcomed Abigail Langois into their family, but he'd at least given Nicola the benefit of the doubt. You couldn't pick who you loved for someone else, but Valerie hadn't been so open-minded. That had made their meetings with Nicola's choice so they could see the children uncomfortable, since Abigail wasn't exactly a big fan of them either.

"Do you know that for sure, or did you check?" he asked as he faced her to avoid an argument.

"David, don't be insulting. She's still here, and she made some new friends this afternoon," Valerie said, and rolled her eyes.

"What does that mean?" He placed his hands on his desktop with only his fingertips touching the surface. The agitation of the last few weeks was taking its toll.

"There was another incident, only this time the cavalry showed up in time. She's out of touch for now."

"What about the children?" he asked, standing up.

"Sit." She waved him back down. The motion irritated him. "Do you think it's a good idea to get mixed up in all that when we're this close?"

"Tell me exactly what happened." He sat, and it made him angry to give Valerie that win. "If you deviated from the plan, you'll be responsible for endangering everything we've worked for."

"I'm not an idiot, and I want this finished as much as anyone. She called this morning after what happened, and Catherine called from the Plaza about what happened after that." Valerie glanced away from him, and he guessed he wasn't going to like what she deemed as the next part.

Catherine, Valerie's assistant, was unquestionably loyal, so he didn't have a problem sending her on sensitive errands. "What exactly did you do?" he asked with much more calm than he felt. In truth his heart raced so fast he was short of breath.

"Ivan followed them to the store," Valerie said, and he closed his eyes as she spoke. By the time she was done he'd clenched his fists and knew the only way to completely calm down now was to punch Valerie until she was bloody, but that was one pleasure he'd never allowed himself. The day he gave in to that darkness would be Valerie's last.

"Do we know where he is now?"

"I've already sent someone, so don't give me any attitude," she said, pointing an imperial finger at him.

"Next time, ask," he said, slamming his fist down. "Don't you think that a representative showing up before we receive a phone call might raise flags of curiosity? If you don't, you're insane. We don't need to have anyone start snooping somewhere they don't belong."

"Then fix it however you think best," she said as she stood and smoothed her skirt down.

"I've got enough to do to add cleaning up after you to my list. From now on, stick to your charities and your responsibilities at the office."

"Don't," Valerie said, her voice a perfect mix of rage and sarcasm since her jaws were clenched. "This is a partnership, and don't forget who gave you a way in."

"It's hard to forget when you're constantly reminding me."

"You were right," the emergency-room doctor said as he worked on Abigail's arm. The bullet had miraculously gone through her bicep and exited without nicking the bone. "It's going to hurt for a few weeks, but you should make an full recovery, with a small scar as a souvenir."

"Next time I'll settle for a T-shirt," Abigail said as she watched the tall detective holding her son. The girls had finally cried themselves to sleep, and each had their head on Finley's lap. She came close to laughing at the expression of shock and figured it was Finley's first experience with children. "Hopefully this won't take much longer and you can go," she said to Finley.

"Don't worry about me, and I'll be around for a while since you've become so popular," Finley said softly, as if not to wake anyone.

"They can sleep through a hurricane, so don't worry," she said, glad when the doctor finished the stitches she needed. "And don't worry about having to babysit us. After this we'll be heading home. I can take a hint."

Finley didn't say anything, but Abigail knew it wouldn't be that simple.

"There you go, Dr. Eaton. I'll get your meds brought down from the pharmacy to save you that hassle, and then you're free to go," the doctor said as he finished her bandages.

"We'll talk as soon as you're done," Finley said, as if uncomfortable doing so with the doctor in the room. "How are you?"

"It's a first for me, and being shot wasn't on my bucket list, so I'll have to add it and write a side note to avoid it at all costs in the future," she said, making Finley laugh. "The drugs make it bearable, but it's going to be a bitch when they wear off."

"I'll keep that in mind since I've avoided bullets up to now."

"Lucky you," she said as she closed her eyes.

Finley stayed quiet and watched Abigail's breathing even out in sleep. They'd been rushed in at her insistence, and Abigail had barely flinched as the young doctor fixed her up. She shifted the boy in her arms and fished her phone out of her pocket to call Roberta for an update. Strangely there was no answer, but she wasn't worried. Some of the police building limited cell services in certain spots, so she'd have to wait.

"Could you send a few people to help me get Dr. Eaton back to her hotel?" she asked Russell when he answered. "I think we should move her to play it safe."

"Did something else come up on the daily special?"

"I'm not sure what you're talking about, but nothing yet. The two shootings are too close together to be coincidence, so I want to be sure. If she witnessed something, retaliation isn't out of the norm had she gone to the police, but she didn't, so coming after her doesn't fit the case unless these guys want to be sure too." The little boy shifted and kicked the younger girl in the head, but she did in fact sleep through it.

"Where do you want to order from?"

"You'll find plenty of places close to the Marquis, so pick one. Once she's safe in a hotel room I'll get back to work. If this follows her home she might not be so lucky next time."

"I'll call you back with what I want," Russell said, and he seemed to have his mouth pressed close to the phone, as if he wasn't alone.

"Do you want me to take care of it?" she asked, wondering if she was actually the one asleep and was trapped in some bizarre dream.

"Yeah, go ahead and pick that up, and I'll pay you back when you get here. Make mine on sourdough."

She was confused, but this wasn't the time to clear it up. "You got it, and I can make the run myself, so forget my request." The day had veered off into the strange, and it still wasn't over. She watched Abigail sleep until the doctor came back with a small bag and a sheet of instructions. He woke Abigail to have her sign her discharge papers and to offer her his personal phone number. Finley laughed again softly when Abigail rolled her eyes when the guy turned to leave.

"You think you can make it out of here under your own steam?" Finley asked when they were alone again. "I need to get you and the children to a new location until you're ready to travel, and hopefully we can talk once you're safe."

"Do you have any idea what today was all about?" Abigail asked as she sat up, clutching her arm. "And we haven't had a chance to introduce ourselves, so hopefully you really are who you say you are."

"I'm Detective Finley Abbott, and I think I've got an idea what today was about. We need to have that talk later on, though." She placed her hand gently on the older girl's back and shook her awake. "I don't want to do that here, so if you're ready, we can go."

The girls stuck to Abigail, and Finley carried the little boy out to her car, where the older girl took over for her. Finley took off once everyone was strapped in, and she circled the streets for over thirty minutes to make sure they weren't being followed. There was no sense moving them if she led danger right back to them. After slogging on this case for almost the four years she'd worked for Russell, she was ready for a break.

"Haven't we passed this spot three times already?" Abigail asked softly, probably not wanting to scare her children more than they already were. "Did you fail the taxi exam and fall on police work as a second choice?"

"I want to make sure nothing else happens to you, so if you don't mind humoring me, we won't be much longer." She took a turn into the park and glanced back more than she looked forward. She didn't see anything familiar, so she headed to the center point of the day's action, the last place she figured these assholes would think to look.

"Hey, Finley," one of the security managers said when she drove to the lower level of the Plaza. Whenever someone who didn't want to be seen arrived at the fabled hotel, they always found someone like him down here to meet them.

"Ready for us?"

"Got you fixed up, and we took care of what you asked for. You should know there was a small fire at the Marquis on the floor you mentioned, and in the chaos we saw a few guys watching to see who headed for the stairs."

"Thanks, man, and I'll let you know how long we'll be by tomorrow."

"Stay however long you need. Boss said for you there's no limit."

Abigail followed, and Finley noticed that her upper lip was beaded with sweat, probably from pain. The room was a suite, and a row of bags was waiting in the main room. At any other time Finley would've enjoyed exploring the space, but this wasn't the night for it.

"A cop with lots of friends," Abigail said as Rick closed the doors. "Maybe my bad luck is over."

"Hopefully so, but until we know for sure, how about you let me help you?"

"Don't you have bad guys to catch instead of babysitting us?"

"If you don't want me to stay, I'll only go as far as the hall."

"You should give my mother lessons, trying to guilt me like that," Abigail said and seemed to hold her arm tighter. "Let's all get comfortable then."

"Thanks for not subjecting me to a long night out there, even if it's nicely decorated," she said as she put the little boy down in the crib that'd been brought up. "You've got a beautiful family, and I want to keep it that way, so please believe you can trust me."

"Right now I've got few choices but to do just that."

Chapter Four

"You understand, right?" Captain Brian Baylord said to Russell as they met at police headquarters with a young representative from the district attorney's office. The young woman with Brian, who hadn't introduced herself, sat quietly and didn't seem to have anything to add.

"If you're asking me to put the brakes on a joint investigation we've been working for this long—that's not going to happen," Russell said as he spread his hands out and shook his head. "Is the commissioner aware of your request?"

"I spoke to him and he understands our concerns," Brian said, pointing between himself and the woman. "Some things that are at times uncovered in these cases are understood incorrectly, and it causes problems to friends of the department. You have to admit that's the truth in things like this."

"In my experience," Russell said, standing up and ready to walk, "the facts lead us where they lead us for a reason. If that's a problem for anyone, then I'm sure someone like you two can smooth things over. For reference, should I get a call from the DA's office, your name is?" he asked, staring at the woman.

"I'm sure you won't need that," the woman said as she stood and calmly walked out. It was smart, since it'd take him a while with a staff as large as the district attorney's office to identify her, if need be.

Russell and Brian watched her go, and Brian wasn't getting to his feet. "Anything else?"

"No, I think we understand each other," Brian said with a smile.

"I think so," Russell said, not believing he'd wasted this much time with this ass, since it was dark when he got outside. When Finley had called, he'd used the ruse of fumbling with his phone to photograph both of the public employees who'd demanded an audience.

He wanted to talk to Finley but would wait until he heard from her and had a better understanding of what all this crap meant. "Hey," he said to Peter Stanley, Finley's partner in his unit, over the phone after texting Peter the woman's picture. When Finley had gone undercover, Peter had volunteered to assist another field office with some technical problems they were experiencing. "Can you find someone for me and keep it quiet?"

"Sure. You got a starting place?"

Peter was almost as good as Finley when the pressure was on. "Check your messages. She works for the DA, supposedly, and he gave his name as Captain Brian Baylord, with an office in police headquarters."

"Give me an hour and I'll give you what I've got."

When he scanned the area again from the spot where he'd stopped, he noticed the woman he'd met with staring at him with her hands buried in the pockets of her coat. "How about I call you, and, Peter, make sure you don't share this with anyone. I'm serious about that part."

"Don't worry—our little secret."

He ended the call and looked the woman straight in the eye. The woman glanced away first, but with a laugh, so he didn't think it was a test of wills. "We're not the only ones with secrets."

"Who are you?" the older girl asked Finley when Abigail excused herself to change out of her bloody clothes. All three children were awake now and surprisingly subdued.

"My name's Finley Abbott and I'm a police officer. See," she said as she held up the gold shield she'd been issued. "I'm here to make sure you're all okay until you get home. What's your name?"

"I'm Sadie, she's Victoria, and that's Liam," Sadie said, her hesitancy coming from fear, Finley guessed. "Why did that man hurt our mom?"

"I'm not sure, but we'll figure it out. I promise."

Abigail came out in jeans and a T-shirt, combing her hair back. It was the first time Finley had realized how attractive she was and how much all three of her children resembled her. They all seemed to share Abigail's reddish-blond hair, bluish clear eyes, and fair skin.

"Come here, my beauties," Abigail said as she sat on the sofa and opened her uninjured arm to them, prompting all three children to run to her. "Everyone okay?"

The question started another jag of crying, so Finley took the opportunity to make a few calls. Forty minutes later a hotel staffer was at the door with bags from McDonald's, which seemed to take everyone's mind off the day's events. Finley set up a picnic on the floor and waited until they were done, knowing she wouldn't be able to speak to Abigail until the kids were asleep.

That took a few more hours, and she waited for what seemed to be a familiar nightly ritual between Abigail and the kids. When Abigail came out again, she was still dressed the same but had removed her shoes. Those bare feet brought back memories of her own childhood and her mom's assurances as she headed to the adventure of her dreamscape, as she put it.

"How's the arm?" she asked when Abigail sat on the sofa across from her and closed her eyes. It was strange that Abigail wasn't a little more freaked out with her presence in her room.

"It hurts like a bitch, actually, and I'm pissed about it, so now that we don't have an audience, you're going to tell me why this happened." Abigail's bluntness made more sense and was easier for Finley to relate to.

"I've got some theories, but can we get through some questions first to see which one might be right?"

Abigail lifted her feet off the ground and folded her legs under her. "Let's see, Detective. Which one of us got shot and needs answers?" Abigail rubbed her face and grunted. She sounded like a woman whose bad day had just crashed down on her.

"Okay, this morning you and the children walked into a total anomaly, and that started a domino effect."

Abigail opened her eyes and stared at her like she'd just said she was there from Mars and was about to suck her brains out with a small straw.

"First of all, anomaly sucks as a description," Abigail said and put her feet back down a little too fast to be from anything but fear.

"And how did you know what happened this morning?" Abigail put her hands up and shook her head. "Wait, I can see you'd know what happened, but how do you know I was there?"

"Dr. Eaton, I'm not going to hurt you, so please calm down."

"Do you know what pisses me off more than anything?"

"Someone telling you to calm down?" she said and bit her bottom lip trying not to laugh. "Or is it the word 'anomaly' for the massacre that happened this morning?"

"We've only known each other a few hours, and already you're a faster learner than my late partner. She never could quite understand that first one, but I don't want to give you the impression I'm a total bitch by speaking like that about someone I loved."

"I get the impression you're a woman who knows what she wants and realizes you have to speak up to get it." She opened one of the soft drinks the kids had left and took a big swig. "How about you ask the questions and somewhere in there we both find what we're looking for?"

"Why me?" Abigail asked.

It was the only question Finley had no answer for.

❖

"Did you get that other location open for tonight?" Linda Bender asked the mountain of a man standing in front of her desk. Boris St. John scared her, but she tried never to show her nervousness around him or any of the other guys so as to not lose any of the hard-earned respect she'd fought for from her first day.

"We opened three more," Boris said as he crushed a handful of pistachios in his fist.

"We've got that much inventory?" She glanced down at her manifest.

"Boss brought in double in anticipation of what happened. He didn't tell you?" He threw the nuts into his mouth and laughed. "I thought you were the teacher's pet."

"I knew he was upping the numbers, but usually there's a break-in period for the women."

"That's not always the case." He placed his hand on the ledgers she concerned herself with more than anyone else in the business did. "Where do you think your bonuses come from, baby?"

"Call me baby again and I'll shoot you in the ass," she said as she knocked Boris's hand off the book. "And what the hell are you talking about?"

Their boss, Yury, spoke up. "These women fight their fate only so long, and plenty of people pay for the privilege of breaking them." Yury had come in while she and Boris stared at each other. "Once the fight's beaten out of them, it's off to the trailers, where the more unimaginative fuckers line up to take care of that itch. Lazy, if you ask me."

Linda now fought off the urge to shiver at that kind of fate. Every so often she had a case of conscience, and only a look at her finances helped it pass. She cursed her late father for deserting the family too soon and leaving her no choice but to accept her Uncle Yury's offer of a job. In their family there was no such thing as charity, even if the death of her father, his brother, had been totally his fault. At least that had always been her opinion, and her education on the family business had cured her of any grief she'd wasted on her father. He'd not only condoned this type of behavior, but he'd also reveled in it.

They traded people like animals and always preyed on the most vulnerable and weak. She was supposed to learn the lesson to never be that fucking exposed. Only the strong enjoyed life and power, so she was lucky to be the eldest of Victor Antakov, and even luckier to be the niece of Yury Antakov.

"Do you disapprove, Linda," Yury asked as he sat in the seat she'd vacated and ran his fingers down the crease of his pants to the knee. As always, he was impeccably dressed in a suit it'd take the women under their control months to purchase, if they had the decency to pay them even minimum wage. They weren't that decent.

"My job isn't to approve, Uncle Yury. It's only to make sure things run smoothly and that our secrets stay within the family." She heard Boris chuckle and came close to shooting him, the consequences be damned, since Yury depended on Boris to keep his operation running smoothly. "Isn't that what you always say?"

"Boris," Yury said, and in an instant the big man was gone. "I sense something's bothering you."

"Don't worry about me. I'm sure you've got plenty on your mind."

She wanted out of this oppressive building that smelled of moldy paper, cigarettes, and dust.

It was the first piece of real estate her grandfather had purchased in his new homeland, and the old warehouse held every one of their sins on all that yellowing paper. To her it was nuts, but the men in her family believed in the ledger. There nothing could be hidden or lost, like in a computer, and anyone who came with thoughts of taking them away added to the lore and dust of the old place when they were eliminated to keep the books safe.

"Spit it out already and cut the shit."

"There's nothing to discuss," she said in the same bored tone she always tried to use at work, since men tried their best to read something into the smallest things.

"Is this about Boris and what you were talking about before?" Yury asked, slapping his hands together.

"Uncle, I more than anyone know I serve and work for you at your pleasure. What you trust me with, you do, and what you have reason not to, you don't. I went to the meeting with Captain Baylor, and I doubt his influence will stop the investigation. That's my opinion, anyway, and you know I don't have those often." She never lost eye contact with him as she spoke, but it had to do more with gauging his reaction for any funny surprises than making him think she cared what he thought. "Men like Boris are the ones with the opinions and snide remarks. All I want is to take care of my mother and family in my father's memory."

"How are your mother and little brothers?" he asked, his cultured and practiced accent digressing to a more Russian accentuation on the word *brothers*.

"Good," she said and smiled for the first time that day. "They're doing well in school, and they both are getting ready to try out for the wrestling team."

"Ah, like me and Victor." He slapped his hands again and laughed. "It's in the genes. Don't forget that. You can't deny your family."

Not if I can help it, fucker, she thought as she laughed with him. Once she had enough money, she was taking her brothers somewhere the Antakov name didn't mean shit. She'd have to leave their mother behind because she was too engrained in the old ways, but she was okay with that. Her brothers were safe for that moment in the private boarding school that was her greatest expense.

"Yes, just like you and Papa. You can be proud." She was tired of the lying, but it'd become the extent of her life, so she plowed on. "Is there something else I can do for you? You usually don't like coming down here if you can help it."

"Boris said one of those women was able to get a message out." Yury's voice was deceptively calm, but she could sense the anger under the surface, like slight ripples in a pool. "How the hell did that happen?"

"Boris is the security man, and from my understanding one of the men got a phone in while we were set up at the construction site on the river." She walked to one of the black filing cabinets and took out a red notebook from the middle drawer. "I'm not sure who forgot the pat-downs, but I sent a couple of guys over to see our Papa Bell and explain the rules again and to warn him about coming by now that he's been exiled."

"Did you have him checked out?" he asked as she pointed out the notation she'd made about the incident.

"Yes, sir, and he swore on his mother that the girl only wanted to talk to her mother, and he didn't see the harm. I turned his life inside out and discovered he was a construction worker with a soft spot for hookers. There wasn't anything sinister about it, and the guys working the sites understand that the next time it's their balls on the line." She put the book away and returned to her seat. "I'm surprised Boris didn't share that with you."

"Everyone has their own agenda. Don't forget that, either." He stood and pulled the lapels of his jacket to adjust the fit. "Take an extra twenty from this month's take and treat yourself to something nice. You've been working too hard, so take a break and come by for dinner. I want to talk to you about a few things."

"I'd love to." She kissed both his cheeks when he came close, glad her day was almost over. "Call me with a date."

Yury placed his hands on her cheeks and stared at her for a long time before letting her go with a kiss to her forehead. "Your papa would be so proud of you."

"Thank you, Uncle. That means a lot to me." She saw the softening in his expression, so she decided to take a chance for once. "I don't want to ever disappoint you or his memory, so I hope what happened today had nothing to do with me. If it did, let me bear the weight of it alone."

He touched a few fingers to her cheeks and shook his head. “Today had nothing to do with you, precious girl. It was a necessary purging, but sometimes we must do unsavory things for new beginnings, and we could all use those every so often. True?”

“True,” she responded and watched him go. “What the hell was that?” she muttered aloud.

Chapter Five

Abigail carefully extracted herself from the girls and checked to make sure Liam was still sleeping before going into the other room to order coffee and something to eat so the pain meds wouldn't knock her on her ass. Her wound was throbbing to the point of nausea, so she was ready to give in to the siren song of the bottle in her purse.

She stopped when she left the bedroom. Finley Abbott was still there, only instead of being the alert guard from the night before, she was asleep on the couch. Granted, she was still fully dressed, including her boots, but the tall cop appeared different with a bit of drool at the corner of her mouth.

It was impressive how quickly she woke up when Abigail closed the door the entire way and it slightly creaked. "Could I offer you some coffee?" she asked as she held the sash of her robe.

"I'll call down for it," Finley said, rubbing her face before sweeping her hair back. "How about something to eat as well?"

"That'll be necessary if I take one of these." She shook the bottle and stopped when someone knocked.

"Did you call anyone?" Finley asked as she placed her hand under her rumpled jacket.

"No, did you?"

"Could you step back into the bedroom, please?" Finley asked, her gun unholstered.

"I could, but let's see who it is first. It's the Plaza—the only danger is how high your blood pressure and shock factor go when you get your bill." She didn't know why she was being so difficult, but she wasn't going to be intimidated into crawling under the bed.

"Please. I promise I won't be long."

"Okay, but after the maid drops off more shampoo we'll have to discuss your overactive imagination."

Whoever it was knocked harder, and before Abigail could torture Finley anymore, the door crashed open and two men came in. It was too late to run, and the pain of Finley pushing her down on her injured arm made her cry out, but it prevented her from getting shot again. Whoever these people were, they came in ready to kill, and she assumed from their frozen expressions when everything was over, they'd never expected someone to shoot back.

Abigail didn't see exactly what happened, but Finley hadn't hesitated, and her quick thinking had saved Abigail again. No way could this be coincidence. Someone wanted her dead and didn't care who was around, including her children, who were now awake and crying again.

"What's happening?" she asked when Finley helped her up and hurried her into the bedroom.

"Get dressed," Finley said, and the order sounded like it was for everyone. "Come on—we can't stay here," she said before she closed the door behind her.

Finley moved fast and removed anything she could find in the pockets of the two guys she'd killed, but not before checking the hall for anyone else. She didn't find a lot, but she pocketed it for later and texted Russell when she was done. It was time to run much farther than New York, if Abigail and her children were going to survive this.

"Ready?" she asked when she opened the bedroom door.

"We're ready," Abigail said, back in her jeans and a hastily buttoned coat with blood on it. "Let's go," Abigail yelled and repeated it when she didn't move.

"Okay, take a deep breath, and I'm not being condescending." Finley closed the bedroom door, knowing she didn't have that big a window to get out of cleanly. Going out with a hysterical woman and three children was a good way to attract unwanted attention.

"We need to go," Abigail said, all her calm gone.

"We will, but I need you to stop crying." She held Abigail by the shoulders just long enough to get her attention. "I don't want anyone to remember us leaving here."

Abigail nodded and finally took her advice of a deep breath. "Let's go. I promise we'll be fine."

The door was hanging by one hinge, and the occupants of the rooms close to them were starting to come out and investigate the strange noises. "Okay," she said when she came back for them. "Use my coat." She took hers off and held it up for Abigail. "When we get into the hall, keep your head down and follow me," she said as she took Liam from Sadie.

She put her badge around her neck and checked behind the door for the location of the stairwell. Her plan was to go up a few floors and hunt for the service elevator. The two guys she'd shot had to be the advance team, so it was time to put some distance between them and whoever else was lying in wait.

"Who's got a cell phone on them?" she asked, and both Sadie and Abigail held up their devices. It didn't take long to crack them open and take the SIM cards out and snap them in half. "Let's get moving."

❖

Yury stood in the window of one of the condos in Trump Tower. He had a perfect view of the Plaza and the swarm of police cars parked out front. If Boris didn't want to pay with a few of his fingers, the incompetence of the last few days had to have come to an end.

"Anything yet?" his hostess asked from the direction of the kitchen.

He really shouldn't be here. To have someone trace him here would derail all the plans he'd made in the last couple of years, but the young woman owned a part of him that he'd never get back, but then he'd gladly given it away. The best place to hide at times, though, was in a city that moved a million miles an hour. Here no one had time to stop and really stare at who was right next to anyone else. For now, Crista Belchex would be his little secret hidden away in this fast-paced universe.

"Something, yes," Yury said as he adjusted his binoculars, "but no phone call. The cops are swarming the place, so maybe for once they're being smart and not leaving any evidence behind."

"You didn't tell me about this morning," Crista said as she came out with two plates. "Get away from the window before you attract unwanted notice and eat." She poured him some orange juice and slid the glass across the antique table. The apartment was furnished with similar fine pieces, but then he knew Crista finally had the time to shop for the things she was knowledgeable about. "What was yesterday about?"

He told her about the lax security and how the girl had made contact with someone they couldn't really trace. The cleanup of their mistakes wasn't usually so public, but the location had served another purpose as well, and she shook her head when he told her what.

"You don't approve?" he asked as he took a sip of his juice. "Don't tell me all this forced relaxation has dulled your instincts."

"I do approve, if it had worked, but it didn't," she said, and he swallowed hard from anger. "Now anyone interested in the business will have a way of tracing this back to someone, so let's pray that doesn't happen."

"No one's that smart," Yury said, but gazing at Crista he knew that was a lie. She was that intelligent, but he doubted there was another like her.

"I hope you're right," she said, and something cold came over him like she'd poured ice water on his head. "If you're not, we might not have enough manpower to fix the damage."

❖

The gawkers disappeared when Finley flashed her badge and barked an order to get back inside. In the stairwell, Victoria hung on to Abigail's hand, and Liam clung to her when she lifted him up on her shoulders so they could take the stairs quickly.

Three floors up, Finley checked before leading them all out, praying she wouldn't have to draw her gun again since she was draped with children. The service elevator was close, and they made it to the basement without picking up any company.

"Will they bring your car down here?" Abigail asked as she held Sadie close to her. The only possessions they'd brought were Sadie and Victoria's backpacks.

"Come over here first." She pointed to a spot near the loading docks but out of view. "Did you call anyone last night?" she asked Abigail but had Sadie in her line of sight. When Sadie started crying instantly, she wondered if children were like this all the time or only in high-stress situations. "I'm not mad, but who'd you talk to?"

"Grandmother called to see if we wanted anything," Sadie said, sounding like she'd start wailing any moment. "I didn't know I wasn't supposed to—" Her tears wouldn't let her finish.

"Sadie, please, I'm not mad." Jesus, she really needed to call in reinforcements and get back to her life and her job. She glanced to Abigail for help, not having any experience in this arena.

"Sadie." Abigail kissed her forehead. "You didn't do anything wrong, baby, but Finley had to know so she can take care of us. When did Grandmother Eaton call you?"

"Last night when you were talking to Finley." Sadie's case of hiccups made the sentence take forever to come out.

"Did you tell her about Finley and where we were?" Abigail asked, as if reading her mind with that question.

"No," Sadie said, but Finley could see that wasn't true.

"Sadie," Abigail said, but Finley shook her head.

The kid already felt bad enough. No sense in making it worse when Sadie didn't have the ability to repeat her mistakes.

"We'll talk about it later," she said, trying to figure a way out that didn't involve her car. "Please stay here." She walked away from them, badge still out, and weighed her options. "Peter," she said, wanting to make the call from a place that was already compromised.

"What's going on? Russell's got me working on some shit that's like black ops, and he said you shot some guy. I work with you for like ever, and the most exciting thing that happened to us was food poisoning."

"Peter, focus for two seconds since I've got no time. I need you to wipe me and tell Russell not to wait up." The truck at the end closest to the Eatons was being unloaded, and the carts full of the dirty linens were lined up ready for loading when it was done.

"Wipe you from what?" Peter asked, and she could hear typing in the background.

"Everything having to do with this job for now, and don't forget about Russell."

"You have to give me some reason why," he said, but he was still typing. "Detective Abbott was some of my best work, including all that background."

"Your memory's getting faulty. I finished this cover while you were at lunch." She glanced behind her, glad to see Abigail was still out of sight. "And I'm not exactly asking you to completely get rid of me from everything. Just wipe me from NYPD's databanks for now."

"Are you okay?"

"There's some major shit going on, and I'm running out of people to trust, so until I can get my witness someplace safe, just get this done for me." She saw the driver of the laundry sharing a cup of coffee with someone in a white smock, so she'd wait until they were done. "Tell Russell I'll follow protocol for once."

"He'll think I'm lying if that's your message."

"I'm not that bad," she said and laughed. She needed to do that, after having taken two lives that morning. She'd never have imagined a complete geek like her would have showdowns and kill the people she chased. She missed the anonymity and seclusion of her office and computers.

"Keep your head down and stay in touch," Peter said and sighed. "I hate that you're out there alone."

"Will do, and I'll be back before you know it."

The delivery guy came back when the staff started loading the carts, laughing with the two workers hauling the dirty linen. On their last trip one of the guys finally asked who she was and what she needed.

She wasn't interested in waving a red flag to heighten their attention, but she wasn't getting out of there unnoticed without giving something away either. "I'm here on official police business, and I need your help." She showed them her badge and explained what she needed. "Where's your next stop?"

"Where do you need it to be?" the truck driver asked. "And will NYPD cut me some slack on my parking tickets?"

"Stop at this address and I'll wipe them from your record—you have my word." She handed him a slip a paper with where she wanted to go.

They all got in the back with a promise from everyone present they'd never tell anyone how they'd left or where they were going. She doubted that under pressure one of them wouldn't crack, but she wasn't planning to stick around in one spot very long waiting for whoever was after Abigail to finish the job.

"Where are we going?" Victoria asked when they started to move and the only light was the few spots peeking around the door where the rubber seal was broken.

"On an adventure," she and Abigail answered together, and Finley heard clapping from who she figured was Victoria.

At least one of us is happy, she thought as the carts slammed forward when the driver hit his brakes.

❖

"You need to go," Crista said as she glanced at her watch. "It's late, and you need to find out what happened."

"You don't want me to call from here, do you?"

"What I need and what I'm getting are two different things." She poured herself a small glass of vodka from the freezer and drank it quickly. It was the one guilty pleasure she allowed herself every day. A life of solitude and waiting were making her want to scream in frustration, but that wasn't something she'd ever allow herself. Her hands twitched at times from the desire to give in. "I've never begged you for anything, but I need you to finish this."

"You don't think I'm trying," Yury screamed, something he seldom did with her. "When it comes to everything now, from the business to the house, it all falls on my shoulders, so don't add to that."

"I'm sorry. You're right," she said, pouring another glass and drinking it. If he wanted any he'd have to get it himself. She could manage only so much domesticity in a day. "We've come too far to lose patience now."

Yury looked at her as if to see if she was being sarcastic, but in reality all she needed was for him to keep his head. The only time he lost his mind was when he lost complete control of his temper. It didn't happen often, that she could remember, but more than one person had died when he indulged his true nature.

"I'll call you from a burner phone when I hear anything. Boris knows the price of failure this time, so I can't imagine him disappointing me." He held her by the shoulders and kissed her forehead. "And I in turn will never disappoint you, so show a little faith."

"Faith in you has never been my problem." She kissed his cheek and led him to the door. "You above all others have been the one constant in my life that I trust as much as the sun rising in the morning."

Yury nodded and walked quickly to the elevator, not wanting to linger and be noticed. His phone finally buzzed in the lobby, so he found a secluded spot and answered. "Why the hell did it take you so long to call me?"

"I was confirming a few things, boss, since they're not going to parade a line of body bags through the lobby," Boris said.

"So you're done?" Relief flooded through him so quickly he fell against the marble wall. It was a miracle his problems were finally buried.

"There were body bags, but not the ones we expected." Boris spoke in a rush, as if he wouldn't understand. "The guys I sent up are dead, and when I sent two more up, the room was empty. Either the lady caught a clue and was ready for us, or she picked a protector."

"Where the fuck is she now?" Had the wall been made of anything else he would've punched it, but a broken hand wouldn't be smart. All he got was silence, and his niece popped into his mind. Boris might've bragged to Linda to get on her nerves, but there was no bragging now. "You don't know, do you?"

"The place is crawling with cops, but I took a chance and left three guys at the doors in the lobby. Up to now we haven't seen her."

"If you need me to explain this to you, I will."

"This isn't my fault, but you know I won't let you down," Boris said, but he'd lost his usual bravado.

"Get it done or start running, because when I catch you, I won't be interested in any explanations or excuses."

He hung up and wanted more than anything to walk across to the Plaza and finish this himself.

Chapter Six

Finley placed her hand on her weapon when the truck stopped and the engine cut off. She was glad all three children had decided to ride with Abigail, since it freed her up in case she had to make a move because of any nasty surprises.

"You sure about this?" the truck driver asked when he slid the back door open. Judging from Abigail's expression, she agreed with him. The address she'd given the guy was a mini-storage facility.

"This is the place," she said as she helped Abigail and the kids out. When she'd rented a unit she'd purposely picked the largest of its kind in the area. Eventually someone could work through the list of renters, but it'd take them months to trace it back to her from the dummy corporation she'd set up. It wasn't impossible, but whoever tried it had to be good.

"If you say so," the driver said, not looking at what she'd pressed into his hand. "You were serious about the parking tickets?"

"I'll take care of you. Let me see your driver's license." She took a picture of his license and the truck's plates. "You can take off. We'll be fine from here."

She punched in the fence code and walked them through the yard to the back corner that wasn't visible from the street. There she punched in another code and walked another block to another massive storage building. The one she'd rented wasn't visible from the street either, for a reason. The truck driver had been helpful, but she didn't trust what the next guy offered him. A big payout was often enough to make people lose perspective.

"Can you give me a hint as to where we're going and what we're doing?" Abigail asked.

The three kids were being especially quiet, and when Finley finished punching in the security code to let them into the large facility next door, they seemed still shocked from the morning's craziness. "Give me a minute." She unlocked the large area and flipped on the lights. The space was pricey, but today made the investment totally worth it. She ushered them all inside and closed the door. "We need to finish our talk so we can figure out what's happened and why."

Abigail turned in a circle, taking in what Finley liked to think of as her secret space that let her decompress when she needed to. "You're a cop?" Abigail asked, gazing at her with an expression of what she guessed was suspicion. "It must pay more here than back home."

"I'll give you my life history as soon as we get through my questions, but I want to help you, and you'll be safe with me."

"I believe you, but I'm reaching my limit of strange things happening to me. If you're not who you say you are, I'm going to lose it and take you out with my nail file." Abigail started laughing and didn't stop until she was crying, which caused all three kids to join her.

"Okay," she said, shocking them into silence, "sit."

The large room held two vehicles as well as an ample couch, and a few computers in one corner. It had everything she needed to either work or run if she had to. Her gut told her it was time to run with this woman, if she and her family were going to survive.

"What are you doing in the city besides eating pizza and going to cool toy stores?" she asked, figuring an easy start was best.

"We come once a year so the kids can visit their grandparents," Abigail said and told her the story of Nicola and Frederick's deaths after Finley had gotten the kids interested in a computer game. "They want their grandkids to know the place where their children grew up."

"But you live in Louisiana?"

Abigail nodded. "Nicola was there working for her family, like Frederick was in Miami. David, their father, didn't trust the expansion of their business to anyone but family, and from what I understood it was going well before their plane went down."

"What's their family business?" she asked as she took notes. She'd never heard of David Eaton.

"International shipping. New Orleans, Miami, and New York are ideal locations because of the ports."

"What exactly do they ship?"

"Nicola never got into that since she said I'd be bored out of my mind, but from her explanations it sounded like they were shooting to be the next FedEx of the seas." Abigail combed her hair back with the hand on her uninjured side and blew out a stream of air.

"Yesterday you were going to meet your in-laws?"

"We were headed to Sarabeth's to meet them, but the shooting sent us running in the opposite direction."

She nodded again, and the earlier conversation with Sadie popped into her head about her grandmother calling her. Shouldn't the woman have called Abigail to check on their well-being? "Are you from New Orleans?"

"Born and raised," Abigail said, staring at her as if trying to read her mind. "My family's there as well, and I'm anxious to get back to them and the routine of my life."

"I want that too, and my job is to make sure none of this follows you home. Right now, though, I can't leave you exposed and let someone take another shot at you." She wrote down a few more things and gazed back up at Abigail. "Did you tell anyone aside from the cab driver where you were headed?"

"No. Sadie loves that place, and I'd promised we'd go after brunch."

"So this was part of your routine while you're in the city?"

"My partner passed away, Detective, but it's my opinion that the things she enjoyed sharing with the children shouldn't die with her."

Abigail obviously wasn't the kind of person who liked to answer one question straight out, but it was time to lose the attitude. "So it was part of your routine while you were in the city?"

"Yes, but I sincerely doubt someone has been trailing me for the last couple of years because I stole a cab from them or something that trivial. I'm the most boring person in the world. Just tell me exactly what you want so I can get us all back to our lives." Abigail had leaned forward and was whispering, but Finley could tell she was truly pissed.

"If you want," she whispered as she swiveled around so her back was to the children, "I can put you on a plane right now, but I'll have someone meet you there. Think about everything that's happened to you and then think about your children."

"All I think about is my children, so don't preach to me. As for the rest, considering all the trouble you've gone to, it won't be that simple to ditch you."

"Witnessing one shooting could be bad luck or a bizarre situation you usually see only in an action movie, but the toy store blows coincidence out of the water. What that means is, I can send you home to what you say is a boring life, and I doubt you'll live out the week." She placed her hand on Abigail's knee to keep her in her seat. "You wanted blunt and honest, so that's what I'm giving you. Someone for some weird reason wants you dead, but I want to help you. Your children deserve to grow up with at least one parent."

"I'm sorry, you're right." Abigail gazed at her children as she spoke, and her bottom lip trembled. "What do you need?"

"Like my boss says, the bread crumbs that'll lead us to the truth."

❖

Valerie glanced up from her paperwork when her assistant Catherine returned from the errand she'd sent her on. So far she'd called Sadie and Abigail over five times, but the calls went immediately to voice mail. None of her messages had been returned, even though she'd stated how worried she was.

"Are you going to make me beg?" she said as she went back to her paperwork.

"Their room at the first place was empty, and so far there's no information from the airlines that they went back. It's like they disappeared from the city, so my guess is she had help."

She closed her eyes and mentally slowly counted to five to dull the anger that being in the dark always caused in her. This time her grandchildren were at stake, so being clueless was unacceptable. "So they're no longer at the Plaza? That's where Sadie said they were."

"The entire building is under security lockdown since this morning, so I have no information yet. My best guess is they're still in the building but have gone silent for some reason." Catherine stayed on her feet and peered down at her with a hopeful expression. No one on their staff enjoyed being on their version of the hot seat.

"You do realize how much I like any type of guessing, right?"

"Yes, ma'am, but we've got all the exits covered, and as of five minutes ago none of them have been spotted. She's got to still be in there."

"My suggestion is to go back and don't return until you know something."

Catherine left with only a nod. Valerie liked that she wasn't one to fill the air with useless chatter, but even that wasn't relaxing the tension in her shoulders. Abigail's sudden change in the routine she followed religiously was only half the equation, so she looked over at her phone to see if there was any communication from another aggravation. David had left early and hadn't answered his phone since.

Their relationship wasn't like any in the Eatons' history, and she wasn't about to go back to the norm of the trophy wife that was seen but never heard. David probably wouldn't mind her acting more like his mother, but not even his mother had done as much as she had for David to assure his success and position. Even if her husband was willing to forget, she wasn't in a forgetful mood.

She stared at her phone, willing it to ring, and it finally did. "Did you fall down a manhole?"

"I've been busy all day so don't start, okay?" David sounded exhausted and breathy.

"You should've had only one thing on your to-do list." She glanced down at her nails and made a mental note to get an appointment for a manicure. "We're in the dark right now, and darkness is where nightmares are born."

"Thank you for the lecture," he said, his words like darts hitting a board. "I would've never figured that out on my own."

"Save the macho bravado for the weaklings it works on. I'm ready for results on this deal."

"Do you suddenly think I'm incompetent?" David said, his voice rising.

"We want the same things, so please be more civil. I'm as upset about all this as you are, but I'm not screaming at you. The thing is, I'm here doing something about it." She ran her finger over the picture closest to her—of their wedding thirty-one years before. Those idealistic young people captured in the shot were long gone. "Since you don't want to say where you were, all I can imagine is that you're starting to find something or someone new to take your mind off things."

"Stop, Valerie, before you make a fool of yourself trying to think beyond your capability."

She was mad enough to have hit him had he been in the room, so she gave herself the satisfaction of hanging up on him. "You're playing with fire, David," she said, staring at the picture, "and I'm just the woman to burn you."

Chapter Seven

Abigail watched Finley load the older Toyota Sequoia with some black duffel bags, but she didn't move from her spot on the couch. The fatigue that had started right after the two men broke through the door was like a dumbbell on her soul, and she had no desire to move.

Instead, she let her mind wander back to her life with Nicola. In the beginning she'd loved how much fun they'd had and how much they'd talked. She'd shared all her dreams with Nicola and had found the support she'd needed to accomplish most of them. By the time she'd finished her residency, they'd already had Sadie and she was pregnant with Victoria, so she'd made the decision to stay home.

For someone who believed so much in family, Nicola had been totally shocked when she'd told her what she'd decided. Her desire to actually raise her children had made something in her partner snap, and the outcome had fractured them as a couple.

As much as she'd loved Nicola, she resented her that much when she started to spend more time away from them on the pretense of work. It hadn't made sense to her then and even less now. If there was truly an afterlife, would Nicola have changed her mind now that she'd had no choice but to go back to work, leaving the children without a parent at home? Her family helped with the kids, and for the most part she was happy. She allowed herself to acknowledge the loneliness at the very end of the day when she went to bed by herself, but she never wanted to do anything about it. The kids and her family were enough.

"Does the baby need some kind of baby seat? And what about the other two?" Finley asked her, and she stopped stroking Liam's hair. "What?"

"The other two?" she said softly and laughed. "They have names, Detective."

"I think you enjoy giving me a hard time, Ms. Eaton." Finley's smile transformed her face. "And you didn't answer my question about Sadie and Victoria."

"Liam, yes. Victoria's in a booster, and Sadie would never speak to you again for even thinking that." She resumed running her fingers though Liam's hair as she glanced at her sleeping girls. "Are we going somewhere?"

"You wanted to go home, so we'll start that way, but we're going to take a more circuitous route." Finley sat in the chair by the computers and rolled it closer. "Once we get there you can't exactly go home, but we'll work something out."

"Can I see my parents?"

"You aren't under arrest, so don't think I'm going to lock you away somewhere. My only concern is you making an easy target, and we won't be as lucky as we were this morning."

"May I ask you something now?"

"Sure, since I'd probably have to gag you to stop you," Finley said, with that same great smile.

"How does a cop afford a 1957 Corvette hardtop?" She pointed to the shiny black car sitting next to the SUV. "I'm guessing at least a hundred grand. Is robbing banks a hobby of yours?"

"May I ask you a question if I promise to answer yours?"

"Sure, if you're not using the time to conjure up a good answer you don't have now."

"How does a pediatrician know enough about Corvettes to guess the year right off, much less the sticker price?"

She laughed, which surprised her, since she'd thought for a while she'd forgotten how to. "My dad's a mechanic, and cars like that one are his specialty. If you need a tune-up I could get you an appointment, since he's usually booked for over a year at a time. So, Detective, it's your turn to tat."

"Tat?" Finley asked as she shrugged.

"Tit for tat. I gave up mine, so let's hear it." She could feel the warmth in her ears as she spoke and blamed it on being punchy.

Finley laughed, but that was all the teasing she dished out. "You probably won't believe me, but it was a graduation present. I make slightly more than a pile of peanuts, so I'd have to save for years for a car like this unless I gave up eating and took to sleeping on the streets."

"Your parents gave you that?" Her tone probably made Finley think she didn't believe her.

"Not my parents, my paternal grandparents. It belonged to my grandfather, and he loves that car. When Gram told him he couldn't drive anymore, he went out and bought a big red bow and took his last drive in it before he gave it to me. No matter how much I'm offered, nothing would make me sell it."

"Do you drive it or let it sit in here so you can rub it with a diaper?" she asked, and laughed again. Some of her dad's clients had that particular hobby, and she'd always thought it strange. It was equivalent to having a woman in your bed, but instead of touching her, you spent all your time braiding her hair.

"Gosh, no," Finley said, and reached for something. She held up a pink baby blanket made of fleece. "This works much better."

"If you named it you're officially a nerd."

"No names for the car, but I'm afraid I still fall into that nerd category."

"You don't shoot like one." She never drank to excess, but right now she'd finish one off if Finley offered.

"When you go through the academy they really don't care what your career path is, but they do want you to be able to take care of yourself." The way Finley carefully folded the blanket gave Abigail the impression she was that meticulous with everything in her life. "My mother sent my instructors plenty of thank-you notes because of their insistence on that."

"All mothers understand worry, especially when it's over their children. I certainly would if one of mine chose your line of work."

"There's that and plenty of luck."

"If you say so," she said and yawned. "Are we safe here?"

"Take the couch, and don't worry about a repeat of this morning. The only people who know about this place are my parents and me. You and the kids are safe."

"For now."

❖

"You need to bring her in now, especially if she has Abigail Eaton and her children with her," Russell's direct supervisor said over the phone.

Russell closed his eyes and mentally counted to three before saying anything. It was bad enough that everyone with delusions of grandeur had called him about this case. He didn't want Washington piling on for shits and giggles. "In the last two days someone has tried to kill Ms. Eaton a total of three times. In my opinion that's excessive for a baby doctor from New Orleans, so excuse me for not following orders. Even if I knew where Abbott was, I wouldn't call her back in."

"Russell, don't give me any shit over this. David Eaton has dinner with Senator Feingold once a month. I doubt Feingold got anything done on the Hill today since he's been too busy crawling up my ass on this. So far he's personally gotten in touch six times, and he wants answers."

"So do I," Russell said as he pointed to his visitors' chair when Peter knocked. "What the hell did Abigail Eaton do to warrant this kind of extreme attention?"

"Mr. Eaton has no clue, and he also has no clue as to how his grandchildren are. His wife is frantic, which means they'll keep Feingold in a froth until they're found. Usually stuff like this bugs the hell out of me, but the Eatons have already lost their children, so having no information about their grandchildren is making them crazy."

"You can give them my word they're fine and safe with Finley. If one of them had gotten hurt she'd have come in and ordered ten times the protection needed." He was ready to hang up, but he waited for his supervisor to make that move. "As soon as I know anything, so will you. You've got my word."

"Don't forget that the second you hang up," his boss said, and then the line went dead.

"Anything?" Russell asked Peter as he gently replaced his receiver.

"The picture you sent of the woman you met with has come up empty. I don't know who she is, but I can tell you for sure that she's not affiliated with the DA's office." Peter placed a file on his desk before he went on. "Captain Brian Baylord is an interesting person who does in fact work for the NYPD."

"What's so fascinating about him?" he asked as he studied the photo of him in dress blues.

"He gave up running the task force on Russian crime to take basically a demotion to managing off-duty assignments in the Bronx. It's not a trade anyone would make without a little shove."

"There's nothing on who might've shoved him out?"

"The two guys I know downtown said there was no story and it really was voluntary."

"That's like saying you volunteer to pick up trash at the Grand Canyon parking lot instead of being president of the United States." He flipped through the rest of the file and sighed. "What's a guy in charge of scheduling rent-a-cops want with this case, and how'd he find out about our involvement so fast?"

"It doesn't make sense to me either when you factor in the mystery woman. I'll keep digging and report back to you," Peter said, taking all the files back.

"Peter," he said, making Peter pause. "If you get a call from my overly diligent supervisor or anyone else—"

"Don't worry, sir. I report only to you. Finley's my partner, so I'm not about to do or say anything that'll place her in danger." He tucked the files under his arm and stood. "I'll run a scan for the woman, so let's hope she's in the system."

"If she's not, we're going to lean on the asshole Baylord until he give us something."

"Do you have any idea how all this fits together?" Peter asked softly.

The young man's demeanor made Russell think he was in the wrong business. "That's what we're working on, so get back to it."

❖

Finley let them all sleep until after nine the next morning and had breakfast ready for everyone. The night before, she'd quietly prepared everything she'd need for the next few days and beyond so they wouldn't stand out in any way. Once they were done eating they'd be free to go.

"You're like a Girl and Eagle Scout all rolled into one," Abigail said as she glanced at the boxes with car seats for the children. "How'd you sneak away and not wake me?"

"I try not to sneak whenever possible, and this time I got away with it since you were exhausted. Would you help me with these?" She pointed to the seats. "Once we're all strapped in, we can go."

"You're driving us home? Is that necessary?"

"Ma'am, I need you to start taking this situation seriously. Do you really want me to drop you at the airport and disappear?" She had the sudden urge to just cuff and gag Abigail and throw her in the car. "I will if you insist, since I can't force you, but what do you think's going to happen when you go home unprotected?"

"This is totally foreign to me, so please forgive me."

"No need for sorry," she said, slicing a box open. "My only interest in all this is keeping you and your family safe."

"You've done an excellent job so far."

They talked as they worked, and when they were all inside, Abigail mouthed "thank you" as she pulled out and locked the unit. This wouldn't be a vacation so they wouldn't make a lot of stops, but Finley was prepared for the road. She had them all lie down as they left, on the off chance someone was watching, but she relaxed once they were on I-78. Before their first stop for gas and food, she'd change the plates on the Sequoia, and the new ones would be in the system should they get stopped. She had a set for every state they'd travel through so they'd blend with everyone else on the road.

"Do you have children?" Abigail asked softly as she stared out the window. "I guess I should've asked before now."

"Up to now I've been married to my job, so it would've been selfish to bring children or a partner into that. My parents always tell me you shouldn't commit unless you can pull your weight."

"That's mighty progressive thinking."

"I don't think it's a fresh idea. My mom and dad have been married a long time, and it works because he's home every night by six, and they sit and talk every evening." Finley remembered well all those chats, hearing about all the guys her dad worked with, and how her parents had held hands through them all. "They both say they enjoy each other's company and still do on their long walks on the beach in Florida since they've retired."

Abigail looked at her and smiled, but it made her appear sadder than if she'd frowned. They were lucky the children were absorbed in the movie she'd started for them. "I'm sorry you're having to go through this alone."

"Thanks to you, I'm not alone." Abigail's face relaxed as she placed her hand on her forearm. "And I'm not cracking up on you. What your parents share—not everyone gets that, so you're lucky to have witnessed it."

"Do you miss being part of a couple?" she asked and winced. She'd never been good at small talk, and her insensitive question proved that. "I'm sorry. Usually I'm not that dense."

"No, it's a fair question, and I do miss a few things," Abigail said but didn't elaborate. "Nothing I'd want to bore you with," she said after a long pause.

That was one of their longer conversations for the next two days. They were a few miles outside New Orleans during five o'clock traffic, but Finley had planned it that way. The family probably was ready to head home, but that couldn't happen yet, so she stopped at a warehouse park she noticed off the interstate. Abigail sighed but didn't say anything.

"I know you think I'm paranoid," Finley said, her eyes on Abigail, but she'd spoken loud enough for all of them to understand.

"Please tell me it's not some dive," Abigail said, but with a smile.

"Let's see what luxuries I can conjure up."

❖

"After all this time you've got nothing," David Eaton yelled into the phone. "Are you forgetting who's responsible for putting you in that pretty office you love so much?"

"Come on, David. The FBI is being tight-lipped about it, but I'm sure they're all fine. If something had happened, Russell would've told me by now," Senator Kurt Feingold said, his voice echoing slightly. "I'm pushing hard, but these people don't report to me."

"You sound like a whiny little girl, so shut up and get me some answers. If you don't, live with the fact you're replaceable."

Valerie closed her eyes when David slammed the phone down. In a way she was impressed with Abigail's little disappearing act, but she was ready to hear from her grandchildren. All the planning and scheming in the world wouldn't matter if they disappeared into thin air.

"Are you ready to listen to me now?" she said when her husband banged his fist down on his desk. David was an instant-gratification kind of man, so situations like this where other people were controlling every move made him insane.

"Today isn't a good day for lectures, so don't make this worse than it has to be."

"You know we'll find her eventually," she said as she stepped behind him and started massaging his shoulders. "There are only so many places she can run, so put people you trust to watch every one of them. While we wait, let's go ahead and file. With everything that's happened, it'll only put us in better position. Let's sell it as temporary, so when Abigail decides to show up we can move with the court's blessing."

"Nothing in life's that easy, so let's wait."

"For what?" She squeezed him as hard as she could, but it didn't appear to faze him.

"I don't want temporary any more than you do, so we wait for the right scenario."

"And if you can't find her?" She let go of him and turned toward the window.

"Like you said, her choices of where to go are limited." He moved to stand right behind her and pressed close to her. "We'll all get what we want. You've got my word."

"And Abigail's got our future."

"Not for long, darling—not for long."

Chapter Eight

"Should I ask who this belongs to?" Abigail asked as she walked through the house overlooking Lake Pontchartrain. It had only two bedrooms but was spacious and decorated in a warm, inviting way.

"Don't worry. We aren't trespassing or getting evicted," Finley said as she put the rest of the children's bags in the guestroom "It's secluded enough that you'll be safe, but close enough to your place to allow us to figure out what's going on."

"My life here has nothing to do with all of this," she said and folded her arms, daring Finley to argue that point.

"Mom," Sadie said softly. "I'm scared, and she's a police officer, so why can't she help us?"

"She will," she said as she hugged Sadie to her and watched Finley walk away. "Finley's right. We'll be safe here, so you don't have to be scared."

It took over an hour, but she managed to calm not only Sadie, but Victoria and Liam as well. Considering everything that had happened, the kids had been really good and were well overdue their freak-out moment. Once they were happy watching TV together, she went looking for Finley.

"What's our next step?"

"We had to run to a safe place so we could go on offense," Finley said as she waited for the printer to stop spitting out sheets. "I say 'we' because I believe this will be easier with you, but you can take a pass if you want."

"Will you be totally honest with me?" Abigail said as she sat on the corner of the desk. "I'll do what I have to, but I'm not one to be kept in the dark. Not anymore anyway."

Finley stared at her for a long while before nodding. "Can we have a conversation that's a little more informative than usual? Hopefully by now you can trust me a little, but I'm working blind and think you can help me. You might not realize you have information, but you might."

"How about you and I make a deal?" Abigail held out her hand, and Finley could've sworn she was in a high-stakes business meeting, but she took it.

"What are your terms?" She concentrated on Abigail's pupils as they widened a little.

"That it's a two-way conversation. I might have answers, but so do you, no matter how blind you protest you are."

"Seems fair, since I've got a feeling we'll be together for longer than you're probably comfortable with." She squeezed Abigail's fingers and smiled. "You go first."

"What do you know about my in-laws?"

The question surprised her, since that's where she'd intended to begin. "I can honestly say the name Eaton has never come up in anything I'm working on. But it seems strange that your mother-in-law would've called Sadie instead of you, or should I ask if you think that's strange?"

"Nicola's family is demanding, and that's when she was alive. Now it's an interesting dance we do because of those three little kids in there."

"Has anyone ever told you that you're kind of infuriating?" she asked, and Abigail laughed. "I take that as a yes."

"I'm sure it's occurred to you that a limited number of people knew where we were the night we ended up at the Plaza. Did you tell anyone?" Abigail crossed her arms over her chest and simply stared at her, as if their thought processes had suddenly meshed.

"Does your mother-in-law have a reason to want to kill you?"

For a second she thought she'd overstepped when Abigail shut her eyes. "She wants the same thing Nicola wanted if I made steps to leave, and that's control of my children."

"Full custody, you mean?" Finley needed a cold beer. This was fucked up.

"I have full custody, Detective. The Eatons want full control." Abigail crossed her arms and shook her head. "There's a difference, believe me."

"And you really don't have any idea what kind of business they're in?"

"You're persistent," Abigail said and laughed. "Maybe I'm a little embarrassed about that since I asked and was told it was beyond my scope of understanding." She sighed. "It was then that I realized love makes you incredibly stupid."

"Maybe that's why I've avoided it all these years." She placed her hand on Abigail's knee. "Let me do some research on the Eatons, and I'll share what I find."

"Do we have food in our little hideout?" Abigail asked, and she nodded. "Good. I'll make dinner and we can review after the kids go to bed."

"If you're tired I can go pick something up."

"I don't mind. Perhaps if you enjoy a little taste of domesticity, it'll help prepare you for the one you won't have any choice but to love."

❖

Abigail enjoyed the few hours of doing something normal after her bizarre vacation. On the drive back home she'd made up her mind that they wouldn't be taking any family trips up North anytime soon. If Nicola's parents wanted to see her children, they could come to New Orleans, and if they didn't like it, they could take her to court. She was confident that any court, especially locally, would side with her.

"Mom, do you think we can go home soon?" Sadie asked, slicing through her daydreaming.

"I do, but we're going to wait until Finley says it's okay. She promised to keep us safe." She put her arms around Sadie and squeezed. If somehow Valerie did have something to do with what had happened at the Plaza, she'd make her pay. "Can I ask you something just between us?"

"Sure, what?" They sat together on the bench in the large window opposite the dining table. The house didn't have a lot of rooms, but it was spacious and nicely designed.

"The night you talked to your grandmother, do you remember exactly what she said and what you said back?" She combed Sadie's hair back and smiled to not alarm her. "You didn't do anything wrong, but it might help Finley."

"She called to see how we were doing and where we were," Sadie said, and Abigail immediately figured out there was so much more to this because Sadie wouldn't make any eye contact. That was Sadie's first tell when something was off.

"Baby, I promise I won't be mad, but you have to tell me everything. It's really important." She kissed Sadie's forehead and held her to make it easier for her to talk without her staring her down.

"I thought it'd be okay because she calls me all the time."

It took effort not to react. "Really? What do you guys talk about?" She was proud of how steady her voice sounded.

"Do we really have to move away? If you don't want us anymore, you can say so, and if we did something wrong, we promise to be better." Sadie's sudden tears broke her heart. "I want to stay with you, Mama. Please."

"Hey," Finley said softly as she put an arm around both of them when she came in, obviously having been eavesdropping on them. "Come on, kiddo. Don't cry."

"But…but," Sadie said, her face red and splotchy.

"Listen, okay," Finley said as she wiped Sadie's face with her free hand and glanced up at her as if she understood the hot rage that boiled inside her. "I haven't known you guys long, but your mom does nothing but talk about you and your siblings. She loves you, and she takes you to see your grandparents because they love you too, but until you're old like me, you've got to live with your mama. That's the rule."

"The rule?" Sadie said, hiccupping.

"Let me show you," Finley said, holding her hand out to the child, and Abigail saw the gesture as Finley pulling her kid from her sea of turmoil. They headed upstairs to the office at the back of the house. The large bookcase was full of computer and software-type manuals, so Abigail had barely looked at it before, so she'd missed the pictures. "This is me at your age." Finley handed a frame over and Sadie studied it intently.

"You've got a black eye," Sadie said, glancing from the picture to Finley.

"Little misunderstanding between me and a boy who insisted on kissing me," Finley said, getting both Sadie and her to laugh. "He had two black eyes, and I got two weeks of detention, so after that I hung up my boxing gloves."

"Is that your mom and dad?" Sadie asked.

"And my brother Neil. We were all together until I went away to college, and I'm positive that's how long you and your posse will live with your mama. But even after you leave for school, you still have to call home. Don't forget that part."

"Thanks for telling me. I didn't want to go, and it was making me sad that I had to."

"Did your grandmother tell you why you'd have to come live with her?"

Abigail was amazed at how easily Finley broke through all of Sadie's walls. Her daughter hadn't processed Nicola's death well, but the therapist she'd taken Sadie to had said the grieving process was normal, and given time and love, Sadie would be fine. "It's okay to say, baby."

"She said it was a secret like our calls were a secret. I'm sorry, Mama. I should've told you. It didn't make me feel good not to, but Grandmother said Nan would've wanted me to talk to her so I'd know about our family. The truth about them, I mean."

Finley hugged Sadie to her, and Sadie cried a little more as Finley looked at Abigail.

If Valerie Eaton were in the room, Abigail would've fileted her with no remorse for tying her daughter in knots. Once it was safe, she'd be going to court to change their arrangement. From now on, until her children could decide for themselves, she wanted supervised visits. She wasn't providing any more chances for the Eatons to take cheap shots.

"Want to get your sister so we can eat whatever smells so good downstairs?" Finley asked Sadie, and the little girl nodded before plastering herself to Abigail. "We need to talk, but it can wait until after dinner," Finley said after Sadie ran off.

"Any hints? I'm so mad I'm about to explode."

"I think there might be something to our theory. Did your partner ever work from home?"

"We have a study she used sometimes. I haven't really touched it much since my life's been hectic, but I thought on my next couple of free days I'd clean it out to make a space for the kids." She stood up and waved Finley downstairs so she could check on her meal.

"Do I have your permission to search your house later?"

"I thought my place wasn't safe."

"There are ways to go about it that won't announce my arrival, and if it's late enough I might be able to spot anyone too interested."

"I want to come." She put her hand up when Finley started to probably protest. "I know I can't, since I'd have to leave my kids alone, and I'd never do that."

"You can trust that I'm not going to leave you in the dark."

She nodded slightly and smiled, thinking perhaps Sadie wasn't the only one Finley had reached with her easy charm. "Good, because there are plenty of pictures up there with stories attached to them, and I'd like to hear them. You've got a lovely home, but I'm a little surprised it's here."

"You can hear my story anytime, if you want, but right now you've got the more interesting one."

Chapter Nine

Finley parked three blocks from Abigail's place, in the drive of a house that was for sale, at two in the morning. After a long search she'd found a place that was not only on the market but staged to give buyers an idea of how the place could look. No one was inside, so after she took the Realtor's sign down, her car appeared like it belonged.

It took almost an hour to reach the house since she made her way through every yard along the way. From two houses down, she saw the car parked across the street. The guy inside was smoking a cigarette, and from the glow of the streetlight she could see where his eyes were glued. Someone was waiting for Abigail to come home.

With the security codes memorized, she made it to the box outside the house and got in through the brain center the company put on every house. In the movies the bad guy always cut the wires and shut the system down, but that was the quickest way to set it off. She was lucky it wasn't in the guy's sights, so she shut it off completely so she wouldn't make any noise going in on the chance someone was waiting inside.

She used the key Abigail had lent her and took a moment to let her eyes adjust. Now the night-vision glasses were easier to use, and a quick scan of the space showed no sign of life. The office was in the back part of the house, but she didn't chance turning on any lights. She didn't bother with the desk either, because if Nicola had any secrets, she wouldn't have been so obvious about it. The computer was her first stop, and she set the code breaker, which would take a bit, depending on the complexity of the password.

She walked through the rooms that surrounded the study, wanting to check their shape compared to that of the study. Then she started with the bookcase to the right of the desk, and as she took family pictures off the shelf she wondered what kind of idiot neglected such special people. Nicola had found a smart, attractive woman and ignored her so completely that Abigail had been saved from having to leave because of an unfortunate accident.

After a few minutes she was able to remove the backing and found a set of ledgers filled with strange writing, so she packed them. They might be nothing, but then why hide them? The next two false backs contained stacks of cash that pinged the part of her brain that screamed something was wrong, but she packed some of it in case Abigail and the kids needed it in the coming months. Cash was truly the only way to leave no trace of yourself. The rest she moved to the kitchen in various places, starting with the frozen-vegetable bags.

The code breaker was still working, so she turned the screen off and left it running, not wanting to wait. She could check it remotely. On the way back to her vehicle she stopped to see if the watcher was in place, and the guy was, still smoking, his attention on the front of the house. She couldn't risk getting the plate number so she studied the make and model and assumed it was no more than a year old, which gave her an idea.

She had one more thing to set, so she broke into the house for sale and arranged one of her laptops so that it seemed like it belonged. If it was found, the loss wouldn't be devastating, just inconvenient. She used the front door in case the watcher had company or his relief was on their way. It was early, but late enough that she'd look like any other homeowner heading to work.

Abigail was up and waiting for her in the office when she got back, wearing the new nightgown and robe they'd bought in Tennessee on their way home. She smiled, wondering when if ever Abigail and her children had shopped at Kmart for clothes.

"What?" Abigail asked as she sat at one end of the leather couch that'd belonged to Finley's parents.

"Your penguins are cute." She pointed to the pattern on the robe, which matched the gown underneath.

"It was better than the kittens Victoria fell in love with," Abigail said as she pointed to the opposite end of the couch. "I know you probably have some more questions, but can we talk first?"

"Sure, about what?"

"Can you tell me about yourself? Like what's a NYPD detective doing with a house in New Orleans?"

She took her shoes off and grabbed a photo album before joining Abigail. The first picture she flipped to was the family shot most people took at their graduation. "This is my dad Shaun, my mom Siobhan, and my brother Neil. The cute kid in the gown is me when I graduated from Dominican. I went to LSU right after, and while I was there I got recruited, but not by NYPD," she flipped the page to another graduation, "but by the FBI. I work in cybercrimes, but when we met I was undercover."

"Usually in crime stories, undercover people infiltrate the bad guy's organizations, not the police." Abigail flipped through the rest of the book and the vacations she'd been on with various family members. "Can you tell me what you were working on?"

"Our policy is to not discuss ongoing investigations, but I need your help. Your late partner had some strange business habits, and even if you know the whole score, you're on the outs now. Someone wants you dead, and whoever that is most probably killed the Eaton siblings. The guy outside your house makes me think that's true."

"Do you believe I know everything Nicola was doing, legal or no?"

"No, I don't, and that's why I'm pissed. Unless I'm reading all this wrong, there's no reason to go after you or your children. Either you saw something or know something you don't realize is important, and you've got to be eliminated before you figure out the truth." She yawned but was too frustrated to sleep. It was totally making her crazy that she had so many loose ends but couldn't tie them to anything.

"Get some sleep, and tomorrow maybe we can put all this together," Abigail said as she chewed on one of her nails.

"No matter what, you realize someone will have to kill me before I let something happen to you or the kids."

"I believe you, but promise not to break your word to me with that excuse. There's plenty more stories you've got to tell."

❖

Yury Antakov slapped the girl he was with hard on the ass when she took too long to get on all fours. He was trying to alleviate his growing frustration with Boris and everyone else on his payroll who couldn't do shit right. Their prey had effectively vanished, and the cops had been lucky lately when it came to finding their lower-end establishments.

A twenty-dollar whore sounded cheap, but with their volume she was profitable. The beauties like the one he was with were more expensive, but their clientele was limited. These bitches knew how to handle a dick and were truly talented at fucking, but usually limited to one man a night.

"Ooh," the woman said when he slid into her from behind and held her tight to him, not moving. If he didn't know better he'd believe her bullshit about size and how he was the best she'd ever had.

"Squeeze it," he ordered, and the command made her tighten the walls of her sex. The pressure was good, and he started pumping in and out hard enough that their skin made a slapping noise when they came together. If she was expecting fast she'd be disappointed. One of the perks of owning bitches like this was he loved fucking.

He held out as long as he could, but eventually he couldn't control his urge and came with a long grunt. She immediately moved to suck him when he pulled out and lay down. Whoever was calling was saved a beating because they'd waited until he finished.

"Tell me you found something."

"Still nothing, boss, but we're working another angle," Boris said quickly.

"Don't start getting creative now. Since you don't have the ability to do what I need, I'm going to put Linda on it. Do whatever she asks, and if she tells me you gave her any shit, I'll gift her with your balls." He almost laughed when the woman sucked his into her mouth.

"I only need a few more days, boss," Boris said, and for a big man he was a good whiner.

"That's what you said a few days ago. Call Linda and remember how disappointed I am before you decide to start thinking for yourself." He hung up and had closed his eyes to enjoy the way his dick was starting to come back to life when the phone rang again.

"You haven't called," Crista said, making him slap the woman across the head to get her off him.

"There's nothing to tell, and you're the one always preaching about security. Don't worry. I've got good people on this, since I'm as anxious as you are to finish." He watched the woman walk to the dresser and stick a spoon in the pile of coke he'd dumped out earlier. To some the drug had become passé, but he liked the fact that only a little took the edge off. He was disciplined enough that this or anything else would never become a problem.

"Then prove it to me," Crista said with what sounded to him like impatience. "You know what needs to happen to move things along."

"We need information first. We get heavy-handed now with your idea, and we'll lose that move when it *can* be used. Look, you've waited this long. You can give it a few more days." He hung up, tired of people bitching at him. "Come back here and suck me. I'm not done."

That went for this bitch and so many other things.

❖

"Nothing on any front?" Russell asked Peter. Another morning not hearing from Finley was starting to worry him. "She hasn't even checked in electronically?"

"She did say she was running with our witness, and if I know Finley, we won't hear anything until she's got something for us to follow up on." Peter placed his laptop on Russell's desk and brought up a series of screens. He'd learned well from Finley not to leave a paper trail if at all possible. "I did do some digging on Brian Baylord, since our mystery woman hasn't popped in the system yet."

Russell put his glasses on and squinted at the screen. The damn fatigue weighing him down was starting to bug him, but he couldn't sleep deeply until he heard from Finley. "What's that?" he asked, looking at a large home close to what appeared to be the seashore.

"Captain Baylord's second home." Peter flipped through more pictures of the place. "It's set up with a corporation as the title holder with his wife on the board, but I found the paperwork he tried to bury with his attorney. I figured this time you'd forgive me for snooping where I shouldn't have. That and a place in Montana are set up the same way, but his prenup negates anything his wife owns in name only now."

"This asshole has three houses?" He thought about how much his wife would enjoy the big kitchen that overlooked the water with its large bank of windows. "I can barely afford our place."

"He's supplementing his salary somewhere, and I'm willing to bet the woman who was there when you talked to him is the key."

"Keep at it, and try finding Finley however you two communicate when you're not supposed to communicate."

"I've tried, boss, but that Plaza thing must've scared her." Peter folded the laptop and picked it up.

"Finley Abbott doesn't scare easy."

"Her witness has three children, though, and she's working without backup."

"Tell her she can trust us, damn it."

"I'll keep trying, and I'll try to get her to call you if I get through." Peter saluted casually as he started to walk out, and that was when Russell noticed Senator Feingold and two cronies.

"Peter," he said, getting him to stop at the door. "Don't leave anything on the hard drive and leave enough of a trail for Finley to find all that stuff."

"Like I said, boss, I've got your back, and for sure I've got Finley's."

"Until I tell you otherwise, watch yourself when you leave here and where you go. I've got enough to worry about."

Chapter Ten

The journals took Finley a week to translate via the Internet, but even after getting through the Cyrillic script, she still couldn't make much sense out of them. They did, though, provide a starting point, since the name at the top of every other page was not written in code. The Hell Fire Club wasn't familiar to her, but she hadn't been home in months, and New Orleans's bar scene was always changing and expanding.

"So you've never heard of it either?" Abigail asked as she held up a few of the translated pages. "What the hell was Nicola up to?"

"Whatever it was, it was certainly lucrative," she said as she tried another search engine. So far she'd come up empty, and it was starting to piss her off. "After counting what I brought back, she had to have close to seven hundred and fifty thousand in cash in your house."

"You think it's drugs? God, I hope not. If it is, I'm a total moron."

Finley glanced out toward the master bedroom, where the kids were watching a movie. All three still appeared entranced. "That's hard to hide, so I believe you would've seen signs of it by now. It's not exactly the kind of business that dies because you do. There'd be remnants, I'm guessing."

"Like someone trying to kill you? Would that be a remnant?"

"Something like that, yeah," she said, and laughed at Abigail's funny sarcasm. "But no one's trying to kill you right now, so let's talk about your in-laws."

"What about them?" Abigail sat across from her on the desk and crossed her legs, and the sight made her think about how long it'd been since she'd been with anyone. Why the hell hadn't she designed the house bigger so she could have a little more privacy than the couch allowed for? As it was she usually woke up with Victoria and Liam draped over her, and she still couldn't figure out how they lay down without waking her.

"How long have you known Nicola?"

"We met in my senior year at Tulane, so about twelve years all together before she died. I'd seen her a few times around campus, but we never really spoke until then."

"It was a miracle she could talk to you at all, considering she was only two at the time."

Abigail poked her with her foot and scowled at her. She was sure Abigail didn't mean it in an intimate way, but Finley felt a twinge of desire. "You know how much I love you talking in riddles. What are you trying to tell me?"

"The Eatons were all born in 2001, at least that's where their paper trail begins, and that can mean one of two things. Either they're in witness protection or they really hated their original surname. They didn't exist before then, so we need some more information to find out why, and Nicola probably shared it with you."

Abigail poked her again. "If you haven't been paying attention, Nicola didn't tell me shit about anything. At no time did she mention having a different name."

She grabbed Abigail's foot and pointed her index finger at her. "No, but she would've maybe talked about her heritage. Remember when Sadie said her grandmother wanted to tell her the truth about their family because Nan would've wanted her to know?"

"The only conversation we had about her name was when I asked her about it. She said it was her great-grandmother's name on her mother's side. I think she said she was Russian, but she didn't say from where exactly."

"That's a good start, and I'm sure it's no coincidence that we believed the case I was working on was related to the Russian mob. They're so closed-mouthed about their business we haven't gotten anywhere." She wished for a few minutes with the FBI computers.

"What exactly were you working on?" Abigail asked.

"After a few tips about women who were being brought into the country illegally for the sex trade, we found a few clues that they might be true. You actually almost got caught in the middle of the best lead I'd gotten when that limo bus was shot up." She swiveled a little and started another search. "One of our guys was able to get into one of their parties." She made air quotes around the word *party*. "He passed one of the women a phone, and we communicated a couple of times by text. She was one of the women on that bus."

"Sex slavery is for real?" Abigail seemed horrified, judging by her expression. "How many people died on that bus?"

"Nine, but in the end they're most likely the lucky ones. Their deaths were violent, but they went fast. The others are stuck in a hellhole somewhere and don't have the right to say no to how many johns they have to service or to what they want." She pressed her hands into fists and tried to clear her mind. "I wanted the people responsible to pay, but all I found was a whole lot of nothing."

"Then it sounds like the first thing to find is this club." Abigail held up the ledger sheet. "If Nicola or her family have anything to do with what you just told me, I want them nowhere near my children for the rest of their lives. If it's true, Nicola has only one thing to be grateful for—that she's already dead."

"Can I be honest about one more thing without you thinking I'm full of shit?" Sometimes the only way to navigate the darkness was with an experienced guide.

"If you think I'd say no to that you're crazy, and I'd never believe that of you. Unlike the people in my past, you actually answer questions and come clean about yourself. You can tell me anything." Finley did, and Abigail gazed at her like she wanted to bolt.

"It's part of who I am, and you deserved to know."

The next day Finley left and prayed Abigail and the kids would be there when she came back. Her next move was necessary if Abigail decided to run without her. From the spot she'd picked she had a great vantage point of the area, and she wasn't surprised to find what she guessed was another rental car. The car in front of Abigail's house most likely belonged to Avis, and a corporation she'd never heard of out of New York had rented it.

When the UPS guy arrived, the man watching took extra notice but went back to his phone call when the delivery man got out of his vehicle with a box. This was what she'd been after, a typical transaction that wouldn't raise any alarms, and the man who signed for it looked familiar. She saw the signature in real time, and it was the right guy. She waited five minutes before he went back inside to see what'd happen.

Her phone rang a minute later, and she smiled when she heard the shower running. She'd asked him to do that to make sure he called from the bathroom, since she doubted it was bugged if someone had gone through the trouble. "Mr. Langois?" she asked and listened to him breathe on the other end. "Sir?"

"Who is this?" Bob Langois asked, and she guessed this was where Abigail had inherited her question-asking technique.

"A friend," she said and spoke to him about what she wanted him to do and why. "Would you be okay with that?"

"You know where? You know what I'm talking about?" he asked, and she winced at the misery in his voice.

"Yes, sir, but we need to keep things safe, so try not to ad-lib." She worried a bit when the watcher got out of his car. "Seriously, follow all my steps."

She made another call and waited. Then she called Bob back after she saw the two vehicles and told him to move. When the watcher tried to follow Bob and his wife Rita, he was boxed in, and no amount of horn-blowing made a difference. The Langois couple got away and drove to the spot she'd asked, and she could still hear the commotion when she waved them into her car. Even if these guys put a tracker on the car, she'd evened the playing field.

"If you're out to get us, we sure made it easy for you," Rita said as she slid into the backseat. "Please tell me you know where my daughter and grandchildren are."

"Yes, ma'am, but we need to get going before we lose our opportunity." She drove off like she was leaving a leisurely breakfast, so no one would take notice. The drive home was meandering, to be absolutely sure, and she sat back and enjoyed the family reunion when they arrived.

❖

Boris St. John sat outside the Langois house, angry at the assignment and angrier at having to kiss Linda Bender's ass. Why

Yury thought the pencil pusher knew anything about finding and killing anyone was a total mystery. If anything, the bitch would use this as an excuse to fuck him over for all the sins against her she thought he'd committed.

The easiest way out of whatever Yury was after was to grab these two assholes and dangle them for bait. If he wanted the bitch who'd witnessed the shooting in New York, and these people were her parents, they'd be good incentive to bring the slut in from whatever hole she'd crawled into. He glanced down at his phone and hit the roof with his fist when he saw Linda's name.

"What now?"

"Call me if they leave."

Linda wasn't one for long conversations. "Why do you want to know? I can follow someone without you telling me how to do it."

"I've got someone lined up to go in if they do, and you just need to call when they're coming back so my guy can get out."

"You sure it wouldn't be easier to go in and take these idiots?" He watched the delivery guy go to the door and the older man take the package. It was nothing, so he didn't mention it to her. "Why drag it out?"

"If you need to have this talk again, call Yury and have it. Until he tells me to do it differently, let me know when they leave."

He punched the roof again when she hung up but quickly paid attention when the couple practically ran out of the house and started the car. Finally an end to all this fucking sitting, and following them would be easy because they appeared frantic. The two black SUVs surprised him, and when he blew his horn to get them out of his way, the driver must've gotten pissed since he didn't move and rolled the window down to flip him off.

When the road was clear the couple's car was nowhere in sight, and after twenty minutes of looking he found it, but they were gone. He prayed for the first time in years that this meant they were in one of the shops, but after glancing in each window he knew he'd lost them. If it was for good, he was screwed. Yury wouldn't accept another fuck-up.

He sat in his car and called Linda and explained what had happened. "Someone must've picked them up. Do you want me to sit on the car in case they come back?" he asked like a whipped dog.

"Boris, I can't tell you the next step to take, but they're gone.

Before anything else, go back to the house and recover the box that was delivered this morning. Call me when you're there."

If he closed his eyes he could almost feel the noose tightening around his neck. "Are you setting me up?" he asked, not expecting her to tell him the truth. He sure as hell wouldn't if their positions were reversed.

"You have my word I'll wait to speak to Yury after I talk to you again. If you want to tell him your side after that, feel free, but you don't have to contact me again."

He laughed because she sounded sincere. "He'd kill you if you admit that to him."

"Would you cry for me?" Linda asked and laughed.

He had no problem imagining her among all those books—a history no one but her most likely ever looked at.

"I'll call you, and no matter what, Yury will never hear anything from me."

He drove back and called Linda to tell her about the pile of ash that contained only small pieces of the box that'd been delivered.

"That's all that's left? The label isn't readable?" she asked.

"The label's gone, along with whatever was in it. The old fucker left a note," he said when he glanced to the counter. "It's addressed to David and Valerie Eaton. Who the hell's that?"

"What does it say?" Linda sounded almost gleeful.

"'I know the truth. Think before you act again since your masks and all that insulation won't save you from the consequences of your poor decisions. You won't have anywhere to hide and will have no secrets left,'" he read, scanning the note again. "'I know the truth' is in all caps."

"Boris, keep the note and have fun on vacation. While you're enjoying yourself, turn your phone on only on Mondays at five in the morning, New York time. If either of us has anything to talk about, that'll be the time to do it."

He stared at the phone, wondering if she was drunk. "Why are you doing this for me? You know what'll happen if Yury finds out."

"Perhaps the time has come when we both can use a good friend. It's the only way to survive the long, dark night."

"Thank you then, friend. I'll call you Monday."

❖

"I'm sorry for how I acted," Abigail said as she sat on the edge of the desk. The house was finally quiet after a long day of tears and laughter.

Finley simply gazed at her from her makeshift bed on the study's couch. Abigail's parents were in the guest room surrounded by the kids on the floor. "You don't have to apologize—it's the way most people react. It doesn't change my responsibility to you and your family."

"You've been really good about that, so just accept my apology and we'll move on. If you don't, I'll feel like an asshole." Abigail sat on the couch, as if she needed to be close to her. "You wouldn't want that, would you?"

She hesitated like she was thinking about it, and Abigail laughed. "No one's all good or all bad. If you're lucky, you find someone who's a mix of both but tips the good more heavily on that scale. That's what I've tried to do."

"So you accept my apology?"

"There's no need, but sure, if it makes you feel better." She was enjoying the way Abigail smiled at her when Victoria came in holding Liam's hand, and when they reached her they held their arms out so she'd pick them up. She'd come to enjoy the nightly visits, liking the open affection Abigail's brood didn't mind lavishing on her. "You guys want to keep the bed warm for me until I get back?"

"You coming back, right?" Victoria asked, rubbing her eyes.

"I'll be here when you wake up, I promise." She sat up and let them use her pillow while she put on her shoes for her appointment. "Be good for your mama."

Abigail followed her downstairs and watched as she strapped her weapon on before putting on a light jacket. "My parents are here now, so do you want me to come with you?"

"If you want, next time I'll be happy to have you come, but new people have a way of making people clam up, and tonight I need chatty. With any luck I'll find out exactly where the Hell Fire Club is and we can move on to the next clue." She pocketed her keys and wallet but really had a desire to stay home. Abigail seemed to want her around.

"Remember your promise to my kids that you'll be back, and thank you for that. Usually they're not clingy with anyone but me and my parents." Abigail stood close to her with a peculiar expression, and she could only guess one thing. It was as if Abigail wasn't wired to make the first move but really wanted to.

"All three of them are adorable in their own unique way, while being complete handfuls for the very same reason," she said as she placed her hand on Abigail's shoulder. "You've done a great job there, and I'm secretly enjoying their attention." She went slowly to give Abigail the chance to move away, but she only sighed when she kissed her forehead, then her cheek. "All this is in no way by the book, but until I know you all will be safe, we only have each other."

"It's not a bad spot to be in, from my perspective," Abigail said as she kissed her chin.

Chapter Eleven

Finley drove to the docks that ran from the French Quarter all the way uptown and found a secluded parking spot close to the warehouse district. She stopped at a garbage can along the way and retrieved the envelope someone had taped to the top. The meeting she wanted to have had to be private, and this was the only way, considering who she was going to see. A bug under a very powerful microscope was the way she thought of who she was seeing.

Two keys were in the envelope; one unlocked the new shotgun house across the street, and the other unlocked the door at the back of a closet almost dead center in the place. "Hey," she said to the big man waiting on the other side. "Thought I'd get lost."

"I'm here to protect you from the giant rats in here," Lou Romano said and laughed as he hugged her.

"Lead on, then, because those things freak me out."

They made small talk as they walked through the long, damp tunnel until they emerged in Emma's, a club named after Emma Casey. None of the FBI surveillance people were allowed in the club's offices, and that was where Cain Casey waited, along with Remi Jatibon. Both women were tall and powerful, and headed very successful crime families in the city.

"Hello, Cousin," Cain said when she stood and embraced her with affection.

"Hello, Cousin," she said as Cain slapped her on the back. Finley's mother Siobhan was Dalton Casey's youngest sister, so she'd grown up with Cain and her family, not seeing them quite the same way Abigail had when she'd told her about this branch of her family. "How's the family?"

"Great—ready for the new addition we're working on. When you've got time I'll sneak you into the house for a visit."

She'd wanted a career in law enforcement catching the sexual deviants of the world, so she'd cleaned up her family tree to get into Quantico, but also so no bureaucrat would pit her against her family. She was happy investigating what she did, since she'd never find Cain or Remi in any of her traps.

"I'd love that, but I really need your help with something, and I don't have a lot of time." She explained what had happened and about Abigail and her family.

"Are you talking about Nicola Eaton?" Cain asked.

"Yes. She died a while back in a plane crash with her brother Frederick."

Remi laughed and nodded. "It was convenient timing since we heard the feds were starting to look hard at their businesses. Their accidents slowed the investigation to a crawl, but their action is still in play."

"Have either of you ever heard of the Hell Fire Club?"

"It's in one of the high-rises downtown, but their membership is private and well-guarded. No one can ever truly keep their mouth shut about a place like that, though, so it's basically the Baskin-Robbins of sex. You pay the fee, and they have every flavor of sex you want to try," Cain said as she tapped her fingers in a random pattern on the conference table. "Nicola was in charge of the everyday business, but the stake wasn't hers. We've stayed clear since that's not our gig, but we keep the same kind of eye on it as anything that might be a problem down the line. If you can bring them down, I'd love you even more than I do already."

"Who owns the action?" she said, smiling at Cain.

"Russian mob, and that too isn't a great thing for our family or Remi's, since they're like termites. They operate in the dark, and before you know it they crumble the foundation of what's yours. Nicola was laying the groundwork here, and her brother was making the moves in Miami." Cain stood as she spoke and poured everyone a drink.

"What about New York?" She was cursing herself for not coming sooner and having Cain hand her a shitload of clues on a silver platter. "Who's in charge there?"

"That I don't know, but look for someone not flashy. Someone financed the kind of skin they've got in the game here, so New York would be a good start," Cain said.

The lower-end workers like the ones killed on the limo bus made both Cain and Remi give her looks of disgust when she explained what they'd found, but perhaps that was in place here too. "The high end's lucrative, but shit like that paves the way, I guess," Cain said.

"Can you put the word out and see if you find someone operating like that?"

"For you, anything," Remi said, hugging her before she left. "And if you need a hand exterminating trash like that, Mano and I will gladly help," Remi said of her twin brother.

"Listen to me, okay," Cain said when they were alone. "You need to watch your ass with these people. I'm the devil incarnate to your employer, but I have my limits. The people running this have none, but they do have plenty of people on their payroll. How much progress have you made?"

"Not much before tonight."

Cain squeezed the back of her neck. "Assume with absolute certainty that someone you work with doesn't have your back. You're my family, so if you need something, call me. Promise me that, or I'll kick your ass if something happens to you. Or I will if I'm still standing after Aunt Siobhan gets through with me."

"Thanks, and I probably will need to call you. I don't want anything to happen to this family. Abigail and her children deserve better."

"Then keep me in the loop. I don't know these people well, but they need to be wiped from the planet." Cain made a slashing motion with her hand. "It sounds cruel, but if they've got Abigail in their sights, she'll never be safe again until you eliminate the threat."

"I don't think the FBI will sanction anything like that," she said and laughed. "Really, Cain, maybe I should call for backup since I don't think this is a one-person job."

"Finley, I can't tell you what to do, but you tip off the wrong person and you'll lose more than Abigail. Can you live with that? Be completely honest since you'll carry that load a long time."

"I'll call. I promise."

"I'm your family, not your judge. You call for whatever reason, and I'll never think any differently about you no matter what you ask."

"If I do ask something like that, it's because I have no other way out."

"There's always a way out, Cousin. You just have to find a way you can live with."

"Is that the secret to your happiness?" Finley asked, relaxing somewhat with the knowledge she wasn't alone in the world.

"One of them, but the main thing is a woman who loves you, children, and family."

❖

Finley came home and poured herself a glass of chocolate milk, something she'd always enjoyed. All the stuff Cain had shared with her was enlightening, but it came with a downside. In her soul she knew Cain was right: Abigail wouldn't be completely okay until these people were gone forever.

"Hey, Finley," Victoria said when she pulled on her pant leg. "Can I have some, please?"

"Me," Liam said from her other side.

"Did you two come down the stairs alone?" She poured two cups and lifted them up to sit on the counter.

"We was waiting for you with Mama, but she sleeping." Victoria was the most talkative of the three, and for some reason she searched her out no matter what she was doing, always with her buddy Liam. He was quiet but consumed everything you gave him with gusto. "Wanna watch TV?"

She carried them both to the den and turned on the History Channel after learning it didn't matter what was on, as long as you sat with them. It didn't take long for the two to fall asleep and another visitor to come down. "You know if they're bothering you—" Abigail said. Liam rolled over, opened his eyes, and put his arms around Finley as much as he could.

"They're no trouble." She ran her fingers through Liam's hair and liked the innocent scent of him. "Cain gave me some information."

Abigail lifted Liam off her, leaving Victoria to her. "Let's get comfortable so we can talk." They put the kids back on the couch, and Abigail pointed to the master bedroom. She'd put Finley's pajamas at the foot of the bed. "I know you're probably exhausted, but I can't wait until morning to know."

Finley told her the entire story while they both sat on the bed, leaning back against the headboard. The best way to have this conversation was equivalent to removing duct tape from any part of your body that had hair—fast. Abigail didn't say anything or make a sound, but tears tracked down her cheeks.

"They knew where the club was and that Nicola was in charge, but they didn't think Nicola or Frederick owned the clubs here or in Miami. They believe it's Russian-mob connected." She moved over and put her arm around Abigail.

"I gave her all those years, her two daughters, and this is what she does? How could she use those women like that?" Abigail wiped her face with fast, impatient swipes. "God damn it. I'm tired of crying, especially for someone I didn't know at all."

She couldn't sit on her hands any longer, so she put both arms around Abigail and pulled her close. She couldn't think of anything to say, so she decided to be something solid for Abigail to anchor to. "You can't blame yourself, and you have to understand the mindset of these people."

"What's that supposed to mean?" Finley tightened her hold when Abigail edged closer.

She moved so she could see Abigail's face but didn't let her go. "Some of the cases I've worked on made me question the existence of any kind of higher power because of the depravity some people perpetrate against the most innocent of our victims. They do it, I guess, for the power, so it's my responsibility to ensnare them on the Web, something that's not that hard, but someone else picks them up and prosecutes them."

"There's a higher power as far as I'm concerned, because you exist, and my children see the goodness in you," Abigail said as she brought her hand up and pressed it to her cheek. "Do you have any idea how that makes me look at you?"

"Don't let the situation color your emotions so that you make decisions you might regret."

The despair disappeared from Abigail's face, and the new expression was something Finley recognized. "Do you remember that I actually graduated from medical school?"

"Yes, and if I had kids we would've met by now."

"I believe I'm smart enough to know what my feelings are and how they developed."

Finley nodded and smiled, but only briefly, since Abigail moved to straddle her legs and kissed her. The smart thing was to let her down gently, but she couldn't push Abigail away. If she did what Cain said and was totally honest with herself, she'd admit she'd found Abigail hard to turn away from the second she saw her. That instant attraction had only intensified once she got to know her.

"Jesus. I've wanted to do that for a while," Abigail said as she leaned back to look at her. "Do you really want to stop?" she asked when Finley moved her and got up.

She walked to the door and locked it. "As long as you know I'm not a—"

"I know. You're married to your job."

She shook her head and laughed. "I'm not a one-night-stand kind of person, so I don't want you to accuse me of stalkerish behavior later on."

Abigail took her nightgown off and moved to lie down. The sight brought Finley's entire body to life and she fell into bed. Neither of them needed much buildup, and it was good to know Abigail was as ready and wet as she was.

"Take this off?" Abigail said as she tugged on her gun strap. She undressed like her clothes were on fire and liked the way Abigail laughed. "Come here."

She lay down, covering Abigail's body with her own, and the contact ratcheted up her desire. The knock on the door came as she lowered her head and kissed Abigail. "Mama…Finley, we're scared," they heard Victoria say, so Finley guessed she had her sidekick Liam with her.

"I'm sorry, but don't think this won't happen again. You're not getting off that easily, Agent," Abigail said as she threw her pajamas at her head after putting her nightgown back on.

"They won't go back to sleep, huh?"

"They sure will, but unfortunately for us it'll be here," Abigail said, kissing her again.

Twenty minutes later they were all on the bed, since Sadie had also joined the party. Finley couldn't help but recall Cain's words again. A woman who loved you, children, and family did sound like the key to happiness. When Liam rolled on top of her, she swore to herself that she definitely would get rid of anyone who tried to hurt these special people and would have no remorse.

None at all.

Chapter Twelve

Linda waited until the next morning to call Yury. "Boris just called you?" Yury screamed, making her pull the phone away from her ear.

"I guess he waited so he had time to run. I tried to warn you about him," she said, glad he couldn't see the size of her smile. "What do you think about the note Boris found? At least he called about that."

"Forget about it and make sure everything runs smoothly. I'll be out for a couple of weeks to take care of this, since everyone has a case of the stupids." The line went dead, and she laughed as she reviewed the email she'd composed that morning. She'd taken a shot the night before and found the clue the note writer put in. The *I know the truth* part of the letter Boris had found had led her to a website and then to an email address.

Her job might've been to manage tons of paper, but she'd become somewhat computer savvy with all her free time. Finally she'd found the perfect opportunity to check off every goal she'd only fantasized about.

The send button felt like a detonator when she pressed it, since she wouldn't be able to explain or take this back if it didn't work. She jumped when the phone rang again, then laughed.

"In case I didn't make it clear before, don't do anything stupid," Yury said.

"You're my family, Uncle Yury," she said in Russian, "and you know how I feel about family. It's everything."

Yury took the phone from his ear and stared at it. He'd never truly trusted Linda, but he owed it to his brother to take care of her and his nephews. "Remember that," he said and slammed the phone down again. His next call wouldn't be so easy.

"I see," Crista said after his explanation.

"Stay inside, and I'll call you when I'm done," he said as he rubbed the back of his neck, tired of all this turmoil. He'd been vicious in his climb to the top and earned himself the right and the respect to relax and enjoy his life.

"Don't expose yourself like that," Crista said, her tone softening.

"I'm an old man now, but I haven't forgotten how to survive. But I worry about you, so stay safe." He closed his eyes and wished he had time to see her before he left for New Orleans. "Don't ever forget what I feel for you, Nicola." He hung up after that declaration but replaced the phone gently this time. It was good to say her name one more time. The day was coming that she'd once again take her rightful place at his side, but the accident had given his child the gift of anonymity from the law. Just like him, Nicola was hiding in plain sight, with a life no one of importance knew about.

"Abigail, New Orleans isn't big enough to hide from me." He made another call and smiled at how quickly he was put through.

"Whatever you need is yours."

He laughed, loving the attitude. This job would be a lot easier than people like Boris had made it so far. "Excellent. I'll see you tomorrow."

❖

Abigail woke alone and a bit cranky from the lingering desire that concentrated in her nipples and clitoris. It'd been so long since she'd needed to have anyone touch her, including Nicola, if she was honest. Something had been so off about their relationship, and it'd made her want to keep her distance even when they had the opportunity to be intimate.

"Thank God for my intuition," she said as she hunted for her robe. "I doubt she refrained from sampling the merchandise available in a big den of iniquity. I'd probably still be on antibiotics."

She heard the loud laughter in the kitchen and smiled when she saw her mom at the stove and her girls next to Finley at the table. Liam appeared content and happy on Finley's lap as they shared a plate of French toast smothered in syrup. It hadn't really hit her how much she wanted this picture—the normal life with a partner, content children, and happiness. Up to now she'd thought she'd had that, but Nicola and what they'd had was a farce, except for the children. It was time to take a chance, so she didn't play it safe and kissed everyone good morning, including Finley.

"Thanks for letting me sleep in," she said, her eyes on Finley.

"You need to be well rested after we've sugared these little monsters up," Finley said, her shirt full of small syrupy handprints. "I have to go out for a while, so you and your parents are on your own."

"Can I talk to you before you go?"

"Sure. I need a shower, if I'm not glued to this chair." Finley kissed Liam's temple before repeating the action with the girls, and Abigail wanted to melt.

Liam hugged Finley with a piece of toast in each hand, adding some more syrup to her outfit, and Abigail laughed. Finley showed her usual patience and opened her mouth when he shared a piece with her. "Be good, you guys, and I'll see you later."

"Are you leaving because of work?" she asked when they were alone upstairs.

"Cain called. The elusive Yury Antakov is making an appearance tonight. He wants her help finding you." Finley stripped her T-shirt off and pointed to the bathroom.

"Let's finish this before you take anything else off. Who's this Antakov guy?" The sight of Finley half-naked made her move closer. Her control had snapped. "Wanting you this much is crazy, especially with all this crap happening, and if you give me some psychological reason why my feelings aren't real, I'm going to hurt you," she said with a smile.

"I would, but I don't lie that well." Finley locked the door again. "When this is done we might not feel so pressed for time, but I want to see if I still want to touch you this much."

She raised her arms when Finley removed her robe, then her nightgown. "It won't be rushed or quiet, so finish telling me what's up," she said, putting her arms around Finley's waist after pulling the drawstring on her pants.

"I got up early this morning, since I was too hard to sleep. And to answer your question, even the feds don't know anything about this guy except that he's high up in the mob that runs almost all the illegal activities the Russians have in New York." Finley kissed the tip of her nose. "I have got a hunch, and Cain's going to help me prove it tonight. If I'm right I'll hopefully close my case and stop whoever's trying to kill you."

"Maybe we should get dressed again so I can concentrate, because that was hard to follow."

Finley laughed but held Abigail closer. The next part wouldn't be easy. "Maybe naked is better. Then you'll know I've got nothing to hide."

"What's your hunch?" Abigail asked, and she shivered in Finley's arms as if she knew the words would chill her.

"From what I read, Yury Antakov carved a business out of nothing with the help of his father-in-law, and it was put together one unsuspecting woman at a time. Considering our investigation, his network is vast and so much more than the upscale places like the Hell Fire Club Nicola was involved with." She leaned back to see Abigail's face. "Think of it like he's got numerous stables, but instead of work horses he exploits vulnerable people in search of a better life. That's easy since they're usually traveling illegally and alone."

"So this is who's coming? Can you arrest him if all you have is a hunch?"

"My hunch isn't that he's coming, which he is, but that I know who this guy really is."

"Tell me already," Abigail said, seeming at the end of her patience.

"He made more money than he could spend in a hundred lifetimes, but he wanted more than Yury Antakov could achieve with all that wealth. So a few years back David Eaton was born, and so were Valerie, Nicola, and Frederick. The Eatons have the prestige and position the Antakovs never would."

"You can't be serious."

"Did you figure out Nicola ran what's basically a brothel?" she asked, not really wanting to be cruel. "I might be wrong."

"But you're not, are you?" Abigail gazed at her as she shook her head. "I have no right to ask, but would you help me explain this to my kids? Please know you don't owe me anything, but don't disappear, okay?"

"My other hunch is you haven't dated because of the cute trio out there, which makes you a wonderful mother. When the time comes, I'll be here. Don't worry about that." She kissed Abigail but tried to keep herself under control. "Maybe we might even fit in a date alone or at a family-friendly place, so don't think it's all about taking your clothes off."

"Just as long as it has a little to do with that."

"Trust me. You're a woman no sane person would ever forget."

❖

Finley spent the rest of the morning and all afternoon in front of three computers, mostly studying the email someone was smart enough to send after reading the note she'd included with the package she'd had delivered to the Langoises. She'd read it over ten times before she'd decided it wasn't a joke and included it with the rest of the information she'd compiled.

"Do you have time to eat before you go?" Abigail asked.

"Not tonight, but I'll be okay. I need to call my boss, but I'm not doing it from here."

Abigail put her hands on her shoulders from behind her, and she enjoyed the scent of Abigail's perfume. "Doesn't he know anything about you except you're from here and work for him?"

"He's met my mother and immediate family, but he doesn't need to know everything about me. What he does need is in here," she held up the flash drive, "so let me get going."

Abigail tightened her hold and didn't let her up. "I don't have any experience with any of this, so please be careful."

"My backup tonight happens to care about me more than anyone on the government's payroll, but I need you to promise me something." She swiveled her chair around and stood, then leaned against the desk so they'd be at eye level. "My brother Neil's the only person who'll come here if something goes wrong, and he'll give you this sequence of words and numbers," she said, handing over a small index card. "Let him do that through the intercom before you let him in."

"Don't do this to me."

"Abigail, please," she said, putting her hands on her hips. "If something happens, you're still in danger, and you can trust Neil to watch over you. Try not to give him a hard time."

"Go, but don't think you can dump me on anyone, even if it's your brother." They kissed, and Finley glanced in her rearview mirror as she left. Today she longed for the safety of her office and computers. Fieldwork wasn't her norm, but no way was she leaving this to someone else.

She headed downtown to one of the large hotels to use a computer in the business center. The file was encrypted enough that it'd take Peter a few hours to open it, but it wasn't the only copy she was sending. Even if Yury had bought someone off, it couldn't be everyone.

"Hey, Chief," she said to Russell and allowed him to vent about everything on his mind. "You've got a right to everything you said, but listen." She told him what she'd sent and what needed to happen first. "Bring a team that you're sure about and hit the warehouse first. It holds the answers about where and who. Try to pick up Brian Baylord at the same time. He's probably got answers, judging from what Peter sent me."

"Are you sure about this tip?"

The email she'd gotten was from someone who wanted out of Yury's trap and was willing to trade all the evidence they'd need to bring the syndicate down, including the code key for the journals. "We can't take the chance not to go. I trust you, sir, but in four hours three other people at different agencies will have the same information. You've got plenty of time."

"Good work, and we'll have a foothold on this no matter who else you invited. Now tell me what you're hiding and why you aren't leading all this. You're telling me you fucking found all the answers. Right?"

"I need these people locked up—that's all. I'll leave the limelight to you." She finished what she needed to do and it was time to go. "Russell, I know you can do this, and Peter's ready to pick up my slack."

"You're up to something that'll put you in the middle of the fire. Keep your head down, and make sure you stick around to make me look good."

"Do this, and do it as soon as Peter's finished. You need to get there while there's still something to find."

Chapter Thirteen

The area around the large building was quiet and dark since three of the streetlights were burnt out, but it didn't seem to matter in the empty industrial park. Since it was the weekend, all the businesses were closed and the streets deserted. Cain had trusted her with this location, so after tonight, she'd develop amnesia.

Finley entered through the back as Cain had asked and was amazed at the number of boxes of liquor inside. She was sure none of it was totally legal, but that didn't matter to her right now.

"At any other time this would be the mother lode of evidence against me," Cain said from somewhere in front of her, almost like she'd read her mind. "Don't worry. I'm sure you're not turning me in."

"I know where to shop if I get invited to dinner somewhere," she said and laughed.

"Come on, smart-ass. Our guests arrive in thirty minutes."

Finley showed Cain and Remi the information and pictures she'd found of David Eaton and his family. "I think this is who you're meeting with," she said, glancing at the shot of David and Valerie at some gallery opening. They looked like the golden couple of the society set. "Not even the FBI has pictures of Yury, which maybe means his family entered the country under a false name."

"This is your show, Finley, so what do you want from us?" Cain asked.

"If I'm right, I need to know why they want Abigail dead. I have a couple of guesses, but I believe they want something she's not willing to give."

"Her children," Remi said, and she nodded.

In both incidents she'd witnessed, the gunmen never came close to aiming at the kids. Their only target seemed to be Abigail. "Exactly, and the way she loves those kids makes me want to hurt anyone who tries to come between them."

"Patience, Cousin, the night is young," Cain said, and laughed as she placed all the information back in the folder.

"Boss, we're ready," Lou said as he put his phone away.

Finley stood next to Simon, Remi's head guard, and relaxed her face to not show emotion. That became more difficult when she was right and both David and Valerie Eaton came in with their own people. Their guards didn't like it when they moved forward and disarmed them. David, or Yury, complained, but Cain told him it was either that or leave.

"What can I do for you?" Cain asked when the Eatons sat across from her and Remi.

She would've believed Yury's story of Abigail if she hadn't known the truth. This guy was charming and smooth, and she clutched her hands into fists until Lou very slightly shook his head. He laid out the help he needed, and it was easy. The couple wanted to find Abigail and would pay a bounty if they killed her for keeping them from their grandchildren.

"We have business here, so it gives us a chance to work together," Yury said. "You have a family, from what I hear, so you understand. My daughter's children have a right to grow up with the knowledge of who they are."

"This woman Abigail doesn't want that?" Remi asked.

"Abigail was Nicola's mistake, and she's too weak to raise Antakov heirs. We need them back, and my husband's giving you an opportunity for easy money if you help us," Valerie said, staring only at Cain.

"I'll help, but I'll do it from friendship. You won't owe me anything." Cain held her hand out to Yury, then Valerie. "Life's easier with friends. How can I reach you if we find something?"

Yury handed over a card and stood to button his coat. The arrogance of the man was easy to see, but Finley realized Valerie wasn't a weakling. This woman would kill Abigail herself if she got the opportunity. "Thank you, Cain, and I'll wait on your call. Simply find her, and I'll take care of what happens so you don't have to take any chances."

"Will do." Cain waved them to the door and had Lou give their weapons back.

That they were leaving pissed Finley off. "Will do?" she repeated when the Antakovs cleared out.

"Stick with what you know," Cain said, holding up her hand. "You understand what has to happen, but it couldn't happen here. They need to be seen somewhere else so this doesn't come back to us."

"They'll never stop coming after her, will they?"

"No, not even if you have enough to put them away for life. Tell me what you want to do."

"I can't ask you for what I need."

"I'm the best person to ask, and Remi will back me up," Cain said, and Remi nodded. "Can you live with that?"

"Trading Abigail and the children for them?" she said with conviction. "Gladly."

The building one block off Canal Street had a line of limos out front, and Finley was amazed that some of the men had dates with them. The Hell Fire Club, which took up the top three floors, wasn't a place she'd bring a date.

"What's on your mind?" Cain asked when she put her binoculars down.

"A lot of fucking's going on if it takes that much room."

"Da taught me early that we'd always have a way in this world because of man's true nature."

"Drinking's one thing, but these women don't have a choice," she said, looking again when another car pulled in.

"That's not what he meant. Man's true nature is vice. Drinking, drugs, women, men, gambling—the list is extensive, and they're always searching for someone to give it to them." Cain started the car but didn't put it in gear. "There's a million ways to make money, Cousin, but what's happening up there and in those hellholes you told me about isn't something I'm interested in, even if I was starving."

"I know you aren't a saint, but you don't have to do this."

"Made up your mind?" Cain said as she reached into the backseat.

"Yes, and that's why you don't have to stay." The weapon Cain handed her was new to her. Though the tommy gun was the stuff of FBI legend, it'd been mostly retired because of size.

"It was Da's, it's unregistered, and when you're done it'll go back into mothballs. I just thought if you want to be sure, this'll guarantee sure."

They didn't have any more time for talk as Cain followed the SUV in front of them and lowered the passenger-side window. Yury and Valerie appeared shocked as the guards around them went down in jerky motions caused by the hail of bullets. Finley didn't hesitate but didn't think of it as murder.

This was justice for people who were not only breaking the law but crossing a line so evil it'd earn them a trip to hell, if it existed. Perhaps their end came too fast, but that darkness wouldn't infect the Eaton children, and it'd take Abigail out of their sights. If there were repercussions, and likely there would be, then she'd be there to keep them all safe.

They drove calmly to a part of town with no cameras, and she was grateful to Cain for her meticulous planning. "You okay?" Cain asked.

"Yes, and thank you." She watched Lou and another guy scrub the car down. "Maybe it's a good time to retire and explore new things. After this I don't think I could go back."

"My benefits are excellent, and I want to meet Abigail." Cain hugged her and kissed her cheek. "Neil will drive you home."

"I owe you, Cain."

"You're my family, so there'll never be debts between us—never."

"You gave Abigail and her children their life back, so I disagree."

"Maybe what you got is a better life you can expand on," Cain said and winked.

"Let's hope," she said, hugging her brother Neil next. "I'm coming home," she said to Abigail over the phone, and that was exactly what it seemed to her now because of the people who were waiting for her.

They would face whatever dangers and happiness that came from this together.

About the Authors

Michelle Grubb (michellegrubb.com) is Tasmanian born and now resides in the UK, just north of London, with her wife. She's a fair-weather golfer, a happy snapper, and a lover of cafés, vinyl records, and bookshops.

Michelle harbors an unnatural love for stray pieces of timber (she promises her wife she'll build her something one day), secondhand furniture shops, and the perfect coffee.

She can play six chords on her guitar, stumble through a song on her drum kit, and if you see her wearing headphones, she's probably listening to Mumford & Sons while dreaming up stories and plot twists.

It goes without saying that writing is Michelle's favorite thing to do. She can be contacted at michellegrubb@me.com.

Carsen Taite's goal as an author is to spin tales with plot lines as interesting as the cases she encountered in her career as a criminal defense lawyer. She is the award-winning author of over a dozen novels of romantic intrigue, including the Luca Bennett Bounty Hunter series and the Lone Star Law series. Learn more at www.carsentaite.com.

Originally from Cuba, **Ali Vali** has retained much of her family's traditions and language and uses them frequently in her stories. Having her father read her stories and poetry before bed every night as a child infused her with a love of reading, which carries till today. In 2000, Ali decided to embark on a new path and started writing.

She has discovered that living in Louisiana and running a non-profit provides plenty of material to draw from in creating her novels and short stories. Mixing imagination with different life experiences, she creates characters that are engaging to the reader on many levels.